CW01509866

Oti Mabuse
Slow Burn

Co-written with Lorraine Brown

**SIMON &
SCHUSTER**

London · New York · Amsterdam/Antwerp · Sydney/Melbourne · Toronto · New Delhi

First published in Great Britain by Simon & Schuster UK Ltd, 2025

Copyright © Oti Mabuse, 2025

The right of Oti Mabuse to be identified as author of this work has been
asserted in accordance with the Copyright, Designs and Patents Act, 1988.

1 3 5 7 9 10 8 6 4 2

Simon & Schuster UK Ltd, 1st Floor
222 Gray's Inn Road, London WC1X 8HB

For more than 100 years, Simon & Schuster has championed authors
and the stories they create. By respecting the copyright of an author's intellectual
property, you enable Simon & Schuster and the author to continue publishing
exceptional books for years to come. We thank you for supporting the author's
copyright by purchasing an authorised edition of this book.

No amount of this book may be reproduced or stored in any format,
nor may it be uploaded to any website, database, language-learning model, or other
repository, retrieval, or artificial intelligence system without express permission. All
rights reserved. Inquiries may be directed to Simon & Schuster, 222 Gray's Inn Road,
London WC1X 8HB or RightsMailbox@simonandschuster.co.uk

Simon & Schuster Australia, Sydney
Simon & Schuster India, New Delhi

www.simonandschuster.co.uk
www.simonandschuster.com.au
www.simonandschuster.co.in

The authorised representative in the EEA is Simon & Schuster Netherlands BV,
Herculesplein 96, 3584 AA Utrecht, Netherlands. info@simonandschuster.nl

Simon & Schuster strongly believes in freedom of expression and stands against
censorship in all its forms. For more information, visit BooksBelong.com

A CIP catalogue record for this book
is available from the British Library

Hardback ISBN: 978-1-3985-4045-3
Trade Paperback ISBN: 978-1-3985-4046-0
eBook ISBN: 978-1-3985-4047-7
Audio ISBN: 978-1-3985-4048-4

This book is a work of fiction. Names, characters, places and incidents are either
a product of the author's imagination or are used fictitiously. Any resemblance
to actual people living or dead, events or locales is entirely coincidental.

Typeset in the UK by M Rules
Printed and Bound in the UK using 100% Renewable Electricity
at CPI Group (UK) Ltd

MIX
Paper | Supporting
responsible forestry
FSC
www.fsc.org
FSC® C013604

To the girl I used to be.
Who dreamed with open eyes, danced
through every storm, and held onto
hope even when the music stopped.

And to every woman learning to
rewrite her story, one step, one
page, one brave word at a time.
This is for you.

With all my love,
Oti

PROLOGUE

My fingers threaded through his as he led me along the long, carpeted corridor of the grand Hotel Paris. Heat sizzled between us as I squeezed him tighter, unable to wait for us to be alone.

'This is my room,' he said, stopping to pat down his pockets, presumably looking for his key card.

I ran my hand impatiently under his shirt, tugging hurriedly at the hem in an attempt to convey how desperate I was to rip the whole thing off and feel his golden-brown skin beneath my fingertips; to run my palms over his abs, which were so well defined that I'd been able to feel them through our clothes as we'd danced together down in the bar, performing the sexiest Argentine tango of my entire life.

'Got it,' he said, whipping the key card out of his pocket and tapping it on the pad.

The door opened and we stumbled inside, laughing softly in anticipation of what was to come. He kicked the door shut behind him and I turned to face him, breathless with longing.

'Come here,' he said, holding out his hand.

I took it, letting him pull me into his arms, shivering involuntarily as he ran one hand down my spine, making my back arch with pleasure. Groaning, I didn't care how primal I sounded – I wanted him, and I wanted him *now*.

'I do not even know your name,' he growled, his voice low and gravelly, sounding older than the twenty-one or so years I guessed he was.

I hesitated. Tonight was the first night of the rest of my life. Or, to look at it a different way, the last night of my old life. I knew I would never see him again once morning came and that we didn't have long together, but regardless I felt I was about to experience something – a significant moment in time – that I would always remember.

'It's Li,' I said. It wasn't *totally* a lie.

'Li,' he repeated. The nickname only my sisters used sounded prettier in his husky, Italian lilt. 'Well if you must be Li, then I will be G. Or you can just call me—'

I kissed him to cut him off, partly because I was desperate to but also to stop him from saying more. The less we knew about each other, the better.

CHAPTER ONE

Lira

Thirteen Years Later

I waved goodbye to one of my favourite couples, Chris and Jenny, closing the front door of the studio behind them with a satisfying click. For the last forty-five minutes, I'd been teaching them a very simple Viennese waltz, involving minimal spinning and a whole lot of standing still while looking longingly into each other's eyes. Neither of them were natural dancers, but it was my job to make sure that, when they took to the dance floor on their wedding day, they had their guests gasping in delight. With a few more lessons, I knew they were going to absolutely nail it.

My heels clattered on the sprung wooden floor as I walked across the studio, giving the bright, modern space a quick once-over. We'd been booked out for an audition that afternoon, so I left the speakers switched on, but turned off the rotating glitter ball – I didn't think the world-renowned Spanish choreographer Carlos Torres, who was apparently casting for a new West End show, would appreciate the multi-coloured beams of light swirling around the room. Much to my family's amusement, I liked to have it spinning above our heads throughout all of my lessons – I thought it brought a touch of the Blackpool Tower Ballroom magic to our humble little dance studio in Castlebury, and put my clients in just the right mood to shed their inhibitions and get caught up in their dancing. It might all be in my head, but nobody had complained so far.

Determined to make the space look as perfect as possible for the casting, I had a quick tidy around. Carlos's assistant had sounded stressed when she'd called to make the last-minute booking, enquiring as to where exactly Castlebury was. When I'd told her it was only seventeen minutes from Victoria on the fast train, she'd complained that nobody was going to show up for a casting 'miles from London'. I'd reminded her that you could spend four times as long getting from one side of the capital to the other on the tube, but she'd refused to accept that the studio was anywhere other than the back end of nowhere.

If we hadn't needed the money, and the prestige of being a venue for world-class choreographers to utilize, I would have told her to stick her booking.

Besides, what did she expect, leaving it until the day before the audition to book a space? Didn't she know that Thursday afternoons were peak time for kids' lessons? As it happened, I'd had to cancel today's toddlers tango, which wasn't ideal, but with the costs of keeping the studio running at an all-time high, I hadn't been able to turn the lucrative opportunity down. Hiring out the space to Carlos and his team was making us three times as much as we'd earn from those classes.

Not for the first time, I wished I had someone to talk things through with when it came to the operational side of the business. I'd long ago given up wishing Mum and Dad would step in and actually make a decision for once – I didn't think it was unreasonable given it was actually *their* business. Most of the time it was great that they left me to run the studio however I saw fit, but sometimes I wondered whether I was going to spend the rest of my life working for my parents, teaching the foxtrot to local pensioners and having a skeleton of a social life, let alone a romantic relationship.

Out in the reception area, I straightened up the cerise velvet chairs and gave the champagne bar a wipe over with a damp cloth. Finally, I updated Chris and Jenny's file with a couple of notes about what to focus on in our next session: *Work on Chris's arms! Remind them to create intimacy with eye contact, even when not in hold!*

I was still sitting at the desk half an hour later when the bell tinkled. I looked up and smiled as Carlos Torres and his assistant, Emily, glided through the door as though they were making a flamboyant entrance stage right.

Carlos was renowned in the industry for being ruthless

and almost *impossible* to impress. I vaguely remembered him from my competing days, and he'd been terrifying even then. Seeing him again, after all this time, instantly took me back to the years I'd spent performing myself. I could even remember how the rehearsal rooms had smelled back then: like dust and sweat and wooden floors. Nothing like the light-filled space, with a delicate spritz of The White Company room spray, you could expect to find at our studio. If Carlos liked it here – and I struggled to see why he wouldn't – maybe he'd use us on a more regular basis.

I slipped out from behind the desk to greet them, trying not to appear starstruck by being in Carlos's presence again – even if I was, just a little bit.

'Welcome to the James Jive Dance Studio,' I said, proffering my hand. 'I'm Lira James, the studio manager.'

Carlos looked at my hand suspiciously, and for a split second I thought he was going to leave me hanging. Then, with a sigh, as though he was doing me a huge favour, he shook my hand limply. Was it worth telling him that I used to dance, too? That he'd sat on a judging panel while I'd danced in front of him, many years ago? That he'd one hundred percent remember my mother even if he didn't remember me? I thought probably not.

'You must be Emily,' I said, shaking the hand of Carlos's even less enthusiastic assistant. 'We spoke on the phone.'

Slim, blonde and sporting a pair of the most magnificent cheekbones I'd ever seen, she looked at me with irritation, as though I'd already managed to annoy her. God knows how – it was probably the 'horrendous' journey out of London I'd forced her to endure.

'How many auditionees are you expecting?' I asked, grabbing a clipboard to scribble down some notes.

'Fifty. If anyone works out where Castlebury is and actually turns up, that is . . .' said Emily, shuddering.

I knew that my home town was hardly at the cutting edge of the dance industry, but it was quiet and leafy and there were enough affluent locals to make running a dance studio viable. And it was a friendly, welcoming place, filled with couples just getting their foot on the property ladder, young families looking for somewhere quiet to raise their children, and the elderly who had lived here their whole lives. We essentially had a captive audience – after all, there wasn't that much else arts-related to do around here. There was an Odeon a short drive away, and a theatre in the next town along, but if you wanted bright lights and excitement, Castlebury probably wasn't the place for you.

Emily looked around at her surroundings, poking her head through the archway separating the bar area from the dance floor.

'I'm sure the idea of auditioning for Carlos Torres will be a huge pull,' I said, smiling at Carlos, remembering what an eye he'd had for detail; how he'd notice if you made even the tiniest mistake, and would then shout at you until you got it right.

Part of me envied the dancers about to audition for him, while another part felt relieved that my life was relatively stress-free now, compared to when I'd been competing at the highest level. When things had gone brilliantly, there'd been no feeling like it, but, inevitably, there had also been the crashing disappointment when they didn't go as well as I'd hoped; the rejection, the constant feeling that I wasn't good enough. In some ways, I missed those highs and lows now that my life was the same every single day. At least back then I was feeling *something*.

'They will need to bring their absolute best today,' said Carlos, showily slipping a sequinned jacket off his shoulders to reveal a black velvet bodysuit tucked into skin-tight black leggings. Stacked Cuban heels competed the look. He'd been world champion several times in his heyday — my mum had once shown me footage of him burning up the dance floor with his Argentine tango — and I bet he still had it in him to blow most professional dancers out of the water.

'Are you casting for something specific today?' I asked, genuinely interested.

'We are looking for our leading lady,' said Carlos, his expression darkening. 'And it is proving more difficult than I thought to find her.'

'How come?' I asked, surprised.

London was teeming with brilliant dancers — how difficult could it be to find the perfect person for the role when you had a reputation like Carlos? Surely everyone wanted the lead in his new show, which I'd read in *The Stage* was going to be called *Slow Burn* and had a sultry, Latin theme, and some dancer from the Italian equivalent of *Strictly* in the lead male role.

'Not one dancer we've seen so far has had enough chemistry with our leading man,' said Carlos, whistling through his teeth. 'None of them are right. I need this pairing to look so hot for each other on stage that they leave the audience breathless and begging for more. So far, not one single dancer has had the intensity required to pull off the spectacular Argentine tango I want them to perform at the end of the show.'

'Well, hopefully the dancer you're looking for will be here today,' I said, reassuringly. It would be a particularly good coup for the studio if he found his lead here – maybe then he'd consider James Jive Dance Studio for every difficult part he needed to fill.

'Shall I get them to line up outside the studio? If they queue to the right, they shouldn't block the entrance to the Waitrose Local. We want to avoid complaints if we can,' I said, ignoring Emily's withering look.

Upsetting the locals was not advisable in a town as small as this. James Jive was an integral part of the community, and the businesses on the high street supported each other whenever we could. Personally, I wanted to keep it that way, and I wasn't sure having fifty girls blocking the pavement was going to ingratiate us with the majority of residents. On the other hand, I imagined some of them might love it – it would be the most excitement Castlebury had seen in months.

'Yes, fine,' said Emily, snippily, tossing her perfect, expensive-looking hair over her shoulder. 'I really shouldn't be doing the door myself, but the girl who was supposed to be here missed her train and there wasn't another one for *thirty minutes*! I told her not to bother.'

'Right,' I said.

'I don't suppose you'd fancy . . . ?' said Emily, eyeing me hopefully.

'I'm afraid I've got some paperwork to do,' I said, apologetically.

It was true, there was always some admin to fill my time with, but really I just didn't want to give Emily the satisfaction of being able to boss me around all day.

At five minutes to two, we were ready to open the doors. Emily was clip-boarded up and looking formidable, which, for reasons I didn't quite understand, the people on the door always seemed to be at auditions. Did they purposely choose the most intimidating members of the team to work front of house, ticking off names so ferociously that the dancers who weren't robust or confident enough would crumble under the pressure and could be weeded out before they'd even begun?

The rest of the casting team had arrived a few minutes ago – two producers and Carlos's assistant choreographer, who, along with Carlos himself, would make up the judging panel. I'd set them up behind the trestle table we used for internal exams, and had made sure they had jugs of water, glasses and little bowls of healthy snacks pilfered from the bar.

After getting the nod from Emily, I let the dancers file in. Pangs of envy curled in my belly, taking me by surprise. I missed dancing – there, I'd said it – *properly* dancing; dancing like my life depended on it. Sure, I got to teach now, so I was still moving my body, coming up with steps, and, of course, when I had the studio to myself, I let loose and danced to my heart's content.

But it wasn't the same.

It wasn't like dancing with a partner, and it didn't come with any of the buzz you got from performing for an audience. There wasn't the tension of competition, of pushing your skills to the absolute limit. There was no waiting for scores to come in, or being crowned world champion – the best in the *world* at something.

I'd been nineteen the last time I'd experienced that feeling, and I was thirty-two now. Where had the years gone, and what exactly had I done with them?

Out of nowhere, lately, I'd had a relentless ache inside me; a nagging feeling that something was missing. Ultimately, it had been my decision to help Mum and Dad with the studio while they travelled the world; to live at home and be the dutiful daughter I'd always been. I'd understood when my mum said she wanted the best for me, a more settled life, not the unpredictable life of a dancer, not knowing where my next pay cheque was coming from. She'd thought I wasn't suited to a life of uncertainty, she'd wanted me to be *happy*, and I was, for a while. But suddenly I couldn't shake the feeling there might be more to life than teaching wedding dances to nice people in a not very exciting town.

Contrary to Emily's predictions, there was quite a queue, and I watched the women file in, their toned bodies exquisite, clattering across the floor of the reception area on a wave of chatter and excitement. The bar wasn't big enough to accommodate more than about fifteen dancers at any one time, so I'd subtly suggested to Emily that she let them enter in groups – when one set of fifteen went in to perform, the next group could be ticked off and waiting in the bar for their turn. My organizational skills had always been second-to-none, which was probably how I'd found myself being manager here in the first place. My former dancer of a mother, a three-time South African Latin world champion, no less, knew I could be trusted to keep on top of things, and I'd never given them any reason to think otherwise.

After helping Carlos's assistant choreographer with the stereo system – a slight tech issue had ensued, but I'd soon sorted it out – the auditions began in earnest. I took my place at the reception desk, using the handily located porthole window to keep an eye on what was happening in the studio, while pretending to be heavily engaged in my 'paperwork'. Carlos's assistant was teaching a set of exquisite steps that I couldn't help mapping out with my feet as I watched – the Argentine tango had always been my favourite.

For one brief moment, I let my mind wander back to a moment in the deliciously decadent Hotel Paris. It had been midnight, or thereabouts. A male dancer with slim hips, dark, intense eyes and the most beautifully sculpted cheek-bones I'd ever seen had led me onto the makeshift dance floor in the hotel bar. I let myself remember how his hips had moved against mine, the way our legs had effortlessly kicked and flicked between each other's as we did a set of the fastest *boleos* known to man.

It had felt like we'd danced together a million times before, and yet it was our first and only time.

I'd thought of him often over the years, and desperately wished I could stop. I knew I'd romanticized it all in my mind, so much so that nothing had ever quite lived up to that night. Or to *him*. And the idea that one single night, thirteen years ago, was going to be the best thing that had ever happened to me was too awful to contemplate.

As ever, the auditions ran over – by two and a half hours! They'd only hired the studio until six, but it was eight-thirty before we knew it and the last group of dancers had only just left the building. Emily was looking even more annoyed than she had been when she'd first arrived – if that was even possible – and Carlos and his team were huddled together, no doubt deciding who they wanted to call back for a second audition.

I stifled a yawn as I put the dishwasher on in the bar and swept the floor in the reception area. I was half-tempted to leave the rest of the clearing up until morning, but I knew I'd regret it when I arrived at 8am to get ready for a day of lessons. Fridays were always busy now that people could work from home – it made it easier for them to slope away from their desks for a sneaky dance lesson. Then there was the kids contemporary class at four, street dance at five and beginners waltz at six-thirty.

Carlos thanked me on his way out, calling me by the wrong name, which I tried not to be insulted by.

'Thank you, Lena, darling. It is a shame your studio is not in London; I would use it again if it was not so difficult to get to.'

I nodded, grateful for the backhanded compliment and resisting the urge to remind him that the studio was only about five miles outside of south London. And did he know how much the council charged to rent a space in central London? Mum would have loved to have had a studio there. She'd never quite taken to suburban life either, having spent her childhood in bustling Cape Town. As my dad had constantly reminded us, Castlebury might not be the most vibrant place on earth, but at least we weren't going bankrupt.

I thought about the day as I finished tidying the studio, running dirty plates and glasses back and forth to the bar, putting the tables and chairs away and emptying the bins, which seemed to be overflowing with protein bar wrappers and empty cans of Coke Zero. It was taking longer than I'd hoped, so I put some Argentine tango music on.

Every so often I stopped to replicate the steps I'd seen Carlos and his assistant teach the auditionees earlier. Having spent most of the last six hours surreptitiously watching the dancers perform the routine, I had pretty much memorized the whole thing. I'd even had the sense that I could do that, too. In fact, with only one or two exceptions, I knew for sure I could do it better.

They'd all picked up the steps easily enough – they were professional dancers, after all, and these things came naturally as long as you kept practising and attending classes and castings. But the Argentine tango was special, and they hadn't been dancing it with their *soul*, the way I knew it needed to be danced.

I turned the music up, performing the steps as though it had been me in front of a panel. I had a vivid imagination and could picture myself there, letting the music course through my blood, moving effortlessly to the beat, bringing alive the story of the tango, the passion I imagined my character was feeling as she tried to lure the object of her affection into bed using just music and dance. I got so into it that, when the music stopped and I looked up, I was almost surprised to see the studio mirror in front of me, rather than the line of judges I'd imagined were watching, enraptured.

I ran over to turn off the sound system. That had been fun, but I had to remember who I was now: Lira James, studio manager, not Lira James, world champion in Argentine tango.

My whole body jerked in shock when I heard a slow clap coming from the reception area. I turned around, dreading what – or rather, *who* – I was going to see there.

I must have forgotten to lock the door. Had someone

let themselves in? I was usually so careful – being alone in a studio at night wasn't the safest, even if the crime rate in Castlebury was practically non-existent. But when my eyes locked onto the gaze of the man standing in the doorway, an unreadable expression on his face, I felt the air leave my lungs.

It was okay. I wasn't about to be murdered; it was just Carlos Torres.

I cleared my throat, embarrassed that he'd caught me dancing the steps meant for the girls he'd auditioned earlier, not for me, just some woman who ran the studio he'd hired. He probably thought I had no business performing his steps, even if it was just for myself; that they weren't mine to execute.

'Again,' he said.

I swallowed hard, assuming I'd misheard him. 'Sorry?'

'Dance those steps again,' he repeated.

I shook my head, mortified. 'I was just messing around. I'm not sure I'd even be able to repeat what I just did.'

'Try,' he said, strutting arrogantly into the studio.

He unfolded one of the chairs I'd just put away and took a seat in the corner of the studio.

'I would like to see you dance those steps again. *Please.*'

I'd never been so confused in my life, but also had never been less able to articulate the thoughts flying around inside my head. Why had he come back here? Why did he want me to dance the steps again? What possible good could come of any of this? It was an understatement to say I was rusty when it came to performing – I could remember the steps, sure, but I was nowhere near as good as I'd been when I was competing, especially under the pressure I suddenly felt consumed by. It would be embarrassing to show him what I could – or more likely *couldn't* – do.

'Did you forget something?' I asked, moving slowly to the stereo, wondering what was even happening here. Could I really dance in front of Carlos Torres again, like I had in the Junior World Championships all those years ago? Would he even remember me if I reminded him who I was? I must look so different now – more curves, the odd wrinkle on my face, my hair relaxed straight instead of worn in the bouncy curls I'd sported back then.

'Yes, I believe I left my phone in the bathroom. And now I am glad that I did,' said Carlos, brushing imaginary dirt off his impossibly tight trousers.

'Glad why?' I asked, still baffled. Did he want me to go and get it from the bathroom? I hadn't got around to tidying that part of the studio yet.

'Because unless my eyes have deceived me, you are the best dancer I have seen all day.'

I scoffed. 'You saw fifty people. And they were all amazing.'

And yet even as I said it, I knew I wasn't being entirely truthful. The Argentine tango was my speciality. In my prime, nobody had been able to capture the spirit of the dance as well as I had. Maybe I *did* have something the other girls didn't.

'You really want to see it again?' I said, my finger hovering over the play button.

'Yes,' said Carlos. 'Quickly, please.'

I started the music and took my place on the dance floor, ready to begin.

Afterwards, Carlos didn't say a word. He went to find his phone and then he came back to collect his bag. I busied myself tidying, assuming I'd disappointed him. He probably wished he'd never asked to see me perform, because now he'd have to let me know I wasn't up to scratch. Mind you, I didn't think Carlos struggled with giving negative feed-back – his brutal delivery was well known in the business. So why was he holding back now?

As he walked towards the exit, he stopped, looking at me over his shoulder.

'This studio – James Jive is the name of it?'

I nodded. 'It's a family business.'

There was a moment of recognition on Carlos's face. 'You are Amahle James's daughter.'

'I am. Mum and Dad own this place.'

'You used to compete, yes?'

I nodded, reminding myself to be proud of my achieve-ments, even if they were a long time ago. 'Junior world Latin champion. Twice.'

Carlos looked confused, as though he was struggling to understand why somebody with as much talent as I must have possessed to win those titles was now teaching tango to pensioners in a small market town.

'Come to Pineapple Studios on Monday, two o'clock. I want to see you dance with our leading man,' said Carlos.

I swallowed hard. 'What?'

He couldn't be serious. If Carlos was choreographing the show, it was going to be an almost guaranteed success. There was no way he'd want a non-pro dancer anywhere near it.

'We are struggling to find him a partner. I think you could be what we're looking for.'

'But I haven't . . .'

My voice faltered. I wanted to tell him I hadn't danced professionally for years; that no leading man was going to want to try out with someone like me. My reputation might have been impressive once, but that was when I was a teenager. It counted for nothing now. I'd probably arrive at the studio only to have him point-blank refuse to dance with me, and I wouldn't blame him.

But by the time I formulated the words of protestation in my head and put them into a coherent sentence, Carlos had left, as silently as he'd arrived.

I sank to the floor in shock as I tried to process what had just happened. He really wanted *me*? He really thought *I* was good enough?

The more negative part of my brain soon kicked in, questioning whether I could face opening myself up to this kind of life all over again. The dedication it required, the competitiveness, the rejection. It meant having to tell my parents that this was what I wanted after all, even after all this time, because what would that mean for them and the business I'd helped them build?

But even though my head was saying no, that it was too late, that I was an excellent studio manager, that I couldn't up and leave just because I fancied being a dancer again, I felt a thrill deep inside of me that I hadn't experienced for a very long time.

I was probably worrying for nothing, anyway – I wouldn't get the part. How could I, when my audition skills were rusty at best?

Yet my heart was singing to an entirely different tune: I still had it. I still had it. I still had it.

CHAPTER TWO

Gabriele

As morning light filtered through my eyelids, I slowly became aware that somebody was lying under the duvet next to me. This was not unusual in itself – I was a single man, of course I had women in my bed on occasion, and it was never difficult to find someone who wanted to spend time with me. What was unusual was that she was still here in the morning. Usually, I made some excuse about having to get up early so that she'd leave and I could sleep in peace. I must have crashed out before I could insist upon it.

My eyes eased themselves open and I glanced, bleary-eyed, at the clock on my bedside table. It was 7.30am. *Jesus.*

I threw back the covers; I *had* to get up. I had already missed my gym slot: 6am was when I worked out longest and hardest, and with the show opening in just three weeks, it was more important than ever that I be in the best shape of my life. After that I had some errands to run, my mother to call and I had to be at Pineapple Studios for midday for a meeting with Carlos, followed by yet more auditions. No, I definitely did not have time to be languishing in bed as late as this.

On the pillow next to me, Jasmine's dark hair fanned out as she stirred. At least I *thought* her name was Jasmine – we hadn't actually talked much the previous night.

I reached over and ran my fingers along her arm, tugging at her hand. She moaned as her eyes opened.

'*Ciao*,' I whispered.

'Hey,' she said, sleepily.

I rolled over so that my naked body hovered above hers. She was here now, looking sexy as hell. What difference would another ten minutes make?

'This is a very pleasant way to be woken up,' she said, pulling me on top of her.

If we were quick enough, I could be at the gym by 8.30.

Several hours later, I tried to look enthusiastic as Carlos ran through the names of the girls I would be paired with that afternoon, but I could not help thinking this casting session was going to go just as badly as all the others. Maybe I was the problem? Maybe it was not that the female dancers could not connect with me, but that I could not connect with them?

Not a single one of the routines I had performed as part of this audition process had felt special enough, which was strange, because all the dancers were professionals – exceptionally talented and capable ones at that. They were perfect, just not perfect for what Carlos and I had in mind. I would be headlining a show on the West End stage for the very first time and I wanted it to be unforgettable; to have the audience flying to their feet, screaming for more. Was that too much to ask? Was I setting my standards too high?

I recognized most of the names from years of competing, and some I had even been paired with before.

'Daniella Thompson?' I said, shaking my head. 'I have told you that is not going to work.'

Carlos put on his best soothing tone. I had never known a man who could go from terrifying to charming so quickly; to be screaming instructions at dancers who were not performing his steps properly one minute, to getting exactly what he needed from you the next.

'She might be our best option, Gabriele. You have said no to absolutely everyone we have put in front of you. We have given you world champions, West End stars, Italian, British, American – you name it, you have danced with them all.'

'But you agree with me, right?' I said to him. 'Not one of these girls has blown us away. Come on, admit it, we are in trouble here. And it sounds like you think we are going to have to compromise.'

23

Carlos sighed. 'I am still hoping not. But Daniella you know very well. You were partners once, you know what makes each other tick, what your weaknesses are.'

'I do not have any weaknesses,' I said. Carlos raised his eyebrows at me. 'Not on the dance floor, anyway,' I added.

Off of it there were many, but that was another story.

Dancing with Daniella again would be fine, even if it was a complicated situation that I did not particularly want to get myself into again. But in my opinion, fine wasn't going to be enough to sell out every seat of every night of our West End run, followed by a European tour.

'And who is this?' I said, poking my finger at the last name on the list. 'Lira James? I have never even heard of her.'

Carlos cleared his throat. 'That is an interesting question . . .' he said enigmatically. 'I want you to trust me on this one. I'm not going to tell you too much because I know what you are going to say. Just dance with her. And then I'll tell you how she ended up on my list.'

I sighed. 'Fine, but she had better be worth whatever it is you're hiding.'

I knew I was being difficult, but getting it right was important, and we were already running way behind on rehearsal time. We needed to find a leading lady and fast, otherwise the entire thing was going to be a disaster, with my name attached to it. If it went wrong, I doubted I would be cast as the lead in a show as big as this ever again.

*

While Carlos taught the steps to the ten girls in another room, I stood alone in front of the mirror that covered the entire front wall of the studio. I went over and over the routine Carlos and I had created, checking every movement, the placement of every hand, of each foot. I had a photographic memory for dance steps – somebody only needed to show me once and they were locked in, which had always served me well for auditions. And it meant I could focus on connection and performance rather than remembering where I was supposed to be putting my feet.

After I had run through the routine several times, Carlos's assistant, Emily, rushed into the room and turned on the music, ramping it up loud.

'Sound check,' she explained. 'We're nearly ready to start.'

I took a few glugs of water and towelled myself down. I would try not to be negative – perhaps the perfect dance partner was in the next room, waiting to audition. Maybe one of them was going to surprise me.

'How are they looking?' I asked Emily.

'Not bad. One or two standouts.'

There was this mysterious woman on the bottom of the list that I didn't hold out much hope for, but at least I knew that everyone else was talented and established. If the chemistry was there as well, we could hopefully make it work, but the problem was, it never seemed to be, not to my standards.

Evocative Argentine tango music pumped through the studio and I used the hairband on my wrist to tie my shoulder-length curls back into a pony tail, getting them off my face, preparing to begin.

This could be the moment the dance partner of my dreams entered the room, and rehearsals for *Slow Burn* could really get started.

Carlos swept in with his clipboard, scraping back a chair and taking a place at the table. Three men in shirts and smart trousers followed suit: the show's producer, director and tour manager.

'Okay, Gabriele, we begin,' said Carlos, picking up his pen, preparing to make notes. 'Be nice, *si*?'

'I am always nice,' I growled at Carlos, keeping my voice low.

Although I knew that was not strictly true.

I stalked into the middle of the dance floor, checking myself out in the mirror one more time. I looked good, and I was going to dance good, too. Whoever was about to come through those doors was about to be flung around the dance floor like they never had before.

The doors opened and in walked the first girl – I remembered her from a show in Italy and already knew that she was not the one, but I smiled at her anyway and pretended I was excited to dance with her again after so long. I was not, but I knew how to fake enthusiasm. Turning on the charm when needed was like second nature to me. Actually feeling it? That was another matter.

*

The ninth girl through the door was Daniella. I knew she was not right for the job either, but given my lack of enthusiasm for the other eight girls I had danced with over the last hour or so, she might very well have to be. The thing was, our relationship was complicated – we had been dance partners then lovers, we had not spoken for years, and now we were kind of friends. Our relationship was all over the place. Plus, I had the feeling she wanted more from me than I would ever be able to give her. She was hot, I had to admit that – a tall, willowy blonde with a great work ethic and a dirty sense of humour. But we did not connect on a deeper level, and I knew our relationship would never progress outside of the bedroom. In some ways that was ideal – who wanted the inconvenience of actually having feelings for someone?! And she was a great dancer – but she did not rock my world. And unless somebody rocked my world, there was always this emotional distance that I could not get past, great sex or no great sex.

Daniella strutted into the studio, as full of sass and confidence as ever.

'Long time no see,' she purred, strutting over to join me on the dance floor.

I nodded a greeting, my eyes sweeping over her body – she was wearing black leggings, a cropped black top and heeled Latin shoes. Her blonde hair was hanging loose down to her shoulder blades, and she had pulled it back off her face at the front with a cute little clip.

As we prepared to start the routine, she whispered in my ear.

'You're looking well, Gabriele.'

I ignored her comment, instead placing my hand on the small of her back, a gesture that was familiar to me after years of dancing together, and more. We should be focusing on the routine and only the routine.

'Fancy a drink at mine after?' she asked, keeping her voice low enough that Carlos and the rest of the team could not hear.

'Let us just dance,' I replied tersely as Emily restarted the track.

'Five, six, seven, eight!' yelled Carlos.

I began to move, my body complying perfectly with what my mind was telling it to do, letting the infectious music transport me to a hot, humid basement bar in Buenos Aires, the sort of place I had been to many times before. Daniella was good. It might even be the best I had seen her dance. And perhaps it would not be so bad if she got a place on the tour – she was talented, and fun. It could definitely be worse. But was the team of men in suits – Carlos excluded, obviously – sitting behind that table really telling me that *this* was the best we could do? Did they not want a sell-out show every night, with standing ovations and five-star reviews? Because I could guarantee that we were not going to get any of those things with Daniella as the female lead.

Afterwards, she exchanged a few words with Carlos and gave him her availability for the next couple of weeks, which he wrote down – without catching my eye, I noticed. He was no doubt thinking the same thing I was, but perhaps was a little more resigned to the fact that it was looking likely she would be cast. As she left the studio and opened the door, she blew me a kiss.

'Come round whenever you're ready. You know where I am,' she purred.

Shaking my head dismissively, because I had more pressing things on my mind, I turned back to Carlos for some reassurance that this was all going to be fine; that if Daniella was the one, we were going to make it work, somehow. Annoyingly, though, he seemed distracted and was not looking at me at all, his attention instead drawn to a point over my shoulder.

'Lira. Thank you for coming to meet with us,' said Carlos, waving somebody in to the studio.

This must be the tenth dancer on the list – I wondered if she was a friend of a friend Carlos had agreed to see as a favour. She could not be that amazing if I had never heard of her, could she?

'Gabriele, meet Lira James,' said Carlos.

I sighed. I was pretty exhausted after a day of castings and, quite frankly, all I wanted to do was leave. Still, I could not be rude to this Lira James. It would only upset Carlos.

I swung around to greet the newcomer, but when we locked eyes she stopped dead in her tracks.

Meanwhile, I felt like every ounce of blood I possessed had left my body, so much so that I half expected to look down and see a murky puddle of it on the sprung wooden floor beneath.

I did not even try to speak, I knew it would be impossible.

It was *her*. Of all people! Lira, Carlos had said she was called, yet I had known her only as *Li*.

She had never told me her full name, nor her last. I would never have been able to find her, even if I had wanted to, and yet here she was, standing in front of me looking . . . utterly beautiful. Even more spectacular than she had that night in Paris all those years ago – thirteen years, to be precise.

My eyes were immediately drawn to the tantalizing strip of chestnut brown skin visible between the hem of her top and the waistband of her leggings, just one of the parts of her body I had run my hands over that night. I remembered marvelling at how soft and smooth she had felt before proceeding to peel off her dress so that I could feel even more of her.

I shook my head, dislodging the image from my mind, trying to stop my face burning up right in front of her. Sure, she might *look* gorgeous with that deliciously curvy body and those dark eyes you could lose yourself in if you were not careful, but getting too close to Lira James, as she was apparently called, was highly inadvisable. It would only end badly, as I knew all too well, and once this audition was over, I could avoid her again, for the rest of my life, preferably, and all would be well.

Except, I remembered how brilliantly she danced; of course I had never forgotten that. And I already knew that, given why we were here – her audition, our dance – she was about to become one very big problem for me.

CHAPTER THREE

Lira

Fuck, fuck, fuck! It was like my brain was too overwhelmed to keep up with what my eyes were seeing, to register exactly who was standing in front of me. There had been a blissful few seconds during which I appreciated this man for nothing more than aesthetics – tall, muscular, shimmering olive skin, long hair pulled back into a sleek, cheekbone-accentuating style that turned his face into the most perfect heart shape.

And then realization had kicked in with a thud. G.

We'd known nothing about each other that night, other than how good it had felt to be together. This was the man who had swept me off my feet – *literally* – and into the bedroom. I'd only been nineteen, and let's just say that the limited amount of sex I'd had up until that point had been *nothing* compared to what would happen in his room that night. But the thing was, by then I'd accepted the reality of what was expected of me, by my parents, my family, everyone – that my flight in the early hours of the morning would signify the end of my dancing career as I knew it and the beginning of a new chapter of my life.

I'd known I'd never see G again, had been utterly convinced, and yet here he was standing in front of me all these years later, oozing star quality and good looks and donning the same self-assured expression I remembered from before, a sort of *"Look, everyone, look at me, look how perfect I am!"* The miniscule amount of confidence I'd managed to drum up for the audition had drained out of me the instant I registered who the leading man was.

How was I supposed to give the dance performance of my life when it felt like I had to remind myself even to breathe?

'Lira James, meet Gabriele Riccitelli. You are ready to dance?' said Carlos, tapping his pen impatiently on his clipboard, probably wondering why I was standing motionless on the dance floor like a startled rabbit, and no doubt instantly regretting bringing me in.

None of this would have happened if he'd given me more information about the show I was auditioning for; if I'd thought to ask. If I'd known it was G – or Gabriele, as it turned out was his name – I could have prepared myself. But okay, I was here now, and it wasn't the best way for us to meet again, with several pairs of eyes watching our every move, but it was still the moment I'd dreamed of for so long, wasn't it? I smiled at him, knowing that any second now he'd smile back and all the anxiety would melt away and we could dance. And then we could talk afterwards, couldn't we? I'd wait for him in the foyer and we could go for a coffee or something. Catch up. Because this was amazing if you thought about it – what were the odds? It was the one audition I'd done in thirteen years and I was going to be in the arms of the man I'd loved dancing with more than anyone else in my entire life.

I took a couple of steps towards him, expecting his gaze to soften, assuming that he would hold out his hand, pull me into him and whisper something in my ear about what a surprise this was, how he couldn't believe I was here in front of him after all these years. Except he didn't do any of these things and was staring at me blankly, his eyes darker and colder than I'd remembered. What if he didn't recognize me at all and was wondering how this woman he'd never seen on the British dance scene had managed to crowbar her way into the audition of the year? Had our night together, which I'd replayed over and over in my mind, meant nothing more to him than another notch on his bedpost?

'Start the music,' Gabriele barked at Emily, his Italian accent much less romantic-sounding than it had been in Paris.

He slunk over to the middle of the dance floor, jerkily holding out his hand for me to join him and still refusing to look me in the eye. Was he really going to make me dance with him in front of all these people without saying a single word? I took a deep breath, calming myself. If he was going to act like an arse, let him. If he wanted to pretend I didn't exist, and that I didn't deserve a place on the dance floor next to him, I would show him that I did.

Come on, Lira! I told myself. *Remember why you are here. This is your big chance.*

If I wanted to impress Carlos Torres and the team of producers I presumed were flanking him on both sides, I was going to need to stop remembering the night I'd spent in bed with Gabriele Riccitelli with *immediate* effect and focus on the task at hand.

Glancing down at my outfit – black leggings, black leg-warmers, a red crop top, my favourite peach satin Latin shoes – I wondered if I'd done enough. Should I have worn something brighter, something more revealing, like the girls I was competing against, who had at least seventy-five percent of their honed bodies on show? And Gabriele's girlfriend – or at least I presumed that's who she was, the way she'd sauntered out, casually blowing a kiss at him and reminding him to come to hers later – was no exception.

I gave myself a talking-to in my head: *I am a talented dancer, even if I haven't been pushing myself to my full potential lately. I deserve to be at this audition – Carlos Torres wouldn't have asked me otherwise. I'm going to absolutely nail this.* If I repeated these mantras to myself enough times, maybe I'd start to believe them.

35

I was aware of every movement of my body as I held my head high and stepped across the wooden floor to join Gabriele. Adrenaline rushed through me when I reached out to put my hand inside his and he yanked me close to him, ready to begin the dance. I was wrestling with my own brain, refusing to let it drag me back to the last time Gabriele had held me like this. This was different. This was an audition, in front of one of the leading Latin choreographers in the world. The memories I'd retained of being in Paris with him had no place here. And I'd danced with male partners before, hundreds of them over the years, some I'd had crushes on, some I'd even been intimate with, and it had never felt anything like this, so why was my body responding this way now? This was a professional environment, this was about a job, my career.

I was not going to let him ruin it for me.

I dared to look up at him, challenging him to look back. He must have read my mind because he finally dipped his eyes to meet mine, but it was like there was no emotion behind them; none of the softness there'd been as I stroked his hair all those years ago and he'd fallen asleep in my arms, satiated and happy. I wrenched the thought from my mind and focused on what I was about to do.

The opening bars of the music rang out across the studio and I tried my best to focus. What was the first step again?! It was like everything I'd just learned in the studio next door had disappeared into thin air, and the other girls already had an advantage over me because they had all been taught the routine last week at my studio, whereas I had pretty much taught myself. My only hope was that muscle memory would kick in and somehow my limbs would move in the right order without me having to tell them.

If I didn't pull it together, this whole thing was going to be a disaster.

The Argentine tango was supposed to be sultry and sexy. This thunderous energy between us might have worked if we were dancing a paso doble — we could have channelled our anger into it, even if we did have to look like we wanted to tear each other's clothes off at the same time — but the tango was different. We were going to have to pretend to be *deeply* attracted to each other.

Fake it, Lira, I told myself. *Do it, now!* Gabriele might well have thought the same thing, because suddenly he was making eye contact with me again, though he looked more like he wanted to kill me than seduce me.

Right now, all I could do was harness the energy that had come from seeing G again. I plastered a — *fake!* — sexy smile on my lips and forced myself to remember the bloody steps, which, thankfully, seemed to be coming effortlessly now, despite how thrown I'd been walking into the studio.

As we glided around the room, as he flicked his legs between mine then lifted me onto his shoulder as though I was as light as air, as I kicked my leg up high and then he spun me around on the spot, as he lowered me to the ground, pulling me close to him for a sweeping back bend, I forgot all the awkwardness that had come before and let the music take over. I connected with him where I could, smiled at him, and he smiled back. Gone was the dull coldness I'd seen in his eyes just moments ago; now they glittered as his slim hips pressed against me in that oh-so-sexy way I remembered from before.

I tried to drag myself back to the present, to what really mattered in the moment: the here and now, the feel of his hand in mine, our strong arms extending to the beat, the palm of my hand flat against his beautiful chest. The steps came naturally, allowing me to concentrate on the feel of the dance rather than what came next, but try as I might, it was like we'd somehow slipped right back to that night in Paris, dancing like we'd never been apart.

Afterwards, we were breathless and sweating. I dropped his hand and looked to the panel to see whether or not they'd approved. They all looked a bit shocked, and I didn't know whether that was a good or a bad thing. Out of the corner of my eye, I was aware of the rise and fall of Gabriele's chest in his tight, white vest. He'd given his all to that dance, too. He was that kind of dancer and so was I – someone who threw everything they had into the ring, every single time. But was it enough?

Carlos cleared his throat and looked up from scribbling away on his clipboard.

'Lira, thank you for coming in. I enjoyed your performance very much.'

My stomach flipped. I remembered now how horrific auditions were – it wasn't a pleasant experience, was it, waiting for somebody to tell you if the absolute best of yourself, the heart and soul you'd just given to that routine, had been enough. Or if you'd managed to accrue yet another failure to add to the long list you already had. And I had to expect to fail this time, surely – I wasn't anywhere near at the top of my game. And yet I'd danced well, I knew I had. And I couldn't help but dream about what it might feel like to land the job and start a new chapter of my life when I'd thought that particular book was closed forever.

'We have a big decision to make,' said Carlos. 'And I think it's fair to say that you've given us all something to think about, Lira James.'

I swallowed hard, daring to look at Gabriele. He was staring straight ahead, his jaw tight, a twitch of tension in his cheek. He didn't want me to get the job, that much was obvious. No doubt there was another dancer he preferred. And as the leading man, he'd probably have the final say.

'We will be in touch,' announced Carlos.

'Thanks for seeing me,' I said, smiling at the panel, and purposely not giving Gabriele the satisfaction of smiling at him, just for him to ignore it. Seriously, who did he think he was? It was for the best that I probably wouldn't be getting the job – even if we could turn it on when a performance required it, it would make for a very unpleasant couple of months if we were at each other's throats behind the scenes.

After I left the studio, I strode towards Leicester Square tube, arms folded around myself, no longer enjoying the

May sunshine. I didn't stop to notice the tourists, the shops I might usually find enticing, the buskers, the taxis, the honking horns as traffic snaked from six different directions at the bottom of Long Acre. I felt so many emotions at once that it was entirely overwhelming, each one so big that I wanted nothing more than to shut down my mind to stop me having to think about anything at all.

I'd danced at a professional level again today, and it had gone . . . *well*? I'd impressed Carlos Torres. I'd proved I was more than a dance teacher at my parents' studio.

And there was Gabriele.

My heart hammered so violently in my chest when I pictured his face there, right in front of me, that I rested my hand on it to steady it. How the hell had we just pulled off a dance that good, given the tension between us? An Argentine tango so heated that my breath had caught in my throat afterwards, and not just because of the physicality of it, but because of the feel of Gabriele's arms around me, the way his hands had spanned my waist, the way he'd gripped me when he'd turned me; it had sent shivers coursing through my entire body. Yep, there was no denying it, he still looked as hot as hell. My legs had felt actually, properly weak when we'd finished dancing, so much so that it had taken extreme effort to thank the panel and walk off the dance floor and look remotely okay while doing this normally very natural task. And now I'd have that agonizing wait for Carlos to call and tell me whether or not I'd got the job.

I wanted to forget about it, to assume I wouldn't be cast,

to be grateful I'd even had the chance to try. But there was part of me that knew Gabriele wouldn't have generated that much heat with anyone else.

What if they were looking for chemistry above all else? Because as much as I didn't want to admit it, we had that in spades.

I pulled out my phone before heading down to the tube. Gabriele wasn't the only person I had chemistry with, I reminded myself, tapping out a message to Jack.

Do you have time for a PT session this afternoon? Could swing by the gym on my way home.

He picked up my message immediately and I waited as he typed a reply.

Sounds good. I'll be waiting for you in my office.

CHAPTER FOUR

Gabriele

After Carlos sent everyone out of the room, I knew immediately what he was going to say. I was going to make him squirm, though. I refused to cut in and tell him what I thought, what I felt about Lira's performance – he was going to have to have the balls to tell me himself. Then again, Carlos was hardly a wallflower.

'We need to cast Lira in the leading role,' he said, looking me directly in the eye.

I bit my lip. Now who was squirming?

'No,' I said. 'Daniella and I know each other much better. We don't have as much time to rehearse as we would have liked. It will be easier that way.'

Carlos sat back in his chair. From across the table, he observed me for a second or two.

'And that's how you want this show to be? Easy? Gabriele, you are coming off the back of huge success in Italy. *Bring the Heat* was the top-rated show in your country, no? As big as *Strictly* is here in the UK. Your celebrity appeal has never been higher and if you want to push your career even further, you are going to have to do something that surpasses even that. Something spectacular.'

'It will be. *Slow Burn* with me in the lead and your choreography – it is going to be a guaranteed success.'

'But not if it's you and Daniella.'

I tutted impatiently. 'You do not know that.'

'We need to give the lead to Lira James, and you know it.'

'She is too inexperienced,' I argued. 'Has she ever even worked professionally?'

Carlos placed his elbows on the table between us, resting his chin on the backs of his hands, his eyes boring into me. 'Maybe she hasn't, but she's the best dancer we've seen by a mile. I know you could feel it, so why are you resisting?'

I wanted to deny it, it was on the tip of my tongue, but that would be a lie, and I did not lie, not ever. Okay, maybe very occasionally, if it was absolutely necessary.

'The chemistry between you two was off the scale,' continued Carlos, clearly not prepared to give up. 'Something special happened as she walked into the room. A moment sparked between you. Have you met her before?'

Butterflies ripped through my stomach. *Porca puttana,* why did thinking about that night still have this strange effect on me? I had slept with countless women since then, some of the most beautiful women in the world, so why was I still hung up on the one night I had spent with her? If I was going to analyse the situation, I would say it was because she had been the one woman who had not been available to me. I had not been able to get what I wanted – she had walked out on me, the one and only time it had ever happened. Not to sound arrogant – although I was acutely aware that I could be – but women loved me. They begged me for more, they begged me to call, they wanted more sex, a dinner date, a relationship I could not give them. But not Lira James. *Li.* She had not been able to get away from me fast enough. Sure, it hurt, but I suspected that had more to do with my battered ego than anything else.

'Briefly, many years ago,' I replied, keeping my voice steady.

Carlos narrowed his eyes at me. 'And . . . ?'

'And nothing. We danced together in Paris, in the hotel bar after the championships. We were teenagers, practically.'

'And was your dance together as good as it was just then?' asked Carlos.

A memory flashed in my mind's eye of the two of us moving in total synchronicity across the carpeted floor of the hotel; of my hands on her waist, her hands running up my back.

'It was better,' I said.

Carlos nodded. He had me and he knew it. 'Rehearsals start the day after tomorrow.'

*

On the way home, I stopped off at Daniella's. She had a flat in Holborn, ten minutes' walk from Pineapple Studios, so it was too tempting not to take her up on her offer. Besides, I needed a distraction. I wanted Lira James out of my mind, and what better way to do it than to have great sex with somebody else?

I rang Daniella's bell and she buzzed me into her building. When I got up to the third floor, she was waiting for me in her doorway wearing, well, almost nothing. Black lacy underwear, a barely-there chiffon dressing gown. Her blonde hair was hanging loose down her back, her hip resting against the door frame.

'I knew you'd come,' she said, as I walked down the carpeted corridor towards her apartment.

She was wrong, of course – before Lira had showed up, I'd had no intention of going anywhere except home. And even now I was torn – I felt like I needed her tonight, and of course I *wanted* her, she was gorgeous, but it was a bad idea to start things up with her again, and I knew it.

I filled the doorway, slipping my arm around Daniella's waist, pulling her into me as though I was either about to take her in hold or take her somewhere else altogether.

'You look as good as ever,' I said, threading my fingers into her hair. It was still damp from the shower and she smelled of some expensive, fragrant hair product she had probably just combed through it.

'I'm all yours, Gabriele,' she said in the seductive tone I'd heard her use myriad times before. I wondered whether she used the same lines on other men, but realized I didn't really care if she did.

She dragged me into her flat and I kicked the front door closed behind me. Then I dipped my head to kiss her and she groaned instantly. Knowing she wanted me this much felt good. I ran my hands down her lean body. She was lovely, of course she was, but why did I suddenly have a longing for Lira? A flash of reminiscence about how I had once skimmed my palms over *her* breasts and then across her flat stomach and then out again over her more generous hips, still strong and muscular, but soft and smooth and voluminous all at the same time.

I grunted with frustration, not wanting to think about her, wanting to be here in the moment with Daniella. I owed her that, didn't I?

I scooped her up into my arms and she wrapped her legs around my waist in anticipation. Her flat was small, her bedroom mere steps away, and I carried her to it, laying her down on the bed, familiar with the layout of her place having been here so many times before.

'I'm glad you're here, baby,' purred Daniella, pulling my vest over my chest. 'Lift your arms.'

She wrenched it off and then began unbuttoning my jeans. Lira's face popped into my mind again and I tried to get rid of it by kissing Daniella hard, burying my face in her neck until finally my lips met hers. She opened her mouth, her tongue moving urgently against mine.

I flipped her over, so that my back was flat on the bed and she was straddling me.

'Take off your bra,' I instructed her.

'Only if you tell me if I got the job or not,' she said, running her fingers underneath the straps, pushing them seductively off her shoulders, teasing me.

'That is not my decision,' I said, feeling a pang of guilt. But if I told her now, it would kill the moment, and the moment was the whole point of my visit.

She reached behind her and undid the clasp, her small breasts sliding out. I reached out to stroke them, focusing on them and only them, then sitting up so that I could suck them, too, desperately trying to lose myself in her body like I usually could.

She stroked my head, pulling me closer.

'This feels so good,' she whispered in my ear.

'Mmmm, *molto buono*,' I lied, laying back down on the bed and pulling her on top of me.

Afterwards, she lay against me, her head on my chest, and I stroked her hair. Secretly, I desperately wanted to leave, but I knew she would be hurt and that even thinking it made me an arsehole, but I just couldn't settle with her here, not tonight. The sex had been great in the end, it always was, but it did not mean I wanted to hang around. She liked to chat after sex, she said, and I knew exactly what about in this case. About the job I knew she was not about to be offered.

'Who was that girl who auditioned after me?' asked Daniella, casually, stroking my thigh, as if to distract me and catch me off guard. 'I've not seen her around.'

I groaned inwardly. For the last fifteen minutes I had managed very successfully not to think about Lira James and now there she was again, popping into my mind's eye. And since I was going to be working with her night after night during the six-week run, not to mention the three weeks of rehearsals before that, I was hardly going to be able to avoid thinking about her, was I?

'She is a former world Latin champion who gave it up to run a dance studio, apparently.'

Daniella stopped stroking my leg. 'Why would she do that?'

'No idea.'

'And what, she's just landed herself an audition right off the bat, after years of being out of the business?'

I shrugged. 'Carlos saw her dance. He hand-picked her to come in.'

Daniella laughed. 'Oh great. He's plucking dancers off the streets now, is he?'

'Hardly the streets. He saw her at her dance studio, when you guys were there auditioning. Apparently, she had picked up all the steps and he was impressed when he caught her practising them after she thought he had left.'

This was weird. I was feeling defensive over Lira, despite me not wanting her to get the job, either. What was *wrong* with me?

'Do you know her, then?' asked Daniella. 'From before?'

'Not really,' I said flippantly. 'We met once, I think, years ago. In Paris.'

There it was again, the dreaded feeling in my stomach, the strange sense of pain I still felt about how all of that had played out; pain over one night of, admittedly phenomenal, sex; pain I was pretty sure I had inflicted on several women in my lifetime, and there would be more to come, I was sure.

How pathetic of me. Basically, Lira had treated me like I had treated many other people, as though I was something to be used and discarded. I would have begged her to stay if I could have. And now here she was, back in my life, and there was no way I was going to let her get under my skin again.

I sat up. Perhaps if I walked, got some fresh air, I would feel better.

'Have to go,' I said, kissing Daniella's wrist before sliding out of bed and looking for my clothes, noticing the look of rejection on her face. I felt terrible.

'Let us hang out again soon, *si*?' I said, feeling as though I needed to give her something. Although I wasn't sure that seeing each other again would help either of us in the long run.

Walking back to the tube, I checked my phone. I had received a message from my mother.

Happy birthday, my darling! Call me when you can.

Damn. I really had tried to forget it was my birthday today. I had never liked birthdays. Actually, that was not strictly true – as a kid they had been fun. I had often spent them in Argentina with Mama and my grandmother while my father stayed at home in Italy to look after the farm. But once I started dancing professionally, once I moved away from home and was travelling from competition to competition and then later from show to show, it became less and less important. Perhaps it did not help that I never told people when my birthday actually *was*.

I called my mother back instead of messaging, suddenly wanting to speak to somebody who knew me, who loved me, and who I adored just as much.

'*Ciao*, Mama,' I said into the phone.

'Ah, my Gabriele. Happy birthday, my sweet boy. How is everything in London?'

'Busy,' I said. 'We start rehearsals for the show in a couple of days, so I am enjoying the rest while I can.'

'Ah exciting. And you have a leading lady now?'

I swallowed, feeling as though my throat had tightened, suddenly. 'We have.'

'And she is perfect, just like you'd hoped?'

That was the problem – she was far too perfect in every way.

'She is an excellent dancer,' I said.

'But . . . ?' said Mum.

She knew me so well.

'But we only have weeks to choreograph four dances and she has been out of the game for years. I am worried she will struggle to keep up. I feel such pressure for this show to be a hit.'

'It will be, Gabi, people will flock to see you, particularly when you come to Italy, but also in London, in Madrid, in Lisbon and in all the other cities you will perform in. You are a star these days and you must not forget it.'

I smiled to myself. I knew all mothers thought their sons were special, but it still felt good to hear it. It warmed my heart that somebody – even if it was my mother – could see positive attributes in me that had nothing to do with the way I looked, or even the way I danced.

'What are you doing for your birthday?' she asked. 'Something with friends? You don't have a girlfriend to tell me about yet, my love?'

I'd reached Covent Garden tube and stood outside, watching the tourists, the gaudily decorated tuk-tuks and the shoppers out with friends, and I felt quite alone. Everybody had somewhere to go, someone to be with. This was why dance had saved me – the dance company would be like my family for the next nine weeks, but then they would be gone, leaving me with nothing and nobody. Again.

'Working, Mama,' I said. 'But that is what I do best.'

'But there is life outside of dance, Gabriele, and you must not forget this. Ah, here is your father. He wants to speak to you.'

I suppressed a sigh, not because I didn't want to speak to my father, but because it always left me in a strange mood when I did and I was already on the verge of feeling depressed. This is what birthdays did to me.

'Fine, put him on,' I said, trying to sound enthusiastic.

There was a rustle on the other end of the line. I heard my father clearing his throat.

'Gabi?' he said. 'Happy birthday.'

'*Grazie*, Papa,' I replied. 'How are you? How is the farm? Business good at the vineyard?'

'Busy. We will have to employ more staff this summer, there is so much to do,' he said.

The familiar feeling of having disappointed my father surged through my body, as it always did when I thought about the family business. In his mind, I should be there in Tuscany now, helping him make and sell wine, not travelling the world doing *this*, a job he'd never fully understood or wanted for me.

'I do need to speak to you, Gabi,' he said. 'About things here, about my plans for the future.'

I tried to laugh it off. 'Okay, but this sounds serious. Can we not do this today, on my birthday, of all days?'

May as well use the birthday excuse.

'Then when?' he hissed.

I felt the stirrings of panic.

'You are not the only one getting older,' he said. 'Soon I will not be able to put in so many hours at the vineyard. As my only son, you should be here, taking over. Remember it will be left to you when I am no longer here. Don't you want to know how things run? Don't you want to support the family business that has paid for your schooling, for your dance lessons?'

'Papa, I—'

I heard a tussle on the other end of the line, my mother's voice. She was scolding my father, telling him not to upset me on my birthday, berating him in his own language, Italian.

'Gabi?' said Mama. 'Do not listen to him today. Now go and have fun on your birthday, yes? Promise me?'

'I promise,' I said.

Although having fun was a promise I was not convinced I could keep.

CHAPTER FIVE

Lira

Jack and I had had an arrangement, if that's what you could call it, for the last year or so, since I'd paid for a course of actual personal training sessions with him at the swanky and extortionately priced local gym I'd signed up to because I could feel my body changing as I got further into my thirties, and not for the better. Of course, I didn't have the pressure of being a dancer anymore – I wasn't competing or on tour, because if I was, that would have come with a much more urgent need to be at my fittest and to look at my absolute best. But how my body worked, how strong it felt – it was still important to me. And Jack had pushed me to my absolute limits during our training sessions, which I'd whined and moaned about at the time, of course, but once I started seeing results, it had all seemed worth the effort.

Then one day, after a particularly intense session, we'd ended up having sex up against the lockers in the men's changing rooms. It had all been so out of the blue that I hadn't even had time to worry about what would have happened if somebody walked in and saw us. Since then, our PT sessions had morphed into sessions of another kind, which I had to say were ten times more enjoyable than pounding it out on the treadmill for forty-five minutes straight.

I knocked on his office door – he was the gym floor manager now, so he spent less time training clients and more time doing admin, which made it believable, I supposed, that I'd need to see him in his office for an extended period of time. According to Jack, nobody had ever questioned why, occasionally, we'd spend half an hour in there with his door locked, although, to be honest, I preferred it when we met at his flat. He'd even been to mine once, when my parents had been away and I knew there was no way either of my sisters would pop in unannounced.

'Come in!' called Jack.

I pushed open the door, closing it behind me. He was perched on the edge of his desk, wearing racing green gym shorts – and they were *short* – and a white polo shirt that made him look like he'd just come off the rugby pitch. His blonde hair was short at the sides and longer on top, and when he reached out his hand I already knew to lock the door behind me – no point in taking chances.

'Come here,' he said softly.

His blue eyes were so familiar now, so warm and safe

and inviting. The opposite of Gabriele's, which were dark brown and as hard as flint. I would not think about him – I was here with lovely Jack, and sure, it wasn't like we ever did anything other than work out or sleep together, but I always enjoyed the time I spent with him. We'd never been on a date and I thought Jack was probably on the same page as me when it came to having no inclination to move things forward. It wasn't true to say I felt nothing for him. I liked him, he was sweet, he made me feel good – hence the urgent phone call to him this afternoon – and the sex was great, but I didn't have those sorts of feelings for him.

He didn't make my insides drop like Gabriele did.

We might only have spent one night together, but it was a night I'd since spent years thinking about, the memory of it as vivid now as it had been then. I shook the thought from my mind – judging by the way he'd acted today, he was not the man I'd imagined him to be. I was here now, and Jack was smiling at me. Jack wouldn't hurt me. And as he pulled me into his arms and kissed me, I managed to put Gabriele Riccitelli to the back of my mind, which was exactly where he belonged.

I moaned softly with pleasure as Jack's hand stroked my back, his fingers dipping lower and lower, disappearing inside the waistband of my leggings, slipping them off over my hips.

'I'm glad you called,' he said, as I trailed my fingertips underneath his regulation polo shirt with the logo of the gym on the front. As you could imagine for a personal trainer, there was not an inch of fat on his body and his taut muscles rippled as I ran my hands over them.

'Just needed to let off some steam,' I said, gasping as he ran his hand from my knee to the top of my inner thigh and back again. I bucked against him, wanting him inside me as quickly as possible so that my focus would remain entirely on the two of us in this room and not on everything that had happened earlier today.

As if reading my mind, he flipped me around so that I was laying on his desk. I watched with pleasure as he ripped off his top, admiring his toned chest underneath. I pushed my fingers inside the elastic waistband of his shorts and pulled him closer.

'These are just *too* easy to get off,' I said, deftly removing them.

Pausing to slip on some protection, he laughed and pressed himself into me. 'You like that, do you?'

'Mmmhmm,' I said, because I couldn't form proper words now that he was inside me.

I hooked my legs around his waist, closing my eyes. It felt better if he was kissing me at the same time, so I pulled his mouth on top of mine. No time or space to think about anyone else now.

Afterwards, I got dressed as quickly as I'd been undressed and blew Jack a kiss goodbye. I held my head high as I opened the door to his office and walked across the gym floor to the exit wearing my dance clothes. A few sideways glances suggested that it looked a bit weird for me to be on a gym floor in heels, and I sincerely hoped nobody had put two and two together and worked out exactly what we'd been doing in that office for the last twenty minutes, but then really, who cared, I supposed. Sometimes I was actually able to put myself first and do things just for fun. And sometimes it felt like everybody else's needs came before my own – and those times usually involved my family.

My phone rang just as I stepped out onto the street and I dipped into the doorway of the shop next door, putting one finger in my ear so that I could hear over the roar of the rush-hour traffic – not that rush hour in Castlebury was anything like it was in central London. In fact the word 'rush' might be a bit of a stretch.

'Hello, Lira speaking?' I said, putting my phone voice on.

I didn't recognize the number, and you could never be too careful, could you? First impressions counted.

'It is Carlos Torres,' said the gravelly voice on the other end of the line. His Spanish accent sounded even thicker on the phone.

My breath caught involuntarily in my throat. I mustn't get excited – he was probably calling to let me down gently, to say that I wasn't at the level he'd need me to be at for a show like *Slow Burn*. But then . . . that dance with Gabriel had been good, I knew it had been. The second he'd held me in his arms again, the moment he'd given my hand a small, sharp squeeze as the steps began, I'd felt it. But whether Carlos had seen it was another matter. Sometimes these things just didn't translate – sometimes you needed to go bigger. It had felt big to me – but had it been big enough?

'We would like to offer you the job,' said Carlos.

I couldn't take it in at first. Did he just say what I thought he'd said?

'Are you serious?' was the only thing I could muster.

'You were the best dancer by far, and your chemistry with Gabriele was phenomenal. We all felt it, and there was no discussion over the matter – it is you we want.'

I leaned against the shop window because I didn't think my legs would continue to hold me up otherwise.

'And Gabriele is okay with this?'

Carlos hesitated a moment too long.

'Gabriele wants what is best for the show.'

'But he's not sure about me being cast in the lead, is he?' I said, saying the words for him.

'He will come around. We need you to begin rehearsals the day after tomorrow. You can do that, right? I assume there is somebody else who can run your studio while you're away?'

'Away?'

'Did I not give you the details of the tour?'

'You didn't.'

The other dancers would have agents – they'd be doing this part for them, the logistics, the negotiation over pay. For now, I had no choice but to do it all myself, and it already felt difficult. How was I supposed to organize things so last minute?!

'I will tell you everything on Wednesday. Come to

Pineapple at two o'clock like before and we will begin. The show opens in three weeks' time.'

'Three weeks?!'

'I told you we were behind schedule. There will be a one-week run in London, followed by five weeks on tour. We will perform in Spain, Portugal and then Gabriele's home country of Italy.'

'But—'

'It is okay, yes?'

This was Carlos Torres. This was a West End run and a European tour. I was the lead female. Of course it was going to have to be okay.

'See you on Wednesday,' I told him. 'And thank you for giving me this opportunity, Carlos. You won't regret it, I promise.'

'I know I won't,' said Carlos, ending the call.

Forgetting I was standing in the street in broad daylight, I punched the air with delight. And then reality sunk in: now what?

On the way home, I'd run through everything in my mind and had come to absolutely no conclusion. What the hell was I going to do about the studio?! The business had started small, with just private lessons and a couple of kids classes on a Saturday. Now it had grown bigger and more profitable than we could ever have dreamed of, and I ran it all pretty much single-handedly. Both of my sisters were successful dancers and off doing their own thing – they rarely, if ever, stepped foot inside James Jive, and when they did, it was like they couldn't wait to leave again. And my parents only swept in on special nights, if we were doing a showcase for our members, perhaps, or if somebody important was hiring out the studio and they wanted to show their faces. Considering our family home was less than a ten-minute walk from the studio, it used to bother me that they didn't come by more. But I'd got used it over the years and quite enjoyed having the freedom to do whatever I liked. Except that secretly I'd started wanting more from my life – and here it was being handed to me on a plate. The problem was, I hadn't shared my dreams of getting back to dancing with anyone – I hadn't even come to terms with it myself, to be honest. And if I just announced it now, they'd hit the roof, wouldn't they? I had responsibilities – as the eldest daughter, I'd signed up for this, I could hardly leave them in the lurch now.

I put my key in the lock and let myself in. Mum was walking down the hallway holding a casserole dish of stew, heading from the kitchen to the dining room.

'You're late, Lerato,' she said over her shoulder, calling me by my full name, a sure sign I was in trouble. 'Your sister is here – I'm glad we can all have dinner together after all.'

'Sedi's here?'

'She is. Now, come eat.'

I dumped my bag in the hall and walked through to the dining room. Our large-ish new-build house was decorated in a unique combination of Mum's South African heritage, from the art on the walls to the colourful rugs dotted around the place, and Dad's love of useless objects, stuff he'd picked up from his travels around the world. He'd been an entertainment director on a cruise ship for many years, it was how my parents had met, and apparently he'd bought something – be it a vase, a candle, or a random ornament – from every single port he'd ever docked at. Now every inch of shelf space in our home was filled with things that nobody knew what to do with, but that my dad liked to look at, perhaps reminding himself of the exciting life he once had.

Sedi jumped up the second I walked into the dining room, throwing herself at me and clutching me tightly to her. I laughed and hugged her back.

'To what do we owe the pleasure? Not bored with Shoreditch already, are you?' I asked, teasing her about choosing one of London's trendiest – and most expensive – areas to live in.

'Hardly!' she said. 'But can't I come and visit my lovely parents and sister now and again?'

'Of course you can,' I said, taking a step back to admire her. 'You look great, as always.'

At twenty-nine, Sedi was a super-successful commercial dancer and always looked like she'd come straight off the set of one of the big-budget music videos she regularly appeared in. She certainly wasn't shy when it came to expressing herself through her clothes – today she was in trainers, designer tracksuit bottoms, a fluorescent yellow crop top and her trademark cap topped off with big gold hoops in her ears. Her hairstyles changed like the wind, but today she wore it in long braids hanging down her back. If I was the *ying* part of the James family, Sedi – or Lesedi, as Mum would call her when she was annoyed with *her* – was the *yang*. When Sedi walked into a room, everybody noticed her. And if for some reason you didn't see her immediately, you'd almost certainly hear her. Her voice was *loud* and she had no qualms telling people exactly what she thought of them – or what she wanted them to do for her. I wished I had half of her confidence.

'Have you lost weight?' asked Sedi, peering at me.

I shook my head. 'Not that I know of.'

'That personal training is really paying off,' said Sedi, giving me a long, slow whistle of appreciation.

Of course she had no idea what my personal training sessions *actually* consisted of, and I fully intended to keep it that way. My sisters were both lovely, but they could never keep anything to themselves, and this thing with Jack, whatever it was, didn't feel like something I wanted to advertise to my entire family.

I walked around the table to give Dad a hug.

'Good day?' he asked.

'It was, actually,' I said, hoping he wouldn't ask why I was in full dancewear.

I usually wore a variation of it to work at the studio, anyway, but there was no way I'd choose something this tight and revealing. I was painfully aware that I was going to have to come clean about where I'd been this afternoon at some point, but this wasn't the right time to broach the subject. I still thought Carlos was going to realize he'd made a huge mistake in casting me, and if that happened, the less people who knew about it the better. I would be dancing at a whole other level, night after night, with one of the most famous Latin dancers in Italy. There was a *lot* of scope for things to go wrong.

I took a seat at the table as Mum brought through an enormous bowl of rice to go with the stew, and Dad immediately began to help himself to a mound of it. I poured everyone a glass of water while Sedi told us about her latest adventures. She regularly travelled across the world working on concerts and shows – one week she'd be supporting a world-famous pop star at Madison Square Garden, and the next she'd be shooting a video for a new rap artist in Barbados. Her life was full of excitement and glamour, plus she got to do what she loved – dance! – almost every day. On which note, I desperately needed her to help me out the following afternoon.

'Hey, DJ,' I said, as casually as I could, using the nickname I called her when I wanted to butter her up. 'Are you sticking around tomorrow?'

'I was planning to – I've got a few days off.'

I bit my lip, deciding I was just going to have to go for it and lie.

'Reckon you could cover at the studio in the afternoon? I've got a doctor's appointment.'

'What's this?' asked Mum, her ears pricking up.

'Nothing to worry about,' I said, 'just some headaches I've been getting.'

This was more of an embellishment than a lie – I had been getting the odd headache, but I suspected it was more about dehydration than anything else, as I was often so busy at the studio I didn't stop to eat or drink. I felt less bad about exaggerating the truth than I would have done about making something up altogether.

Sedi groaned. 'Do I have to?'

'It would be great if you could?' I said, smiling sweetly at her.

Did she really begrudge me an hour or two off? I'd run that studio six days a week for more than a decade, and had rarely taken a holiday. Everyone made such a huge deal of it when I did that it put a dampener on the whole idea of taking a break in the first place. And it was one afternoon; surely she could manage that? And then I'd have to work out what I was going to do for the rest of the rehearsal time and tour, because clearly I couldn't rely on my family to help out.

'It's not often I come home – I'd planned to spend the day in front of the TV with my feet up,' moaned Sedi.

I stifled the urge to snap back at her. She was so entitled sometimes, and was never willing to put herself out for anyone else, probably because she'd never actually had to.

'Surely you can do this for me, just this once?' I said. 'You've literally taken about two lessons so far this year.'

'To be fair, that isn't her job, Lira,' said Mum, sticking up for Sedi as usual.

'Sure, but we can help each other out, can't we? Isn't that what families do? I need to be able to take time off occasionally – all I'm asking is for a couple of hours off to go to the doctor.'

'Fine, but you can't be gone long,' said Sedi, looking pissed off. 'And you'll have to tell me exactly what to do because I just want it to be as easy and stress-free as possible.'

Of course she did. That summed up Sedi – swan in, do the minimum amount of work needed, and swan out again. And sure, dancing was hard, she didn't get every job she wanted – but it felt like everything else simply fell into place for her.

I tried not to let it bother me, and the last thing I wanted was to get into an argument. It was just that, without even realizing it, Sedi had hit a nerve. My sisters had left home the second they could – Sedi moved away to dance college up north and my youngest sister, Nolo, went to New York to dance at sixteen. Meaning it had just been me, Mum and Dad at home for years now, with me spending most days at the dance studio and Mum and my sisters helping out only when I practically forced them to. Dad oversaw the financial side of things, but he wasn't a dancer, which, fair enough, meant he couldn't help out with lessons, but he rarely even came to the studio these days, and I did the reconciling of takings at the end of each day myself anyway, and all the budgeting and ordering in of stock. They probably had no idea that, although they'd 'strongly advised' me to stop dancing when I was nineteen, I'd felt actually, properly bereft for ages afterwards. It might have felt like the right thing to do at the time – I'd won the World Championships, had fulfilled most of the goals I'd ever had, and it had made sense to walk away while I was at the top of my game. But what if I'd given it up too soon?

'Come to the studio at one on Wednesday,' I said to Sedi. 'I'll need to leave at quarter past, so that'll give me time to talk you through what's happening and who to expect.'

Sedi tutted, just as her phone pinged with a message. She slid it out of her pocket and read it, the trace of a smile crossing her lips.

'Good news?' I said.

She shoved her phone away. 'Not really.'

I waited for her to elaborate. She didn't. And then I mentally ran through a list of every single dance teacher I'd employed over the years, hoping one of them would be able to cover my lessons while I went off on tour. Because the way this evening had gone down, it was clear that nobody around this table would be willing to step up.

CHAPTER SIX

Gabriele

I tried to arrange my face into a relatively approachable expression as Lira walked into the rehearsal room the next day, but, honestly, it was a struggle. I was in a terrible mood, made worse by thoughts of my birthday and the sinking feeling that I should probably have had people to celebrate it with; people other than my mother who cared when it was. I was pretty sure my dad only remembered because she reminded him. And then, of course, Papa had gone and made everything worse by bringing up the vineyard.

I knew I was in a privileged position, with wealthy parents and a thriving family business. And I knew my father thought I was being selfish, pursuing a dance career when really I should have been by his side, learning the wine business, preparing to take over the farm when he retired.

But the truth was, I had no real interest in that world; I never had. I'll admit it sounded idyllic, making wine in the hills of Tuscany, shipping it to some of the best restaurants in the world, employing a whole team of staff. But all I'd ever wanted to do was dance. And I knew that my time was limited; that a point would come where I would have to fulfil my familial duty.

Maybe then I would feel ready – I hoped as much, anyway. I just kept praying that I had time to achieve everything I wanted to in the dance world first. At least headlining a West End show was about to be ticked off my list.

'Morning,' said Lira, greeting Carlos first and then, reluctantly, dragging her eyes to me.

I wished I had pretended to be doing something that required me to keep my head down, because, God, why did she have to look so damn good all of the time? Today, she was wearing a leotard that left little to the imagination, and a flippy little miniskirt that may as well have not existed for all the coverage it gave. Her skin was glowing, and then there were her slim, muscular arms; the pretty face I had tried so hard to forget. Those cheekbones, those eyelashes, the lips that were almost begging you to kiss them. I felt an ache in my groin and almost groaned out loud, not because I was turned on by her mere presence – which I *was* – but because I was frustrated with myself for feeling this way. How did she manage to do this to me?

'Morning,' I grumbled.

'Let us begin,' said Carlos, pulling up his chair so that the three of us were sitting in a circle so small I could nudge my knees against both of theirs if I wanted to. Clearly I did *not* want to, on either count.

'So. Dances. As well as the group numbers, which we will start rehearsing tomorrow when the entire company are here, we will need four duets.'

'Four?' said Lira.

'Is that a problem?' I snapped.

'Not at all,' she replied, just as snippily. 'Which four were you thinking?' she asked, purposely turning to Carlos.

'We have decided on a soft and romantic classic American smooth waltz, a fun and sexy salsa, a very slow and seductive rumba – and then, of course, the highlight of our show: a fiery and dynamic Argentine tango. You will know some of the steps already from the audition.'

'Sounds wonderful,' said Lira, shifting in her seat.

I felt a shot of smugness at the fact she looked uncomfortable with the idea of four duets. I wondered which aspect of all of this was bothering her most. Surely, she should be grateful to have the gig at all, given her lack of recent experience. And if I'd had my way, it would have been Daniella sitting here instead of Lira, even if I knew damn well that our performances would have been nowhere near as sensational.

'We are very short on time now, as you know,' warned Carlos. 'Of course, I will oversee things, but you will have to polish and rehearse the numbers you have together in your own time. Evenings, weekends, whatever it takes.'

'I do have some commitments to the dance studio ...' said Lira, looking anxious.

'What dance studio?' I asked, playing devil's advocate. I knew she worked in one; it was where Carlos had met her.

'I run the James Jive Dance Studio in Castlebury,' she said, barely looking at me. 'It's my family's business.'

'So get somebody else to cover,' I said.

Did she need me to spell it out for her? Her dance career came first, surely.

'That's a big ask,' she said. Then, when she saw Carlos looking alarmed, she added, 'But I'll make it work.'

I turned to face her. 'You do know what a big opportunity this is, correct?' I said. 'And that, if it had been up to me, you would not have been cast at all?'

'Gabriele ...' warned Carlos.

'No, Carlos, she must know how lucky she is to be here. Especially, when she has not danced seriously for years. There is a lot riding on this for me.'

'And there isn't for me?' she countered. 'Of course I'm grateful for the chance. And I will work harder than I've ever worked in my entire life to make this show – this *partnership* – a success. All I'm saying is that things at the studio are more difficult than they seem. I—'

'I really do not care what you do with the studio,' I said dismissively, wondering if I could stop being such an arsehole any time soon. 'I seem to remember you have two sisters – let one of them help, because you are needed *here*.'

71

Great. Bravo, Gabriele. Now she would know that I had retained everything we had shared that night in Paris, about her family, about mine. There had not been a lot of time to talk in between exploring each other's bodies over and over again, but what I had learned about her, I had remembered: her mother was South African, she had met Lira's father while performing in a show on a luxury cruise ship and she had fallen pregnant very quickly; Lira is the eldest of three sisters. That was all I knew.

'I *will* be here, but I don't need you to tell me how to run my business,' countered Lira.

'Enough!' said Carlos, clapping his hands together. 'We do not have time for this clash of personalities – you dance beautifully together and that is what you must recreate time and time again on stage. Whatever the problem is between you, sort it out.'

I sighed dramatically. 'Relax, Carlos. We will make it work.'

'And talking of problems, we are struggling to find somewhere for you to rehearse. Unfortunately there is no studio space available here for you to practice your duets. Perhaps that is something you can figure out between you?' suggested Carlos.

Emily, looking as harassed as ever, chose that moment to scurry into the room.

'I've rung every single studio in central London and nobody has evenings and weekends free at such short notice,' she announced breathily.

'We should have booked this earlier!' I exclaimed, flying out of my seat. 'Why are arrangements only being made now?'

'Calm down, Gabriele,' said Carlos. 'We will find a place for you.'

'We could use my studio in Castlebury?' suggested Lira.

'How would that work? And where the hell even *is* that?' I asked her, the irritation obvious in my tone.

'Twenty minutes from Victoria on the train,' said Emily, rolling her eyes.

'On an *overground* train?' I asked, confused.

'You can *do* the train, can't you?' said Lira. 'Or is it only chauffeur-driven limousines these days?'

I gave her a withering look. 'I am perfectly able to use public transportation. I would simply prefer not to.'

'Well, sadly, we don't all have that privilege,' she quipped.

'Right, we must begin. Let us start with the American smooth,' said Carlos. 'Emily – music, please.'

Emily scurried over to the sound system and I suddenly wished I was anywhere else but here. I had been so excited about this show, but the proximity to Lira, the realization of how much time we would have to spend together *alone* in a studio was becoming more and more difficult to manage.

I stood up, moving into the centre of the dance floor, feeling the music in my body as it piped out of the studio's speakers. Lira joined me on the floor and we stood opposite each other, looking at one another without speaking, listening to the track, letting the ideas come.

'Why don't we start separately and then come together?' suggested Lira. 'Like this: you over there, me over here.'

She directed me to the far-left corner of the room, while she took her place on the right.

'Something like this?' I asked, marking out some steps.

She followed suit, executing them perfectly.

'Each step should move us closer together,' said Lira.

'Always keeping eye contact,' shouted Carlos, who was watching us with crossed arms.

And as she moved closer to me, and we added in step after step, I found myself longing for the moment I could feel her body pressed against mine again. *Porca miseria!* This was not a good start, and I had a feeling that things were going to get much, much worse.

CHAPTER SEVEN

Lira

When I arrived back at the studio after rehearsals, Sedi was lounging on one of the armchairs, chatting with somebody on video call.

'Oh, hey,' she said to me before flipping her eyes back to the screen. 'Lira's back.'

'Who's that?' I asked, wrapping my cardigan around my body.

I'd worn loose black trousers and trainers to leave the studio earlier because I'd told them I was going to see my GP. Stupidly, though, I'd completely forgotten to change back after rehearsals and now I dearly hoped that Sedi wouldn't notice I was wearing a skirt and a leotard underneath my thankfully oversized knitwear.

'Nolo's on the line. Here, look,' said Sedi, flipping the

screen around to show my youngest sister, who was sitting cross-legged on her bed. I was usually delighted to talk to her, just not right at this moment.

'Wasn't expecting to see you,' I said, taking a seat next to Sedi, forcing her to shuffle over to make room.

'Missed you, too,' said Nolo sarcastically. 'Anyway, I can't chat for long, I've got rehearsals in forty minutes.'

Nolo was currently living the dream – although she assured us there was still much more she wanted to achieve. She must have read the Misty Copeland autobiography about fifty times and was the most focused and ambitious person I'd ever met. Nothing – and I mean nothing – was going to get in the way of what Nolo wanted, which naturally made her just the tiniest bit selfish, but we forgave her because she had lots of other amazing qualities and none of us were perfect, were we? She was a member of the New York Ballet Company and had moved out there when she was a teenager. Ballet had been her passion since she was two years old – I still remember me, Sedi and Mum waiting outside while she took her first class – and she'd always been brilliant at it. She was brilliant at most things, as it happened, including life, generally, in my opinion. She didn't have a problem saying no to Mum. She had no time for boyfriends and yet somehow had men begging to go out with her, and on the odd occasion she said yes to dating someone, *she* was the one who broke *their* hearts because they wanted to get serious and she didn't. Today, she looked every inch the prima ballerina in her tight black vest, black leather jacket and relaxed hair pulled back into a sleek bun. Nolo was leaner than me, and taller, with a smaller chest and narrower hips and a long, slim, elegant neck. Sedi was curvy like me, but because she was tall, too, nothing seemed quite so obvious.

It was like I'd come from a different set of parents (I hadn't – I'd checked!).

I'd grown to love my more curvaceous figure over the years: my wide shoulders, my rounded hips, my nipped-in waist, the fact I was only five-foot-four. I'd come to terms with my body and how it looked and what it was capable of – which was quite a lot, actually – and how I felt *inside* my skin. The self-doubt had lessened now, and when I was on a dance floor, I felt sexy, attractive and desirable. Off it, not so much, but that was a work in progress. Unless somebody like Gabriele came along, tearing all the good work I'd done on myself to pieces, setting me back not just one step but several.

It had taken months for me to forget about him – or at least to not think about him every waking moment – and now here he was, cruising into my life looking beautiful, still, and dancing with me in the breathtaking way he always had. But this time I would remain strong. I would be cordial, but aloof; friendly but guarded. We would work together for rehearsals, the London run and then the performances in the European cities I couldn't wait to visit, and then I would walk away from him. Because, after all, I'd done it before, which meant I could do it again.

'Everything okay with the doctor?' asked Sedi, giving me a concerned look.

'All fine,' I said, brushing her off. I really did not want to have to make up a whole bunch of details about my non-existent appointment. I felt bad enough about lying to them as it was.

'What doctor? What's going on?' asked Nolo, leaning into the screen to peer at me.

'Just a routine check-up, nothing to worry about,' I said, cringing inside.

Part of me wanted to tell them the truth there and then, but I was holding back until I was certain I wasn't going to mess everything up and get fired from the show in my first week of rehearsals. Plus there was the small matter of the studio – how was it going to run without me? I'd always prided myself on keeping everything ticking over with as little fuss as possible – perhaps it was eldest child syndrome, but pleasing my parents and making things easier for my siblings had always felt like a priority. And they were grateful for the work I put in at James Jive, I knew they were – it allowed them to go off and pursue their own dreams. Somehow, I was going to have to find a way to keep the studio running while I was working on the show. There had to be a way around it and the last thing I wanted was for them to worry. We all relied on the money the business pulled in – living in Shoreditch wasn't cheap and Manhattan even less so, and if the studio wasn't packed full of lessons and classes, that probably wouldn't happen.

'So, how's life?' asked Nolo.

I shrugged. 'Same old, same old.'

How could I even begin to tell them how much had happened in the last forty-eight hours? It would be Gabriele they'd be most shocked about – I'd told them about him in detail over and over again, the three of us only teenagers at the time I'd met him. I had been the most experienced when it came to guys, but in the end even Nolo, who had only been fourteen, had told me in no uncertain terms that I was going to have to get over it; that there were plenty of other boys out there in the world, and that if it had been meant to work between us, it would have done.

I wondered what they'd say if they knew I'd just been dancing in his arms at Pineapple Studios.

Nolo narrowed her eyes at me. 'Something's wrong. Look at her, DJ.'

Sedi looked at me. 'Oh yeah, I see what you mean. Come on, spill,' she insisted.

I wanted to be vulnerable in front of them, to ask their advice, to scream from the rooftops about this amazing job opportunity I had and ask them what they thought, and what they imagined our parents might say. But talking with my sisters about my feelings wasn't something I could do right now; not yet. Not when it came to this.

'There's nothing *to* spill. And if you're done staring at me, you can tell me how it went today at the studio,' I said to Sedi, changing the subject. 'Did the toddler class go well? Did everyone turn up for their private lessons?'

Sedi looked utterly bored as she reeled off the details of how everything had played out at James Jive while I'd been gone. Apparently, she'd sacked off teaching the toddlers a samba and had taught them street dance instead – fair enough, but I really hoped I wasn't going to get a ton of complaints from disgruntled parents tomorrow.

But as she talked and Nolo joined in, my mind kept wandering back to earlier that day; to Gabriele, who had made my entire body fizz with excitement every time he took my hand. Luckily, there wasn't a lot of contact in the American smooth, but what was I going to do when we started working on the rumba? There couldn't *be* a more intimate dance. And then, of course, there was the Argentine tango. And the fact was, it didn't really matter what I was feeling inside, I had a job to do. We were going to have to work closely together to create the routines of our lives; the very best dances we'd ever come up with. The chemistry Carlos had seen at my audition was going to need to be recreated again and again and again, for *weeks*; for the rehearsals, then in front of a paying audience at the London shows and the European tour.

It would be fine, I reasoned – we could turn up the heat on stage and then, afterwards, we could dial it down again, go our separate ways, back to our hotel without giving it another thought. Except, the idea of staying in the same hotel as Gabriele again made my cheeks turn a shade of pink that they definitely hadn't been two seconds ago.

Aaargh, I *had* to get over this! He was arrogant and

obnoxious – what had I ever seen in him?! I forced myself to focus on listening to Sedi and Nolo gossiping about their careers, realizing I didn't feel the usual pang of envy. I was doing it too now. I was a professional, working dancer, just like them. And I could not let this opportunity slip through my fingers.

After Nolo had rushed off to rehearsals and Sedi headed back to Mum and Dad's, I put in some calls to every single dance instructor I'd ever worked with. By the end of the evening, I had tentatively filled all the teaching slots for the next nine weeks, keeping the reason for my absence vague, and warning them that there was a chance the whole thing might fall through. If it *did* all work out, Dad did the wages, so at some point I was going to have to come clean to him, otherwise the dancers would never be paid, and my own salary would need to be reduced while I was away on tour and not physically working at the studio. But it felt good to have a plan in place and, starting from tomorrow, rehearsal times were all covered.

I smiled to myself, taking a moment to acknowledge that I was really doing this; that there was no going back now.

The entire cast spent the following afternoon at Pineapple Studios learning the choreography for the group dances. Knowing how time was likely to run away with us, Gabriele and I had agreed to rehearse our duets again tonight at James Jive. I was shocked he'd agreed to leave the confines of London, to be honest, but I didn't question it for fear that he would change his mind – I needed all the time I could get to learn the steps, which were far more complicated than anything I'd been used to lately.

Gabriele had stayed late to work with Carlos on a dance I wasn't involved in, and I had some admin to do at the studio, so I gave him all the details and told him to follow on.

He looked distinctly irritated as he swung through the door just after 7pm, all swagger and brooding good looks.

'That train is much too slow,' he said.

'Hmmm, can be,' I said, refusing to engage. In the absence of any more central rehearsal space, he would just have to get used to it.

'I'll be with you in a second,' I said, keeping it casual, tapping away on the keyboard as though he was disturbing me, when actually I was only pretending to work.

'So,' I said. 'Shall we pick up where we left off with the Argentine tango?'

'Sure,' said Gabriele, strutting onto the dance floor as though it was he and not my parents who owned the place.

I made sure the front door to the building was locked and followed him, surreptitiously watching him in the mirror. He'd already put his bag down in the corner, pulled out his water bottle and was drinking from it, his Adam's apple bobbing up and down as liquid flowed down his throat. I used my phone to select an Argentine tango track, letting the hauntingly high notes of the violin ring out across the studio. My finger hovered over the button for the glitter ball. I didn't think Gabriele would appreciate me switching it on – he didn't seem in a particularly joyful mood (was he ever?) – and my head was already all over the place with rotas and changing session times and wondering how the hell I was going to do all of this without upsetting my family.

Gabriele walked into the centre of the room and I joined him there, standing opposite, definitely *not* looking at the biceps bulging out from the arms of his T-shirt. And absolutely *not* thinking about what it would be like to run my hands over them, to see if they were as rock-hard as they looked.

I lifted my head, making eye contact, my heart hammering in my ears so loudly that I could barely hear the music, although thankfully I could still feel it in my body.

First things first, we needed to find the character of the dance – this was where I could shine. I might not have been dancing in Gabriele's league for many years, but I had been creating routines all day every day, and since we could only use limited steps with our clients at the studio, I had a ton of ideas built up in my mind already.

I restarted the track so that we could listen again.

'What do we think the story is?' I asked Gabriele.

He paced around the studio a little, as though deep in thought. 'It's about lust,' he said.

I swallowed hard. He was right, of course, the music lent itself to it, but was this really a good idea, for us in particular?

'Lust between two people who cannot be together because of their external circumstances,' he added.

I nodded along, as though I was perfectly fine with all of this. Which I was, from a professional point of view – unrequited lust worked perfectly for a really sharp Argentine tango.

'Why don't we begin apart, maybe mirroring each other,' I said. 'One behind the other.'

Gabriele nodded, getting into the position I'd suggested. 'For two or three beats.'

I mapped out some steps. 'Something like this?'

'Yes,' he said, his eyes sparkling with enthusiasm. 'And then I will come to you, place my hand on the back of your neck, spin you around and lower you to the ground.'

'Let's try,' I said. I had to be confident that I could do whatever he asked of me; that I could match him step for step.

As I faced the mirror, he walked around me. I didn't have time to acknowledge the spark that ran through my body as he placed his firm hand on the back of my neck and spun me around, because before I knew it I was bent backwards, inches from the floor, and then almost as quickly flicked up again to standing, as though I was as light as air. I remembered the story – lust that must be avoided at all costs. My instinct was to move away from him, then, as though I was trying not to give in to the feelings coursing through my body, and I took a few walking steps forward, like I was trying to brush him off. His instinct was clearly to follow me, as suddenly he was behind me, his breath warm on the back of my neck, his arm wrapped around me.

'*El Cruce*,' he commanded, as I let him turn me around to face him and then take me in hold for the traditional tango cross, crossing my feet in sync with his gentle pivot as he led me across the floor.

'Let's go again from the beginning,' I suggested, and he nodded his approval.

While I went to cue up the music, I watched him rubbing the small white towel he carried with him over his face and neck. And then I tore my eyes away, thinking that the less I actually looked at him, the better.

As the music played, I began to let myself relax into it as we repeated the steps, over and over, finding our rhythm, adding in more complicated moves, even trying a lift. I let the music wash over me as I followed his lead, trying my hardest to forget that this was Gabriele in front of me, imagining another dancer in his place. Someone I had absolutely no feelings for, whom I was having to force a connection with under great duress, for the good of the performance. Before I knew it, we'd been rehearsing for over an hour and the routine was beginning to take shape.

'You seem pleased with yourself,' he commented, as he glugged at his bottle of water and I did the same.

I swallowed my mouthful hard, nearly sending it down the wrong way. 'How do you mean?'

'In your opinion it is going well?'

'I think we're making a good start, yes,' I replied, bristling.

What was he getting at? There was no way he could

deny that the dance was beginning to come together, and I was coming up with lots of ideas of my own, which he'd seemed to like.

'Then this just shows your inexperience,' he said. 'We have a long way to go, and only two and a half weeks before opening night to do it.'

Okay, then. Clearly, I'd been lulled into a false sense of security. He was being difficult for the sake of it. Was this how it was going to be the whole time? Was he like this with everyone, I wondered, or was it just me he had a problem with?

I'd only ever had one proper dance partner before – Tomas. We'd competed together throughout childhood and our teenage years, and he was like the brother I'd never had. We bickered, sure, but we never spoke to each other the way Gabriele was speaking to me right now, like he hated me; like he wanted me to mess up so that he had somebody to blame if things didn't go exactly to plan.

'Have you got a problem with me getting the job?' I asked him, deciding that being upfront and direct was the key if this was ever going to work. I was prepared to lay it all out on the table if he was.

'Why would I have a problem?' he asked, his mouth contorting into the sort of sneer that indicated, yep, he had a *massive* problem.

'You tell me,' I said, doing a quick sweep of the studio, gathering up the cups that I and the other dance teachers had left dotted about the place throughout the day. Coffee was the main way I managed to keep myself alert and energized for each and every lesson. 'Has it got something to do with your girlfriend? Only, I know she auditioned just before me, and I see she's been cast in the ensemble. I'm guessing you'd much rather be dancing with her in the lead instead of me. Is that it?'

He spluttered, looking at me aghast. 'What girlfriend?'

'Daniella, I think her name is. She blew you a kiss on the way out of her casting?'

I tried to keep judgement out of my voice, but I had found it a bit ridiculous – if she was going to see him later, why did she need to make such a big deal about it as she left the room? She'd caught my eye on the way out, as if to warn me not to have too much of a good time because he was hers and so was the job. Obviously, the latter had turned out not to be true.

'Daniella is not my girlfriend. She is my former dance partner.'

'Didn't look that way,' I said, trying not to sound bothered.

'Anyway, why would it matter if I *was* dating somebody?' he asked, raising his eyebrows at me, goading me.

'Obviously it wouldn't,' I said. 'I was simply trying to work out why everything I say seems to irritate you.'

'I had not realized you were such a delicate flower, Lira,' he said. 'Perhaps you ought to go back to teaching your wedding dances. I am sure everyone is *molto* nice to you there.'

'They are, actually. And for the record, speak to me as

your equal, or don't speak to me at all. Now, shall we run what we've got one more time, before you have to get your train? The last one leaves at ten past ten.'

He shuddered. 'I would hate to be stuck all the way out here for the night.'

God, he was annoying. He was nothing like the man I remembered from Paris, who had been sweet and attentive and had acted like he never wanted to let me go.

I jabbed at my phone to press play on the music and took my place on the dance floor, waiting for Gabriele to join me.

'Five, six, seven, eight,' I said, impatiently.

We began to dance, both of us easily remembering the steps we'd rehearsed. Irritatingly, every time we found ourselves attached at the hip or the forehead or the nose, as was traditional in the Argentine tango, I forgot all about how much his attitude was driving me mad. Instead, I kept remembering how otherworldly it had felt when we'd been in bed together and he'd been pounding into me so intensely I'd thought I might have been about to pass out.

CHAPTER EIGHT

Lira

I opened the door to Sedi, who continued to forget her house keys no matter how many times we all reminded her.

'Twice in a fortnight – we should be honoured,' I said, teasing her and standing aside to let her in.

'Yeah, well, I thought I'd make an effort to come home while I'm in London. I'll be flying to Australia at the end of next month, so I won't be seeing you at all for weeks after that, you'll be pleased to know.'

I pulled her in for a hug. 'I always love seeing you, you know that.'

'The feeling's mutual, I suppose,' she grumbled. 'God, I'm hungover,' she said, heading for the kitchen. 'I need a pint of water!'

'Out last night, were you?' I asked, calling after her.

It didn't surprise me. Sedi's social life was about a hundred times more exciting than mine and always had been. Sure, all three of us had spent most of our time dancing in our teens, but Sedi, more than either Nolo or I, had managed to balance that with copious amounts of drinking and partying. And there were boyfriends, *lots* of them. She wasn't the luckiest when it came to love, and by her own admission, she had dubious taste in men, but I'd always admired her for going after what she wanted, for not being afraid to upset people, whether that be some guy she was seeing or our parents. Sedi would never have found herself in the position I was in: pretending to run a dance studio while secretly rehearsing for a West End show. It sounded ridiculous even in my own head. I needed to tell them, and I was going to do it today. My stomach twisted itself into knots in anticipation, although I wasn't quite sure why. They'd be happy for me, wouldn't they?

I followed Sedi into the kitchen, where she was gulping water directly from the tap like a thirsty dog.

'Gross,' I said, teasing her.

'Sorry,' she said, wiping her mouth with the back of her hand. 'Desperate.'

'Just don't let Mum catch you,' I warned her.

Mum was a stickler for manners, but she also forgave Sedi anything, and boy did Sedi know it.

'Where were you last night, then?' I asked, thinking I might as well live vicariously through Sedi in the absence of any social life of my own.

'Just at a dinner,' said Sedi, suddenly going all coy.

'Somewhere nice?'

'Mayfair.'

I whistled, impressed. Then I peered more closely at Sedi – I was pretty sure she was blushing.

'Why are you looking at me like that?' she demanded, pulling the black cap she was wearing further down over her face.

But I was not to be deterred. 'Were you on a *date*, DJ? Because you've gone all red.'

Hiding my smile, because it wasn't very often I got to embarrass Sedi – though it happened much more regularly the other way around – I went over to the worktop and carried on peeling the potatoes for the roast we'd be having in a couple of hours' time. It was Sunday, so no rehearsals today, which meant I didn't have to pretend to be somewhere I wasn't. And roast beef was Dad's favourite – maybe when I told them what I'd been up to, I could at least get *him* on side. He wasn't explosive like Mum and Sedi, but he was also very practical, and he'd be worried about how the studio was going to keep afloat without me overseeing every single little thing. I wasn't sure whether he'd be up for stepping in and doing more – apparently he and Mum also had an announcement to make today. It could be anything. They were free spirits, our parents, and at any given time it was impossible to know what they were going to do next – it could be setting up another business or moving to the Outer Hebrides. I thought there was very little that could surprise me about those two.

'It wasn't a date,' said Sedi. 'Now what can I do to help?'

She must really need to change the subject if she was offering to cook.

The roast turned out well and everyone was tucking in. Everyone except Nolo, that was, whose face was on an open laptop screen placed in a corner of the table. I'd always found this ritual my mum insisted on a little strange – once a month, Nolo had to 'join' us for dinner. Since New York was five hours behind, our mealtimes never matched up with hers, so we tended to eat while she talked, and then when we'd finished, we'd ask her lots of questions or – only very occasionally, in my case – talk about ourselves.

Things were going well for Nolo, as they always seemed to be. The dance company were about to go into production with a new show and for the first time in ages, this didn't send me into a tailspin about how lacklustre my own life was in comparison. It hadn't felt great to be envious of my own sisters – I wanted the best for them, of course I did – it was just that I'd wanted good stuff to happen to me, too. And suddenly it was and, yes, I wanted to share it with them. Maybe I'd test the waters first.

'So I've been thinking . . .' I ventured.

Sadly, Nolo was so caught up in telling us the minutiae of her Manhattan life that she seemingly hadn't even noticed I'd spoken.

'So yeah, our neighbours are this really cool couple – he's an actor and she works in PR for Google and they keep having—'

'I think Lira was about to say something,' interrupted Dad. 'Were you, Lira?'

Fuck. Now I was actually going to have to say it, wasn't I?

'Lira has been thinking, apparently,' said Sedi with a smirk.

'It has been known,' I replied, stalling for time, but I could feel all eyes on me expectantly.

'So I know I've been pretty much running the studio single-handedly for the last, well, thirteen years ... but there *might* be some other things I *might* want to pursue. Like, for the next eight weeks or so.'

I swallowed hard. Was I really doing this?

Mum put her knife and fork down with a clatter. This was not a good sign.

'What kind of "things", Lerato?' she asked.

'It's just a hypothetical question at this point,' I said, immediately losing my nerve. I glanced nervously at Dad, who I thought was most likely to come up with a reasonable response.

'Why don't we hear her out before we jump to conclusions. Go on, Lira, you were saying?' said Dad.

Aaargh! Could I *un*-say it, maybe? Could I just get up and walk out of the room and make them forget any of this had ever happened? But I'd started this, and so I could hardly bottle it now, much as I wanted to.

'I've been offered an opportunity that I don't feel I can turn down. And I wondered if I could have some time off?'

Their faces said it all, but I garbled on regardless – I'd started now, hadn't I? 'And don't worry, the teaching side of things is sorted, I've got cover for all the classes, teachers we trust and have worked with before. I just wondered if maybe you could all be on hand to help keep things ticking over – the admin side of things? Popping into the studio to check everything is as it should be, that kind of thing?' I ventured.

'What? Why me?' asked Sedi, in indignation.

'Why *not* you?' I countered. 'I know you're going to Australia soon, but there's a bit of time before you go?'

'But this has always been our agreement, Lira. As the oldest child, you told us you were more than happy to manage James Jive for us and to make sure it was a success. It's in all of our interests that it continues to do well,' said Mum, glaring at me.

Everyone's interests except, perhaps, mine.

'I was happy. *Am* happy. And it *is* doing well,' I insisted. 'I think you'll agree that earnings are up year on year. All our classes are full, and there's a waiting list for private lessons. I've never let you down and it's not my intention to do that now. It's just eight weeks, guys. We can make that work, can't we?' I asked hopefully.

Met with silence, even from Nolo, who was frowning at me through a screen, I realized I'd under-estimated how much of a shock this would come to them. I supposed that's what happened when you did everything anyone ever asked of you – I might have been keeping the peace at the time, but what had I been setting myself up for in the long term?

'Lira, what's brought all of this on?' asked Dad. 'You've never complained before.'

I suddenly felt a lump in my throat – why were they being so difficult? Didn't they think I might want a change, and wasn't that okay? They hadn't even asked what it was I was planning to do!

'Maybe I don't want to be just a dance teacher my whole life,' I said, keeping my voice steady. Except for Dad, my family were all so loud and boisterous and opinionated that I felt my needs fade into insignificance when I was with them, but I was determined not to let that happen this time. I was confident in myself, I could stand up for what was right.

'What do you want to be, then?' piped up Nolo. 'Because if it's anything to do with dance, you've left it far too late. You'd be retiring soon, anyway.'

'Thanks *so* much for your support, Nolo,' I said sarcastically.

She always had to play the age card – it must be delightful to be the youngest sibling and to have absolutely no familial responsibility.

Mum turned to me, her face a mixture of confusion and determination.

'Lira, you are so good at managing the studio. How could I ever trust it to somebody else? And I need you more than ever now, because *our* big announcement is that me and Daddy are going on an extended trip and we're going to need you to hold the fort here. You will have to run this house while we are away, as well as look out for your sisters. We are counting on you.'

My stomach dropped. I took a large sip of water, hoping to suppress the nausea that had begun to flood my body. *Extended trip? More responsibility?* There was no way I had time for all of that, not now.

'What trip?' I asked, my voice husky with emotion.

Mum and Dad looked lovingly at each other – yes, I reckoned they were the only two people still madly in love with each other after thirty-two years of marriage. I'd never even seen them bicker, let alone full-on argue. Whatever it was they connected over, it had been constant and unwavering – Mum fired Dad up and Dad kept Mum grounded. And they both liked to do exactly what they wanted – and who was there to stop them? Not their children, and definitely not me.

'We're going on a six-month cruise,' said Dad, beaming. 'Remember that's how your mum and I met?'

'How could we forget? We've heard the story about a hundred and fifty times,' said Sedi.

'So, what, it's like a world cruise?' asked Nolo.

'Exactly,' said Mum excitedly. 'Although it's not all pleasure – we'll be working, too. Your father and I will be executive entertainment directors on a brand-new high-spec cruise ship. The money is excellent, so we thought we could put it into the studio when we get back – maybe give it the revamp we've been meaning to for a while?'

'Great,' I said, trying to summon up enthusiasm from

somewhere. While this was wonderful news for them, and coming from a good place on their part, it was, of course, terrible news for me.

'We are so excited,' gushed Mum, going all dewy-eyed as she pictured her trip. 'We get to visit my home in South Africa, plus Fiji, Australia, New Zealand, Argentina, so many places we have always wanted to see. And it will make things so much nicer for me if I know you're all safe, and that Lira is looking out for you like she always does. You *can* still do that for us all, can't you, Lerato?'

I swallowed hard, feeling as though I might start sobbing on the spot. Really? Me in charge? Again?

'Lira doesn't exactly look happy with the idea,' said Sedi, narrowing her eyes at me.

'You're twenty-nine years old. Why exactly do you need taking care of, again?' I asked, trying desperately to keep my cool, although I could feel my temper begin to flare.

Because here my parents went again, essentially saying that they would be out of contact for six whole months. If there was an emergency, sure, they'd want to know, but otherwise I was on my own as far as they were concerned. I should be used to it by now, and yet I didn't see why I should have to be. Sedi and Nolo were grown adults.

I surreptitiously pulled my phone out of my pocket and sent a hasty message to Jack. This was bad, bad, bad and if I didn't get out of here immediately, I was going to tell everyone what I really thought of them, and that definitely wouldn't help my case in the long run. Perhaps they didn't realize how long they'd been taking me for granted, as-suming I'd be here at their beck and call forever, ready to step in whenever they needed me. What about *my* hopes and dreams? Had a single one of them even thought of that?

Can you fit in a session?

I watched as Jack read the message and began typing immediately.

I'm at home. Come over.

I didn't need asking twice, and pushed back my chair, leaving my unfinished meal on the plate. I was acutely aware of everyone's eyes on me as I left the room without a word.

Jack opened the door to his apartment and pulled me inside, pushing me up against the door once he'd closed it.

'To what do I owe the pleasure of this unexpected visit?' he asked, taking my head in his hands and kissing me hard before I could answer.

When we paused to take a breath, I answered him. 'Awful family dinner. Needed to get out of there.'

He nodded. 'Fancy a glass of wine? You can tell me all about it.'

I shook my head, taking his hand and leading him to-wards the bedroom.

'Talking about it won't help, but I think I know what will,' I said, laughing.

I glanced over my shoulder at him, expecting him to join in, but he wasn't smiling at all. In fact, he looked all serious and a bit pissed off. I hesitated – did he feel like I was using him, or something? And in a way I was, if I was honest with myself. But that was how it had always been between us – just sex. No commitment, no drama. Had he expected me to change my mind? Had he changed his? I'd assumed I wasn't the only PT client he gave extra attention to, but what if I'd got it all wrong?

'You okay?' I asked.

'Sure,' he said, laying down on the bed, watching me as I began removing my clothes.

Whatever he'd been feeling when I skipped his offer of his drink seemed to have passed, but I made a mental note to ask him about it. Just not right now.

Letting my jeans fall to the floor, I crawled coquettishly on top of him, trying to ignore the memory of the shouts of '*Come back, Lira!*' and '*What are we supposed to have done?!*' ringing in my ears – I hadn't been able to get out of there quick enough. Clearly, my family had decided what I was and what my life would look like, and as far as they were concerned, it was convenient for them to keep it that way.

'How can I help you forget about your dinner?' asked Jack, looking me up and down appreciatively as I straddled him.

'I'm sure you can think of something,' I said, leaning forwards and taking my weight on my hands so that my breasts were brushing against his face. I knew he liked it when I did that.

'Mmm, so good,' he said, taking one nipple and then the other into his mouth.

And yet, as I closed my eyes, enjoying the sensations coursing through my body, gyrating on top of Jack to indicate how much I wanted him right now, it was Gabriele's face that popped into my mind's eye: *his* dark wavy hair that I suddenly wanted to feel between my fingers; *his* cool, brown eyes I wanted watching me.

I gasped, not in ecstasy like Jack probably imagined, but because I was shocked that I'd gone there, after all this time, after how hard I'd tried not to think of him in that way.

I popped my eyes open again, slid off the remaining underwear I had on and tried my absolute hardest to focus on Jack and only Jack.

CHAPTER NINE

Gabriele

Press coverage for *Slow Burn* had begun to trickle in and every single article mentioned my name and the fact I was the longest serving – and apparently most popular – dancer on an Italian show called *Bring the Heat*, which had secured the highest number of viewing figures on a Saturday night ten weeks in a row. I knew that the shows we were performing in Venice, Florence, Rome and Milan had sold out already, which brought with it a huge amount of pressure. Which, in turn, probably explained why I currently felt stressed and on edge the entire time.

'What's wrong, baby?' asked Daniella, coming up behind me while I was grabbing some alone time at the back of the studio during a particularly tough rehearsal session, trying to get my head together.

Baby?!

She started massaging my shoulders and, while there was no denying it felt good, I didn't want to give her the wrong idea. I shifted forward in my seat, hoping she'd get the message.

'I'm not really a massage guy,' I mumbled.

She dropped her hands and came to stand in front of me with her hands on her hips.

'Let me help you.'

'Let you . . . help me?' I said, confused. What could she possibly help me with?

'I want to relax you,' she said, crouching down in front of me. 'Why don't you come over to mine tonight and I'll cook? We can have some wine, some fun . . .'

I tried to give her a genuine smile, but really I just wanted to be left alone. I had specifically come to the back of the studio so that I did not have to speak to anyone. Next time I wanted to be alone, I was going to have to lock myself in the bathroom.

'I have to rehearse tonight.'

'Tomorrow night, then?' she said, looking hopeful.

'I have to rehearse every night.'

She stood up, seemingly irritated by my answer. 'Rehearse what?'

'My duets.'

I glanced involuntarily over at Lira, who was going through some steps with Carlos in another corner of the studio. I was fascinated by her easy-going nature. She had

Carlos doubled over with laughter, and he never laughed; he was serious like me, usually. I had known him for years and I had never heard him roar like that before – what had she *said* to him?

Daniella followed my gaze, landing on Lira.

'I hope she's going to take this more seriously once we're out on tour. As dance captain, I'm going to have to keep a close eye on her.'

Carlos had appointed Daniella dance captain for the show, meaning she would be in charge of ensuring the choreography continued to be carried out exactly as we had rehearsed, and would deal with any problems when Carlos was not there. I was sure she would do an excellent job, but, at the same time, I had a feeling that she was going to be particularly hard on Lira.

'How long ago was it you knew Lira?' she asked.

'Thirteen years,' I told her without thinking. Would it seem odd that I had remembered it so precisely?

Daniella laughed, seemingly relieved. 'Where's she been since then, then? Because I googled her and nothing came up, except something linking her to that provincial dance studio.'

'It is a very nice, well-run studio space,' I said, having no idea why I was defending James Jive or whatever it was called, when I had previously been bemoaning the fact it was outside of London myself. Also, why was Daniella doing internet searches on Lira?

'Everyone thinks I should have been cast in the lead,' said

Daniella. 'The entire cast is talking about it. We're just not sure she's cut out for a show of this calibre.'

Thankfully, Carlos called across the studio before I could answer, because it was a guarantee that Daniella would not have liked what I had to say. 'Gabriele! Come over, please. Lira has suggested a new step that I think looks very slick. Come give us your opinion.'

Carlos was not an easy man to impress, so if she was managing it, she must be doing something right.

'Better go over,' I said to Daniella.

'My door is open for you any time you want,' she said in a low voice as I passed her.

I made a decision there and then to keep things strictly platonic between us, at least until the end of the run – I wanted things to be as drama-free as possible so that I could focus entirely on my performance. There was no place for feelings in this company. And yet, as I approached Lira, who was wearing skin-coloured leggings and a micro crop top – which, somehow, held her substantial and perfectly-formed breasts solidly in place, despite the apparent lack of actual fabric – I felt a rush of something inside me yet again. Was it that her taut stomach was on show? Was it the slim wrists and delicate fingers that made the intricate arm work we had choreographed look so spectacular? Or was it that I suddenly wanted to skim my hands over every inch of her body again, a sensation I had never fully forgotten?

'Let me see this step you have come up with, then,' I said, putting my hands on my hips belligerently.

She showed it to me. Annoyingly, it was exquisite.

'Do it again,' I said, watching her.

Then the next time through, I joined in.

'I like it,' I said, addressing Carlos rather than Lira.

'It was all Lira's work,' said Carlos, smiling at her proudly as though she was his protégé. I would not be surprised if he had shared the Cinderella-type tale of how he had found her with the press – I supposed it did make a pretty good story.

I nodded at Lira – it would have been rude not to – but I could not bring myself to say anything more. She was watching me with those big, brown eyes of hers, perhaps wondering what she had let herself in for, going on tour with me, when the only thing I could seem to emote around her was sullenness.

'I'll leave you to it,' she said, right on cue.

Seconds later, I heard her chatting to Luca, a guy I had worked with a couple of times and who had seemingly taken Lira under his wing. He was just about the only cast member I had not heard bitching about her.

She laughed again, a rumbling belly laugh I had never heard in Paris because, well, everything between us had felt too intense to be funny. This was a side of her I had never known existed. I wondered briefly about the other parts of her I would never get to know.

'Do you want to tell me what is going on?' asked Carlos. 'Between you and Lira? I have seen you be distant with people before, but nothing like this. Did the two of you have a relationship?'

'Hardly. It was a hook-up. Years ago.'

Carlos nodded calmly. 'You have hook-ups all the time from what I hear. What makes this different?'

I glanced across at Lira, hoping I might find the answer there.

'*Lascia stare*, Carlos. It is not different. It was a shock to see her, that is all.'

He looked at me like he did not believe a word coming out of my mouth. 'Have you talked to her about it?'

'There is nothing to talk about! We spent a few hours together, so what?'

'I do not want you doing anything to jeopardize the show. Speak to her, and soon,' insisted Carlos.

'Fine. Not a problem,' I said.

Of course, I had no intention of doing any such thing. Talking to her would make no difference. I would still have to catch a train out to God knows where tonight and spend two hours dancing with her in a deserted studio, with her looking . . . the way she did.

Suddenly, she was beside me. I really hoped she couldn't read minds.

'We should probably rehearse the rumba tonight,' she said, sounding a little hesitant.

Hardly surprising – the dance was slow and intimate and I was not convinced I trusted myself to do that alone with her. Not yet, not until I had got rid of all of this chaos in my head.

'You know, I was thinking that we could skip training

this evening,' I said. 'I am a little burnt out. Missing one session will not hurt. We can make up for it at the weekend.'

I knew how dedicated she was to making the routines perfect, and that this would disappoint her. I was disappointed in *myself* – jobs always came first, so why was I struggling to put things in perspective this time?

'We're cutting it fine as it is. We need every second together if we're going to have the duets ready to go for opening night,' she said snippily.

Carlos clapped his hands. 'Let us run the group salsa, please, everyone!'

The funky opening bars to the track played out and I reluctantly took my place on the dance floor, willing myself to be the professional I knew I could be.

I almost went back on what I had said about rehearsals as the feel of Lira's hand in mine as I rotated her around the room settled me, our arms crossing and uncrossing, followed by the thrill of spinning her faster and faster. I was lulled into a false sense of security that it would all be okay.

But then I accidentally looked into her eyes and I was gone again. I felt like I was losing my mind.

'I really need a break tonight. Tomorrow we do the rumba,' I said.

'Whatever,' she said, pulling away from me the second the music stopped.

For a second – and I had no idea what possessed me – I held onto her hand tightly, not wanting her to go, not like this. But then she tugged harder, wrenching herself away, giving me a dark look as she stalked off to the changing rooms. Great – she was really upset. And if Carlos found out about this, he would not be happy.

Deciding some fresh air was what I needed, I stepped out on the street, leaning against the damp, dark walls lining both sides of Langley Street. There was something calming about being out here and I breathed in the thick London air – the gloominess was a sharp contrast to the energy, bright lights and noise inside the studio. Deciding my current mood could not continue, I scrolled absent-mindedly through the contacts on my phone, an endless list of people from the dance world and women whose faces I could barely remember. I chose one at random – Alexandra. I had a vague memory of spending a pleasant night at her place somewhere in West London.

It is me, Gabriele. Are you free tonight?

By some stroke of what I could only call misfortune, Lira and I happened to leave rehearsals at exactly the same time that afternoon, and since we were both headed towards Leicester Square tube, I could hardly avoid talking to her. My meet-up with Alexandra was not until later, so I was heading home for now, and Lira would be going to Victoria to catch her train to Castlebury. We would have a few tube stops together to endure – surely I could make safe conversation with her for that short amount of time?

'Not changed your mind about rehearsals, then?' said Lira, hoisting her bag over her shoulder as we turned onto Long Acre.

'It is important to look after ourselves when on tour,' I said, sounding worthier than I had intended to. 'A night alone is just what I need and then I will be back on full form, I assure you.'

This was not entirely a lie. The casting process had exhausted me and I recognized the familiar feeling of burnout bubbling beneath the surface of everything I did.

'We should really try to talk about what happened before . . . in Paris,' said Lira, her voice faltering a little, as though she was only saying this because she thought it was what she *should* say, not because she wanted to discuss the past any more than I did. I wondered whether Carlos had spoken with her too.

'What is done is done,' I said, hoping that would shut it down. 'I do not think it would be helpful, not when there is so much at stake.'

'That's exactly why we *should* talk about it. Don't you think it's affecting the show? We can barely look at each other, let alone speak. Why don't we try and have a conversation about it? It can't get much worse, can it?' said Lira.

'I disagree,' I said defensively. 'I think we are managing very well under the circumstances.'

'But what *are* the circumstances?' she ventured as we waited to cross the road. I had no means of escape unless I wanted to step out in front of traffic or turn back in the direction I had just come from. The traffic was tempting.

'I am not sure what you mean,' I said, hearing the dismissive tone in my own voice and knowing I was being difficult, but seriously, she wanted to talk about this *now*?

'Because I only have fond memories of that night,' she said. 'I mean, it was a challenging time for me, but—'

'Challenging how?'

My interest was piqued. Was she talking about us?

She hesitated, as though struggling to decide whether to say more or not. I thought this might be the longest conversation we had had since she waltzed into that audition room a few days ago, and I was intrigued.

'Everything was about to change for me that night,' she explained. 'And I was trying to get my head around it, make peace with it, but then you asked me to dance and—'

'Hey, guys!'

Before we were interrupted, I had been about to ask Lira what she meant by everything changing for her. Irritated, I turned to see Daniella, who had somehow shoehorned her way in between the two of us and was grinning up at me. I should be thankful; I had been trying to avoid having this conversation and now Daniella had given me the perfect excuse. So why did I suddenly want to hear more about what had been going on in Lira's life back then?

'Heading to the tube?' asked Daniella chirpily, either oblivious to the tense atmosphere or pretending not to notice.

'We are,' said Lira, thankfully stepping in. 'Where do you live, Daniella?'

And as the two of them began to talk, I wondered what

Lira had been about to tell me; whether I would ever find out and whether it would explain what happened the night she left me in a hotel room without so much as a goodbye.

CHAPTER TEN

Lira

The evening before our dress rehearsal, and with less than forty-eight hours until opening night, things felt strained to say the least. Our four duets were choreographed, but they still needed work, and Gabriele wasn't convinced our Argentine tango was strong enough. We'd arrived at James Jive about an hour ago, after a day of rehearsing with the rest of the company at Pineapple, and we'd already acknowledged that we were going to have to rehearse all night if we had to.

For a brief moment, I let myself wonder about where he might sleep if he missed his last train. There was no way I could take him back to the house – Mum and Dad hadn't left for their cruise yet, and, ridiculously, I still hadn't told them about the show. Sedi had headed back to Shoreditch the morning after I'd stormed out of the dinner and I'd tried to arrange a video call with her and Nolo to explain, but Nolo had been at long rehearsals most days and Sedi had been in Paris for an audition and we hadn't been able to agree on a time. As for Mum and Dad, I'd had plenty of opportunities to say something, and I'd apologized for my outburst at lunch, but neither of them had actually asked me why I wanted to spend less time at the studio, and what it was I wanted to do instead. Knowing them, they were probably hoping it would all just go away – actually talking about problems wasn't really a thing in our family.

I'd locked up the studio for the night and had read over the notes left for me by one of the freelance dance teachers I was secretly employing to cover lessons while I was at rehearsals. I'd put them all on the payroll, so at some point Dad was going to notice, but hopefully it wouldn't be until he and Mum were mid-Mediterranean, by which point the *Slow Burn* London run would be in full swing and I could deal with their disappointment from a distance. I mean, how bad could it be, right? Maybe it was all in my head, anyway – when they found out why I couldn't run the studio for a while, they might be over the moon for me, excited that my passion for performing had been unexpectedly re-ignited. Anyway, whatever happened, it would be worth it – I'd never have imagined I'd be heading up a West End show in just a few days' time. My fears about being dropped or not living up to Carlos's expectations were waning with each passing day, and I was confident that I could actually pull it off. And if I could just hold off my family for a little bit longer, I would be able to focus on giving the best performance of my entire life on opening night without worrying about what everyone thought. For possibly the first time in my life I was being completely and utterly selfish and putting my own happiness first – and it felt pretty damn good.

I took a sip of water, reminded myself we very nearly had this routine down, and walked into the studio where Gabriele was waiting for me on the dance floor.

I flicked the music on and took my starting position for the Argentine tango, as I had a hundred times before.

'We need one more lift,' said Gabriele, suddenly.

'Really?'

Wasn't it a bit late to be adding something else in? The routine looked great as it was.

'I will try something this time; something I saw online and think we should try to recreate. Go with it, okay?' he insisted.

'Fine,' I agreed.

'I want us to dance like we are in Argentina,' he said, taking my hand and looking into my eyes. 'Remember that I learned this dance from my grandmother, my *abuela*. There is an aggressiveness to it over there, a violence. Many years ago, it was illicit, forbidden, lower class, and even today it must still have that intensity. We must dance like our lives depend on it.'

I nodded, falling into the walking step, *la caminada*,

letting him lead me across the floor. We knew each movement like the backs of our hands, and yet, in some way, the steps felt brand-new each time we performed them. With what he'd said about Argentina in our minds, this time I felt him commanding me. I felt heady, breathless, like I never wanted our dance to stop.

And then, taking me by surprise, Gabriele fell to one knee, running his hand down my thigh until he reached my ankle, at which point he placed it over his shoulder. I knew what he was about to do and had no choice but to go with it, praying I could balance as well as he seemingly thought I could. With my leg hooked over his shoulder, he placed his hands around me and rose to standing, taking me with him. My pelvis was pressed so hard into his face, I was surprised he could breathe, but he appeared to have enough oxygen to spin me around twice before lowering me gently back to the floor.

'Embellishment!' he shouted.

I lifted my foot off his shoulder, extending it out as far as I possibly could before whipping it around behind me and sinking into a deep lunge.

'Good,' said Gabriele, pulling me up to meet him, our foreheads touching now, his long eyelashes tickling my cheekbones as he blinked.

We picked up the steps we'd rehearsed, the *boleos* becoming faster and faster, sharper and sharper, until the music came to a crescendo. For our final move, he lifted me again and I kicked my foot out behind me before swinging one leg back through his legs, finishing up in the splits on the ground. Then, with one hand, Gabriele lifted me high into the air, and as soon as my feet touched the ground again, he put his hand on the small of my back to support me as I fell into an extreme back bend, my right fingertips trailing on the floor behind me.

I stayed very still for a beat or two, my blood pumping hard through every part of my body, before he hauled me up.

'Did that work?' he asked, breathless himself.

I nodded. It had felt risky, but I knew it would look fantastic. 'Yes.'

And then, as I looked into his deep brown eyes, and he looked just as intensely into mine, something happened between us; the thing I'd been missing, a softness to his gaze, a searingly addictive feeling curling up from my feet into my stomach and my chest. It was as though his defences had dropped away and I could see the real Gabriele again, the one I'd known briefly all those years ago.

The music was still playing, and of course it was romantic and evocative, so maybe that was what tipped us over the edge. Or perhaps it was the heat from his palm, which was still placed firmly on my lower back making me feel safe and seen.

I wanted him to keep it there forever.

Was it me or were our mouths drawing closer together?

His head dipped a little, as though he might be about to kiss me. Letting myself go with the intense need for him that suddenly overwhelmed me, I rocked my weight forward onto my toes, pressing my chest into his strong, wide one, lifting my chin, ready for him to press his lips against mine. He was centimetres away, then millimetres. Our chests were rising and falling as we looked into each other's eyes. My heart was racing so hard I was sure he could feel it.

And then he pulled back.

'Li . . .' he said.

'It's okay,' I whispered.

I knew what he was going to say. We couldn't. We shouldn't. I went to take a step back, too, but instead he pulled me into him again, sliding his free hand underneath the wrap miniskirt I'd ill-advisedly decided to wear, slipping it deliciously between my thighs.

And then he kissed me.

He actually did it this time, and I didn't have time to think, I just reacted, arching into him, a moan escaping from my throat that I hadn't even realized was there. I'd wanted this so much; for years and years I had dreamed about it, daydreamed about it, and now it was happening. I let myself go with it, giving everything of myself to him.

'Lira, what are you doing to me?' he growled, picking me up again, like he had during the dance, carrying me effortlessly over to the mirror with his strong arms, resting my back against the cool glass.

I gasped with pleasure. 'This feels so good.'

I slid down the mirror, planting one leg on the ground and curling the other around his waist, wanting his whole

117

body close to me. My hands were tangled in his hair, his tongue was filling my mouth. It was like every single cell in my body was on fire. And then, over his shoulder, I saw something – or should I say *somebody* – peering through the window of the studio.

I put my hand on Gabriele's chest, pushing him lightly away.

'Somebody's out there,' I said.

'They will soon get bored and go somewhere else,' he said, not moving, stroking my cheek instead, looking at me with those hypnotic eyes you couldn't ignore even if you wanted to.

But whoever it was didn't go away, they rapped on the window and then they moved to the front door and knocked on that, too. Frustrated, I checked my watch – it was nine-thirty in the evening. Who on earth could it be at this time? Unless one of our clients had forgotten something and had swung by to see if we'd found it.

'I'd better go and see who it is,' I said.

Gabriele groaned as he released me from his hold.

'Fine. But hurry back.'

I laughed lightly as my foot dropped to the floor. Was this really happening?! I straightened my skirt and patted down my hair, which I was sure would now be all over the place after Gabriele's hands had raked deliciously through it. I smiled to myself as I ran out into the reception area, immediately realizing exactly who it was at the door, because they were currently yelling drunkenly through the keyhole.

'Lira?! Are you in there? It's me, let me in!'

It was Sedi and she sounded off her face. I stepped away from the door like it had burned me.

'One second!' I called.

I rushed back into the studio, where Gabriele was leaning enticingly against the mirror, slightly flushed, looking at me as though I was going to fall right back into his arms and carry on where we left off. I'd have liked nothing more, but this was an emergency.

'It's my sister!' I explained, hearing the panic in my voice. 'You're going to have to sneak out the back door.'

He looked at me, confused. 'Why would I need to sneak out?'

Seriously, could he just move?! There was no time for this! 'Because I haven't told anyone about the show! And if she sees you here, she'll know something's up and I'll have to explain to my entire family what I'm doing and—'

'Your family don't know you have been cast in *Slow Burn*?' he asked, seemingly incredulous.

Of course it would sound weird to anyone else. Nothing about what I was doing felt remotely normal, but I'd got myself into it now, and tonight was *not* the time for the big reveal.

'No. They don't. I'll explain it at some point, but right now, you need to go.'

Sedi hammered on the door.

'Tell me now,' said Gabriele, infuriatingly refusing to vacate the premises.

'It's complicated.'

'Who do they think is running the studio while you are at rehearsals? And what is going to happen when we go on tour – who is going to look after it then?'

'I've hired a couple of dance teachers I know, all of whom I trust implicitly. Plus, I'll be available on the phone 24/7 if they need me,' I added, aware of Sedi becoming increasingly frustrated out on the street. 'And by the way, I don't need your judgement on the matter!' I picked Gabriele's hoodie off the floor and threw it at him. 'The back door's this way. I'll show you.'

He shook his head, grabbing his bag and his water bottle, and followed me across the dance floor as I opened the fire door at the back of the studio and stood aside to let him through.

'This leads out into an alleyway. Head that way and you'll meet the main road. Turn left for the station,' I said.

'Way to make a man feel wanted,' said Gabriele, snarling at me as he brushed past.

Clearly, I'd upset him, but my main priority was letting Sedi in and making some excuse about why I'd taken so long to get to her. At least she wouldn't be quite so astute given her drunken state.

'Sorry,' I said, flinging open the front door. 'Couldn't find the key.'

'Hmm,' said Sedi, pushing past me. She staggered straight into the studio, looking around with an eagle eye.

'Was there somebody else in here with you?' she asked slurring her words. 'I heard another voice.'

I shook my head. 'How much have you had to drink, Sedi?'

She ignored me, pointing her finger at me ominously and then twirling it around in a drunken fashion. 'Have you had a man in here, Lira?' she teased. 'Have you been up to no good in the family dance studio?'

'Absolutely not. I was just choreographing some steps for one of my wedding couples. You must have been seeing double.'

She scoffed. 'They're doing an Argentine tango on their wedding day? Ha! A recipe for disaster!' she declared. 'Got any Prosecco open?'

'Haven't you had enough?' I said, already sounding like the sort of parent I never wanted to become. The problem with Mum asking me to keep an eye on Sedi and Nolo was that, for their entire lives, they'd been given everything they'd ever wanted on a plate. My parents rarely denied them anything, and so when I said no to something, they tended to ignore my protestations and did exactly what they wanted to anyway. If only I possessed half of their sense of entitlement.

'Why are you telling me what to do?' whined Sedi.

'I'm not, I'm just advising you,' I said, knowing it was pointless trying to get through to her. If she wanted more alcohol, she was going to have it, whether I approved or not. 'There's an open bottle of white wine in the fridge – should be nice and cold,' I said to appease her. 'Why are you in Castlebury, anyway?'

'Wanted to see Mum and Dad before they go on the

cruise, didn't I?' said Sedi, fumbling around, unscrewing the bottle and pouring a too-large measure into a glass.

While I watched her, I let myself acknowledge what had just happened with Gabriele.

We'd kissed. It had felt amazing. And it absolutely could not happen again.

CHAPTER ELEVEN

Lira

The day of our first performance had come all too soon. My heart immediately felt as though it was stuck in my throat when I walked into the theatre to prepare for opening night and was directed to the backstage area and the dressing room I'd be sharing with the other girls. Only Gabriele had his own dressing room, and so he should – he was the star of the show; it was his photo on the posters, it was his reputation at stake. In some ways, I should feel much less pressured – I was an unknown in this industry and I had nothing to lose, because if things went badly, I could revert to running the studio. Except, I would know how it had felt to dance like this again, and I suspected that going back to my own life would no longer be enough.

I took a moment to acknowledge the fact that, in a few short hours, I would be performing with a professional dance company in the heart of Theatreland, minutes from Covent Garden and in one of London's beautiful old theatres, complete with sloping floors and ornate balconies and red velvet seats. When I passed a door leading into the auditorium, I peeped inside, almost tearing up when I saw how magnificent the stage looked, with its red velvet drapes hanging dramatically to each side and the huge lighting rig suspended from the ceiling. This morning we would be having a light check before taking a break and returning late afternoon for a warm-up. I was confident in the work we'd done, but tonight's performance would be a chance for Carlos and the producers to gauge how each dance – and the show as a whole – landed with the audience and make any necessary changes before the all-important press night.

The feeling of euphoria at the prospect of dancing in front of an audience again was quickly replaced by a sickening sense of fear. I didn't feel ready, certainly not for my duets with Gabriele.

We'd simply run out of time and, although we hadn't repeated the grinding on the mirror from a couple of nights ago, mixing business with pleasure was never a good idea, and we should have saved all of that sexual tension for the stage, not succumbed to it in one moment of madness. Plus, he'd been cold with me since then, suggesting I'd thrown him out of the studio because I was embarrassed to be seen with him. That was far from the case, as I'd tried to explain, but he hadn't been interested in listening, choosing to brush me off instead.

And so here we were, even more awkward around each other than before. I supposed the only saving grace was that it hadn't gone much further than a – spectacularly *exquisite* – kiss. Oh, and that Sedi seemingly had no idea that anyone – let alone him – had been with me that night. I hadn't lied to her exactly, but nor had I told the truth.

I seemed to be doing a lot of that lately.

As I walked down a corridor, a warren of carpets and doors that led to the dark, underground bowels of the theatre, the door to a dressing room flew open and Daniella appeared.

'Oh. Hello,' she said, as if she was surprised to see me. I had the same call time as her and the rest of the cast, so why was she pretending otherwise? Then her startled expression turned into something else – a smirk, perhaps; I wasn't sure. 'Gabriele's in there if you're looking for him.'

She pointed to his name on the door.

'I'm not,' I said, smiling tightly and carrying on.

I knew I had to talk to him sometime, but it didn't have to be now. My head was full of nerves and the steps that, in a couple of hours, I would have to perform. I couldn't allow anything to throw me even remotely off.

Annoyingly, because I wasn't really in a chatty mood, Daniella fell into step beside me as I headed for the communal dressing room. I couldn't hear any of the usual chatter from the other dancers, so we must be the first in.

'What is it with you two?' she asked. 'You and Gabriele?'

I swallowed hard. How much did she know? Surely he hadn't told her?

'I've no idea what you mean, and honestly all I want to think about right now is the show,' I said, trying not to sound defensive.

Apparently, Daniella was not to be deterred.

'Because I hope you know how lucky you are to have been given this role. It's unheard of for a dancer as inexperienced as you to be handed something like this on a plate.'

'Of course I realize what an opportunity this is,' I said, put out by her tone. What was she suggesting here?

'As dance captain, I will be watching you closely, as I will every other member of the cast. And if you're not on your absolute A-game every single night, we're going to have a problem.'

Was she threatening me? I bet she'd love it if I messed up and had to be replaced by either her or one of her adoring hangers-on, a group that included Carlos's stuck-up assistant Emily, and who seemed to be gossiping together – sometimes about me, no doubt – every time I looked at them.

'Trust me, there won't be a problem.'

Daniella looked at me sideways.

'Some advice, for what it's worth. Gabriele needs to be

focused on the show, not on some new romance that probably won't last more than five minutes, anyway.'

I shook my head, reminding myself to keep calm, that she probably had no idea what she was talking about and was fishing for clues. Little did she know that romance wasn't even an option – I was hardly going to make Gabriele fall madly in love with me, was I? There was some unresolved lust between us, that was all. And it wasn't worth risking my reputation – or the wrath of Daniella.

'There's absolutely nothing happening between us,' I lied.

Then I found a small section of the mirror that I could make my own and began to unpack my make-up from my bag, trying my best to ignore Daniella, who was still hovering next to me.

'He doesn't do relationships, anyway. You know that, don't you?' said Daniella, leaning her back against the mirror, refusing to go away.

'Why would I care either way?' I said, scraping my hair back into a bun.

'There's a spark between you, anyone can see that. But if you think it would ever be more than that, you're mistaken. He'd never give you what you want.'

'How would you know what I want?' I asked, turning to her, wishing more than anything that she'd just leave me alone and go away.

She shrugged – she'd rattled me and she knew it.

'Don't say I didn't warn you,' she said.

I tutted as she walked away, looking at myself in the mirror, knowing she had a point, even if I could have done without her rubbing it in.

Luca chose that moment to poke his head around the door.

'Is it safe to come in?' he asked, raising his eyebrows hopefully.

I smiled. 'It's only me in here, so sure.'

Luca scooted inside.

'What did she want?' he asked. Daniella had probably just flounced right past him.

'Quizzing me about Gabriele. Warning me off him,' I said.

Luca rolled his eyes. We'd developed a pretty close friend-ship considering we'd only known each other for three weeks. He was Gabriele's understudy, so we'd rehearsed the duets together as well as the group dances. I loved Luca, but was it bad of me to hope that I'd never actually have to dance with him on stage? He and I shared a laugh together, and we enjoyed bitching about how snippy some of the other dancers could be, but I knew we didn't have a fraction of the chemistry on stage that Gabriele and I did.

'She's clearly in love with him,' said Luca, flinging him-self into a chair and watching me lay out my make-up and hair products for later. 'And you're making her insanely jealous.'

I laughed softly to myself. 'I don't think anyone's ever been jealous of me in my life.'

'Rubbish,' said Luca. 'You're beautiful and you know it. And so does Gabriele.'

'He doesn't.'

'Oh so that's why he looks at you like he wants to rip your clothes off, is it?'

'That's hatred you're picking up on, not desire.'

'I know what I see,' said Luca infuriatingly. 'Come on, you can tell me, we're friends now. You've slept together, right?'

I bit my lip. I desperately wanted to tell someone, to say the words out loud, to hear the opinion of another person instead of listening only to the relentlessly punishing voice in my head.

'Ages ago. We were kids,' I said.

There. It was out there now. I was almost too scared to look in the mirror because I would see Luca's facial expression reflected back at me and I would be able to tell what he thought of it all. And Luca was the kind of guy who said it as it was.

'Knew it! And there's something more recent. Isn't there?!' he demanded to know.

'No.'

'Do not lie to me, Lira James. No couple has that much of a connection on stage without shagging, or at least wanting to.'

I sighed, checking over my shoulder. For all I knew, somebody could be skulking around outside, and if one of Daniella's henchwomen overheard, the entire cast would know all there was to know about mine and Gabriele's sex life – or lack thereof – within minutes.

'Fine. We kissed. A few days ago.'

'And now what?'

'And now I'm trying not to do it again.'

Luca sat up straight in his chair. 'What's stopping you?'

I turned to face him. 'Isn't it obvious?'

'Er, not really?' said Luca, looking genuinely perplexed.

'Daniella said we shouldn't mix business with pleasure.'

'Probably not, but everyone does. We're dancers – who else are we going to meet if not each other? Also, I wouldn't necessarily listen to anything Daniella has to say – she has an ulterior motive, as discussed.'

'Also, Gabriele is hardly the relationship type. There's no point in us having some casual fling that will only make things awkward afterwards.'

'Has he actually said that's all he wants?' asked Luca.

He didn't have to. It was obvious, wasn't it? 'Not in so many words.'

'Well, I wouldn't make assumptions, Lira. I don't know him *that* well,' said Luca, getting up to leave, 'but he seems like a bit of a deep, sensitive soul to me. If he's not into relationships, it's probably because he hasn't met the right person.'

'Hmmm,' I said.

'Better go and get ready for the light check,' said Luca. 'But, Lira, maybe it's worth taking a risk? What's the worst that could happen if you let things take their natural course?'

I shuddered. 'I dread to think.'

I watched Luca leave the dressing room and turned back to look at myself in the mirror. Did he have a point? I'd never really thought of Gabriele being sensitive before, but what if underneath all of that confidence and bravado there was someone more vulnerable, someone who was just as scared of falling in love as I was? I thought briefly of the moments after we'd slept together in Paris. He'd fallen asleep with me tangled in his arms, and even as he'd drifted off, his breath slowing and softening, I remember noticing that he didn't loosen his hold on me. I'd never felt like that after sex before, so contented, so safe, so *wanted*. He hadn't seemed like a womanizer then, but he was only twenty-one; perhaps he'd grown into it. In fact, if I thought about it, it had been me who'd set a precedent that this was simply a casual hook-up, not him. I'd known we were only destined to be together for one night, or at least I *thought* I'd known, and as a result, there had been none of the usual *will we or won't we see each other again*? We wouldn't, and that was that.

My flight had been at 6am that same morning, my taxi due to arrive at 3.

And so, an hour after watching him drift off, I gently removed myself from his arms and got dressed in the bathroom, throwing my remaining things into my suitcase and sneaking out of the room with only a very brief glance back at the beautiful man sleeping naked in the bed. My life was

131

going to be different from then on in, and it was pointless taking any of the old along with me.

It had felt like all or nothing. And in my case, seemingly, it had been nothing.

CHAPTER TWELVE

Gabriele

I stood stage right, waiting for the show to begin. It was Carlos who would be most anxious this evening – finally his vision would be coming together in front of a paying audience. After tonight, he would have to finely tune the production based on the things – good and bad – he observed on opening night.

My job was to make sure that the only things he had to say were good.

I turned to Lira, who was standing quietly behind me. She looked a little unsure, as was to be expected after so many years away from the stage. For the first time in a long while I wondered if we had done the right thing by throwing her back in at the deep end like this, with nowhere near enough rehearsal time. She was an amazing dancer, and of course – although I was loath to admit it – our chemistry was exactly where it needed to be, on stage at least. Off stage it was . . . complicated. We had not found the time to talk about our kiss, nor the fact she had ushered me out the back door of her studio afterwards because she did not want to be seen with me – my ego had been bruised by her all over again. As a result, there was an unspoken tension between us that I imagined both of us were finding unhelpful for the performance of a lifetime we were expected to give.

'Are you ready for this?' I whispered to her.

She nodded. I was not sure if I believed her, but I supposed I would have to take her word for it.

Through the tiniest gap in the velvet curtains, I could see a snapshot of the audience, a thin sliver of faces, some avidly reading their glossy programme, others chatting to the person sitting next to them. I could feel the atmosphere all around me – the excitement, the expectation. It was everything I loved about live theatre. Now, all I had to do was deliver what had been promised.

'Is it a full house?' asked Lira.

'I cannot quite see,' I said. 'But Carlos said that all the seats had been filled, yes.'

I turned to face her, softening my voice, wanting to be supportive, to reassure, despite not quite knowing where I stood with her after the other night.

'You are going to be brilliant out there,' I said softly. *'Magnifico*. Trust me.'

She nodded her appreciation and we shared a smile of

solidarity, an understanding that we would both go out on that stage and give it our absolute all. She looked stunning in her costume for the opening dance, a long, navy blue satin dress with spaghetti straps and a slit so long it ran all the way up to the middle of her thigh. Her make-up was perfect for the stage: polished and simple, except for her mouth, which was ruby red and glossy. For a second, I imagined plunging my own lips against hers and then I got myself in check. What the hell was wrong with me, thinking like that moments before we were about to set foot out on stage? I was seriously calling my own professionalism into question.

'I'm worried about the rumba,' she said, biting her bottom lip and unfortunately drawing my attention to her mouth over again.

We had added in a new move that morning, at Carlos's request. It was risky, but I knew she could do it.

'Do not be afraid,' I said. 'If one of us makes a mistake, the other will cover. We know each other well enough for that.'

And I meant what I said, even if there were many parts of her that were still a mystery to me. I could feel her ambition, her attention to detail, how much she wanted this second chance at a dance career. What I did not know was why she had given it up in the first place; why she seemed so scared to be honest with her family; why she had walked out on me that night in Paris. But these questions would have to be answered another time – we had work to do now.

The house lights dimmed and the audience hushed and settled. I dropped my head, closing my eyes for a second, grounding myself.

Let this performance go well. Let the audience love the show. Let me dance like I have never danced before.

The opening bars of the Argentine tango rang out across the theatre. This was not the duet Lira and I would end the show with, it was a group number, a recreation of a sizzling-hot night-club scene in Buenos Aires, a city I knew and loved. Lira and I were first to step out from behind the curtain; for forty-five seconds it would be just me and her, all eyes on us before the rest of the cast joined us and we became a company of dancers, all with the same common goal: to wow, to entertain.

I reached behind me and took Lira's hand, squeezing it once before stepping out onto the stage, leading her behind me, becoming the character I was playing for this dance. The lights went up on stage, covering us with an intense beam of light as I pulled Lira into me, running my hand down the side of her body as she bent backwards, trailing her hand on the floor, my other hand supporting her back. As she came back to standing, I took control, snapping into hold, beginning the routine we had rehearsed over and over, willing it to go well.

The steps that ended the show nearly two hours later – if you included the interval – were some of the most dramatic of the entire production. Lira was balancing on my shoulder, I was spinning her around, then she slid off, spiralling into my arms. I caught her, seconds from the ground, and held her there, suspended in motion, before pulling her up to meet me, her hand on my cheek – an almost kiss – then her final back bend.

The lights went down, and for a second or two we did not move. We had done it. We had got through the show with minimal mistakes. It could not have gone better, not on a first night. Whether the audience had liked it or not, I was not entirely sure, although if their whoops and whistles throughout the show were anything to go by, it had felt like they had.

Performing was in my blood, it was what I *lived* for, and I rarely felt nervous, but perhaps tonight had been the closest I had got to it. It was a strange feeling headlining a show, knowing that no matter how perfectly everyone else performed, if I did not deliver, the whole show would be criticized in the press and there would be nobody else to blame. My stomach had been fluttering all day, and now I knew what people meant when they said they had butterflies in their bellies.

The stage lights came up again and Lira and I pulled apart, turning to face the audience. For a beat or two there was a loaded silence, until thunderous applause broke out, and I breathed a sigh of relief. Lira and I turned to our respective sides of the stage, inviting the rest of the cast to join us. The applause would not stop, and there were more enthusiastic shouts of *Bravo!* and *More!* – that would be the friends and family, no doubt, although, of course, there was nobody here for me. My parents were in Italy, and the only friends I had in London were the ones involved in this production.

When the whole cast were in place, I took a step forward alone, taking another bow. I straightened up, spotting that some of the audience were on their feet – lots of them, in fact. This was always a good sign. Perhaps that was why I got carried away and turned to take Lira's hand, pulling her with me so that we could take one final bow together. This moment was supposed to be mine, but it felt wrong not to share it with her – I would not have danced so well with anyone else, I knew that emphatically.

And then together we turned and walked backstage, giving the audience a final wave as we disappeared behind the curtain.

The adrenaline rush when you come off stage is indescribable, and tonight was no exception. The whole company was in high spirits and everyone was jumping around, hugging each other. Carlos threw his arms around me. Lira kept beaming at me as though she could not quite believe we had pulled it off.

'Yes, Gabriele! Bravo! They loved you out there!' enthused Carlos.

And then he turned to Lira. 'And you, my dear! A star in the making!'

Strangely, I did not feel even a prickle of envy or competitiveness. I knew how well I had danced, and of course I had wanted Lira to match me, otherwise what would have been the point in hiring her? The two of us were electric together and I wanted the world to see it.

Having checked my phone in the middle of all the festivities backstage, I noticed that I had several missed calls from my mother that I really should reply to. I glanced around the room – the cast were not going anywhere: we had much to celebrate. I slipped out of the bar, heading back to my dressing room, closing the door behind me. I took a moment to look at myself in the mirror, nodding to myself in appreciation. The small improvements to be made would be unnoticeable to anyone but me, Carlos and the most highly trained dancers. Lira had taken only one wrong step, and I had soon spun her back around the other way with a flourish, hoping to draw the eye to our arms and our elegant necks, rather than our feet.

I sunk down into a chair, letting myself relax for the first time that evening. And then I pulled out my phone and called my mother.

'Darling! How did it go?' she gushed. 'I have been searching for reviews to see how it went for you.'

I rolled up the sleeves of my shirt, hot now in the enclosed space of the dressing room.

'They will not be out yet, Mama. The theatre critics will not see the show until press night tomorrow.'

She laughed. 'Well, then you must tell me the second your first review comes out. Remember how I used to make scrapbooks of all your newspaper cuttings?'

I smiled to myself. 'I do. I should look back at them sometime; remind myself of how far I have come.'

My mother and my *abuela* had always been my two biggest champions. Spending summers in Argentina with them had ignited my passion for the Argentine tango, way before I knew I wanted to dance for a living. As a child, I learned the steps the proper way, on the streets of Buenos Aires, where the music and the steps felt like they were in my blood, and where, every night, locals would play music and perform the dance in its rawest, dirtiest form.

Being half-Argentinian gave me an advantage over other dancers, no matter how accomplished they were at every other dance. The Argentine tango was special – it penetrated your soul, and you either got it or you did not, and if you did not truly understand its roots, the dance would never take an audience's breath away.

Lira felt it. Perhaps it was her South African heritage that allowed her to tap into the music like that. I had never been to her mother's home country, but I imagined the passion for music and tradition there ran just as deeply as it did in Argentina.

'How is Papa doing?' I asked, vaguely thinking I ought to get back to the party.

'We do not need to speak about that now,' said Mama. 'This is your special night, you go enjoy it.'

'Why, were you planning to tell me something that would stop me enjoying it?' I said, my heart sinking. She may as well tell me because it would be on my mind now, anyway.

Mama sighed. 'Papa is not so well. I worry about him, you know that. He is trying to do too much on the farm and comes home every night looking so tired and grey. He barely has an appetite, not even for his own wine.'

I raked my hand through my hair. This did not sound good. Food and wine were two of my father's greatest pleasures, and if he was not enjoying them, it must mean that something was wrong with him.

'When was the last time a doctor checked him out?' I asked.

'You know how stubborn he is,' said Mama. 'Perhaps you could talk to him? Even better if it could be in person. I was hoping you could come home for a night before the European tour begins?'

'That is in less than a week, Mama. I will see you both when we come to *Firenze*.'

'But that feels such a long way away, Gabi. What if . . .'

I swallowed hard, dread seeping through me. What was she suggesting?

'What if what?'

'Nothing.'

She thought something bad was going to happen before I could see him, I could hear it in her voice. Heart problems ran in his side of the family, and if he was pushing and pushing himself all of the time like she said he was, who knew what state his health might be in. Why did he not hire more staff? Take a step back, run things from the sidelines?

I knew why. He was too proud to ask for help. If he

got very sick, I would have no choice but to go home to Italy and run the wine business for him, which was exactly where he had always wanted me to be. It was wrong of me, but I wondered if he was purposely not helping himself so as to force my hand.

'Leave it with me, I will see what I can do,' I said, already running through my schedule in my head.

There might be more rehearsals, finessing our routines, press interviews, plus performances six nights of the week. I was torn between wanting to make a quick visit home, for my mother more than my father, if I was honest, and wanting to say no, that I could not, that it would not be possible.

Lately, when I went home, I worried that something would happen while I was there and that I would be trapped, never able to leave. Which was a terrible way to think of your family home, and I always felt very guilty about it afterwards, because I loved my parents dearly; I just did not want to live with them in the middle of nowhere. Despite the vastness of the land we owned, the rows and rows of vines, the olive farm, I felt strangely claustrophobic when I was there, and was always, *always* desperate to get back to the city, whether that be my apartment in Milan or my rented place in London. The further I was from the hills of Chianti country, the better I felt. It was easier to have physical distance between my dance career and the family business; it was what had always worked best.

'I don't mean to make things difficult for you, Gabriele,' said Mama, feeling bad now, no doubt. 'I know how busy you are. Forget I said anything.'

I had dragged it out of her, I supposed, but still – she could have made something up. The last thing I felt like doing was celebrating now.

I ended the call and put my head in my hands, trying to clear my mind. Perhaps my mother was being melodramatic; she did have a tendency to overreact. And my papa was a grown man – if he felt unwell, he needed to go get himself checked out, and I did not see how I could force him to do so, or why I should have to.

A knock on the door jolted me out of my melancholy.

'Come in,' I called, probably more tersely that I should have done.

The door was eased tentatively open and Lira poked her head around the frame.

'Hey,' she said.

She was glowing. Happy. And why would she not be? She had just danced the gig of her life and had pulled off the almost impossible, just as Carlos had reassured us she could.

'Hey,' I said, sitting up.

'Am I disturbing you?' she asked, hovering in the shadow of the half-open door.

I waved her inside. 'It is fine. *Prego entra.*'

She let the door close behind her and suddenly we were alone in the stagnant heat of my windowless dressing room, her eager, open face lit up by the bright bulbs dotted around the edge of my mirror.

'How did you think it went?' she asked, crossing her arms and then uncrossing them again.

She was nervous; it was adorable.

'Almost perfection,' I said.

She laughed. 'Always so modest.'

'You would do well to sell yourself more, Lira. Who else is going to do it for you?'

'Maybe,' she said, a slightly wistful look in her eye, as though I had hit on something that felt important to her.

Her family, I guessed. If she was keeping the fact she was doing the show from them, I could only presume they were not supportive of her career choices. But how could they not be when she danced as beautifully as she did? Were they not proud of her? But then I thought of Papa and how he had never said he was proud of me, either. Quite the opposite at times.

You are throwing your life away on a stupid dance job! Call yourself a man? A real man would run the family business, like a good son should.

'I was thinking we should rehearse the rumba a little more, if you can find the time,' she said. 'I messed up that step. And one or two of the lifts felt a little clunky.'

She was exactly right, and I could not help but be surprised at her attention to detail. I'd barely registered it myself, but thinking about it now, one of the lifts had felt more difficult than it should have been.

'What are you doing tomorrow daytime?' I asked her.

'I thought I would celebrate by working like a dog in the studio all day,' she said, with a wry smile.

'You are joking?' I said.

'Half-joking. I do have a couple of lessons to do in the

morning – the cover teacher has a medical appointment she can't get out of.'

'Shall I come to James Jive after that? Say 1pm? We can run through the dance for an hour or so and then head back into London together for warm-up.'

'Sure,' she said, frowning a little. 'You're agreeing to come all the way out to Castlebury for an hour without complaining? Who even *are* you?'

'Hilarious,' I quipped.

Her smile was infectious. Way to get me out of my bad mood.

'I guess I should get back,' she said, tipping her head towards the door.

I nodded. 'I will be out in a few minutes myself.'

As she opened the door, I almost called out, asked her to stay. Everything felt better and brighter when she was here, and as she closed the door behind her the room felt dull and cold again.

I had not thought about family responsibility once while she had been here, only about the show and her exquisite skin that I wanted to lie on top of and somehow melt into. Had that subconsciously been why I had agreed to trek out to her hometown tomorrow when I should have been re-laxing, getting ready for that evening's performance? Did I think I was in with a chance of kissing her again? That was hardly going to happen in broad daylight, was it, and we were not even focusing on the tango this time, although the rumba was definitely almost as sexy.

I got up from my seat, took a deep breath, put the anxiety about my father's health to the back of my mind and flung open the door. This was my night as much as it was everyone else's, and I deserved to revel in it, no matter what was going on back in Italy.

CHAPTER THIRTEEN

Lira

I arrived at the studio early the next morning, mainly to avoid the chaos the house was in. Mum and Dad were off on their luxurious-sounding cruise the following day, and there were flung-open suitcases and copious amounts of washing strewn across every surface, and my mum was in one of her agitated moods. I'd learned over the years that it was best to stay out of her way completely at such times.

It felt good to be back in the familiarity of the studio, where I felt like my normal self again and was instantly reassured that everything was running smoothly, despite it no longer being my only priority. I did a quick stock take, cashed up from the day before and ran through the bookings for the following week. The stand-in teachers had done a great job of keeping things ticking over for the last few days, but there were little details that needed straightening out; bits of tidying they either hadn't noticed needed doing or hadn't had time to do. And although I'd been keeping on top of my emails, there were still a plethora of new ones to reply to: enquiries about private lessons, mainly, as well as people wanting to join the waiting list for the kids' classes. I'd have a week's reprieve now that the London performances were about to start – I could work in the studio during the day and head to the theatre for late afternoon, just employing additional teachers for an hour or so at the end of each day if I needed to.

Minutes before I was about to start my first lesson of the day, I got a strange text from Mum, asking when I had a break today because she needed to talk to me. I presumed it was just about the plans for while they were away, but whatever it was, her tone felt off.

I told myself it was probably because she was still in the middle of packing and I punched back a message.

I'll be free at 12.

My second lesson of the day was with one of my favourite clients, Adrian. He was a high-flying city banker who had always wanted to learn the waltz, and he'd come up with a plan to surprise his wife – who was a keen dancer herself – on their twenty-fifth wedding anniversary. An eager student, Adrian picked up the steps relatively easily, even if his delivery needed a little – okay, a ton of – work.

'That was brilliant, Adrian. Your best yet,' I said, running over to turn off the music.

Adrian beamed at me, sweat dripping down his face. He'd definitely got fitter since we'd been having our lessons, and apparently he'd dropped two whole collar sizes.

'I've got the best teacher. How could I not improve?' he said, taking a tissue out of his trouser pocket and wiping his face with it. 'Right, I'd better get back to my desk before anyone notices I've taken a two-hour lunch,' he said, grimacing.

I laughed. He worked from home a couple of days a week, which, apparently, had revolutionized his life. He now had no qualms about slacking off for an hour or two during the day – and if he made up the time and still got the job done, who cared?

I thought, perhaps recently, I'd come to the same conclusion myself. I'd always felt like I needed to be involved in every aspect of the studio, making it my business to check and double-check everybody else's work, because it was *my* responsibility to make sure everything was running smoothly. But since performing had come back into my life, and I'd been sneaking off myself when I needed to, I'd realized that I didn't need to micro-manage everything. The other teachers had coped perfectly well without me and, sure, there might be the odd dirty mug littered around the place, and the bins might not have been emptied for a couple of days, but nothing terrible had happened.

The studio hadn't fallen apart without me.

'Let's book your next session in,' I said, heading for the reception desk and my computer. 'Not long until your anniversary party!'

'Don't!' said Adrian, leaning on the counter while I checked my diary. 'I'm beginning to think this was all a really bad idea.'

I gave him a scolding look. 'Your wife is going to be blown away when she sees what you can do. It's just nerves getting the better of you. I one-hundred-percent believe you can pull this off and make your wife's jaw drop in amazement.'

'God, I hope so,' said Adrian.

Behind him, the door opened and I looked up, surprised to see several members of my family piling into the studio – Mum, Dad and a pissed-off-looking Sedi. Strange. I really hoped they weren't planning to stay long because Gabriele was coming at one, and I needed them all to be out of here before he arrived.

'Hi, guys,' I said, wondering if I looked as confused as I felt. I could count the number of times all three of them had been in the studio at the same time on one hand.

I quickly booked Adrian in and told him I'd see him soon. Mum turned on the charm, as she did so brilliantly, asking him how long he'd been dancing and how wonderful that he wanted to surprise his wife. Adrian seemed enamoured with her on the spot, just like everyone was when she was at her most sociable. I only hoped this indicated she was in a good mood – Mum's bad ones were not to be messed with.

The bell above the door jangled as Adrian left and I came out from behind the desk. Sedi was already slumped in one of the armchairs looking fed up. Mum was casting her eagle eye over the studio, no doubt ensuring that I was keeping the place clean enough for her exceptionally high standards.

'I wasn't expecting to see all of you,' I said, glancing at Dad.

If they were so stressed about packing, had they *both* needed to come? Maybe they just wanted to run through arrangements for when they were away on the cruise. Perhaps Sedi had volunteered to help out after all. I glanced at her – she didn't exactly look happy to be here, so that seemed unlikely.

'We're hoping you can explain this,' said Mum, standing right in front of me with an angry expression replacing the warm one she'd given Adrian a few seconds ago.

She passed her phone to me ominously. I looked down at the screen and my stomach dropped. Fuck. It was a message from her Italian friend, Lucia, who ran a high-end dance-wear boutique in St John's Wood.

Is this your daughter?! You didn't tell us she was dancing with Gabriele Riccitelli!

Accompanying the message was a screenshot of a piece in the *Metro*, announcing *Slow Burn* and mentioning my name as well as Gabriele's. It wasn't even a review – and stupidly I hadn't even considered that my name might be mentioned in the papers before press night. And I knew there wasn't much crossover with the commercial dance world or the New York ballet scene, so I'd assumed *Slow Burn* wouldn't be on my sisters' radars, either. This was my fault for not telling them sooner; I'd had plenty of opportunities. I supposed this was what you got for avoiding difficult conversations. Now I'd found myself in a situation that was going to be far more confrontational than it would have been if I'd been straight with them from the beginning.

'Looks like you've been lying to us for months,' said Sedi, sulkily.

'Lying?' I said, looking up in her direction. 'What have I been lying about, exactly?'

'About being in a show!' hissed Mum. 'What, did you audition for it? When did you get cast? A long time ago, I presume. Why didn't you tell us?'

I could hardly get a word in edgeways with everyone screeching at me, could I?

'We're very disappointed in you,' said Dad. 'We trusted you to run this business to the best of your ability, but instead you have been going off and leaving it in the hands of – well, *who*, exactly? Whoever it was, they could have done anything. Taken anything. Now I'm going to have to go through the accounts to make sure there's no money missing.'

'Wouldn't it have been a good idea to look at the books

anyway? Before you go away?' I suggested, rather unwisely and a tad more snippily than I'd intended.

Dad gave me a look – I rarely talked back to him, but I was feeling cornered and maybe they *did* need to hear a few home truths about themselves, while we were at it. He was a self-proclaimed financial director, but he hadn't even noticed that there were three extra staff members on the payroll this month.

'Anyway, I did try to tell you all at lunch the other day, but as usual, none of you would listen,' I said, feeling anger swirl in my stomach, a sensation I usually tried my best to avoid. 'And not one of you followed up with me about it afterwards.'

Mum tutted. 'You've ruined our cruise. How can we go now, with the mess you've left us in?'

I groaned out loud.

'Mum, you're totally overreacting.'

'Do not tell me I am overreacting! This is the business your father and I have slogged our guts out over for years. And you come in and you . . . you . . .'

'*Run* it for you?' I said, knowing this would tip her over the edge, but not letting that stop me. If Mum thought she'd been heading up this business single-handedly, she was seriously deluded.

'How dare you?!' said Mum.

'You've got some cheek,' said Sedi.

Sedi. I'd have thought she'd have my back no matter what. So much for sisters sticking together.

'How come *you're* so wound up about all of this, anyway?'
I asked, turning on her, not getting it. She'd be off around
the world soon anyway – why did she care what happened
to the studio as long as she didn't have to do anything with
it?

'No reason,' she said, giving me a shady look.

'I told Sedi that if you are incapable of running the
studio, she will have to step in and do it for you,' declared
Mum.

I laughed. I couldn't help myself.

'Mum, there's no way Sedi is going to do that. Sure, it
would be nice for her to help out more. But run it? Never.
Anyway, teaching cover is all sorted.'

'So you don't think me capable?' Sedi demanded to
know.

'You're perfectly capable – it's just that I know it's the last
thing you'd want. And I've never known you to do *anything*
you don't want to do.'

'Well, there's a first time for everything, isn't there?' she
shouted.

'Do not yell at me!' I replied, even louder than she had.

This was all getting *way* out of hand. My emotions were
suddenly veering dangerously out of control and, although I
willed myself to stay strong, to stand my ground, my throat
tightened as I felt the tug of tears. I absolutely did not want
to cry in front of this lot, because then they'd know how
much they were getting to me, and I had a sort of desperate
need to maintain my reputation as the together, reliable

member of the family. The fixer; the good girl. Except that nothing about the way I'd handled this felt good.

I'd said things to Sedi that I'd only ever thought in my own head, and I wasn't surprised she was angry, because I should have just asked her to help instead of accusing her of being selfish now, years down the line. It wasn't hers or Nolo's fault that they'd had it their own way all this time – it was our parents' place to say no to them on occasion. And, I supposed, mine.

'Let's talk about this sensibly,' said Dad with a huge sigh.

He hated things not being in order, and that included emotions. I knew that, and he was trying to calm things down in his own way, but I couldn't see how he could, because it felt like my whole career was at stake here. My happiness, my *life*, really. And I had a point to prove that they just did not seem to be getting.

'Shall I start by telling you how all of this happened?' I suggested. 'And then you can carry on vilifying me if you still want to.'

Mum huffed and grumbled, but she did take a seat, and Dad perched on the arm of her chair.

'I'm waiting,' said Mum, crossing her arms.

I proceeded to tell them the whole story – about Carlos, his audition, him catching me dancing. That Gabriele was looking for a particular connection with a partner – that we knew each other vaguely from the World Championships. I obviously missed out the mind-blowing sex bit.

Afterwards, they seemed a little appeased – at least I

hadn't gone chasing it, they said, that was something; the job had literally presented itself to me, had dropped into my lap.

'We thought you were happy here at the studio,' said Dad. 'We didn't think you wanted to dance anymore.'

I bit my lip, wondering how much to say; how honest I could be.

'I *am* happy. But I'm also wondering if I might also want . . . something more?'

'Well then you should have spoken up!' said Mum. 'You're making us sound like terrible parents.'

'Of course that's not what I'm saying,' I said, raising my voice again. What was happening to me?! 'And yes, I am partly to blame. I should have been more open about how I was feeling. But it's not like I've been faking it this whole time — I really enjoy running the studio. And you have to admit, I do a good job.'

I looked at them, daring them to say that I didn't. Mum nodded reluctantly.

'Of course you do. And we appreciate it, we always have.'

Okay, this was good. We all appeared to be calming down.

'But I'm still young enough — just about — to do something else with my life. And I miss dancing, I miss it with my entire soul. You know how that feels, I know you do. And now I've got this chance to do this exciting thing and I couldn't turn it down,' I explained.

Hopefully, in a minute, somebody would say congratulations. That they were proud of me, pleased for me. But the longer the simmering silence went on, the more I realized that they were too worried about how this would impact *them* to celebrate my good fortune. My being cast in a show was nothing more than an inconvenience.

Mum and Dad stood up, followed by a disgruntled-looking Sedi. I wasn't sure how long we'd all been bickering, but if it was close to one, there was a good chance Gabriele could rock up at any moment. He'd have no idea what he was walking into and I didn't want him knowing how difficult things were for me – I thought he'd probably find it all quite pathetic. I doubted he was afraid of telling his parents exactly what he did and didn't want to do.

'We'll leave you to it, then,' said Mum.

'I think that's best,' I said. 'Oh, and it's press night tonight, if you wanted to come, Sedi. Shall I put your name on the door?'

She shifted uncomfortably, her gold hoops sparkling in the light.

'I had made other plans,' she said, huffily.

I was seriously lost as to what I was supposed to have done to *her*. Why was she acting as though I'd wronged her, when all I'd done was follow my dreams – something she'd been doing since she was old enough to talk? I felt sick as I watched all three of them leave with none of the usual hugs and kisses. I'd never seen them so angry with me – and I'd never been so mad at *them*. I knew it must have come as a shock, but I couldn't believe they hadn't been even the tiniest bit happy for me.

Exhausted by the effort of trying to keep it together, I took Sedi's place in the armchair, where finally the enormity of it all hit me. I tried to take a deep, calming breath, but instead it turned into a sob, and then another, and before I knew it, I had tears streaming down my cheeks. I'd get up and find a tissue in a minute, but for now it actually felt quite cathartic. Maybe trying not to cry when you felt shit wasn't good for you after all.

I was wallowing so much that I wasn't aware of the studio door opening until it was too late.

'Lira? What is wrong?'

Gabriele strode over to where I was sitting, looming over me with a look of concern on his face. He crouched down so that his eyes were in line with mine and I squirmed under his gaze, not wanting him to see me like this. I must look horrendous.

'I'm fine,' I said, sniffing wildly. 'Honestly.'

'You do not look fine,' he quite rightly said, rummaging in his bag and pulling out a packet of tissues before thrusting one into my hands.

I took it gratefully, wondering how I could blow my nose with him staring at me – hardly an attractive sight, was it? I dabbed at it instead, which, of course, had little to no effect.

'Want to talk about it?' he asked softly, his brow creased with what I could only guess was sympathy. I hadn't thought him capable of such an emotion, so if anything useful had come out of this mortifying episode, perhaps it was the knowledge that he did have a heart after all.

'Not in the slightest,' I said.

I wasn't one to get emotional in front of other people, preferring to use my dancing as a way to express how I was feeling. But even if I *had* been that way inclined, I was pretty sure that opening up to Gabriele Riccitelli would be the last thing I'd consider. There were several reasons for that, the most pressing being that it felt important to keep him at a professional distance. Our working relationship already felt fragile and precarious. If I suddenly started blubbing to him about my personal life, who knew what might follow?

I jumped up, brushed myself off and excused myself to go to the bathroom where I hoped I could compose myself, and as quickly as possible.

'Back in a second,' I called to Gabriele, rushing into the inner echelons of the studio, glad to be away from his sweetly worried face.

The James Jive bathroom was a spotless, calming space with large full-length mirrors – a necessity for any dancer – and nice toiletries that I'd persuaded Dad to spend a bit extra on because they gave the studio's facilities an elevated feel.

I ran the cold water and put my wrists under the tap, cooling myself down. Then I splashed my face with water, hoping to flush away any sign of tears.

I wasn't sure what I was crying about, anyway – my family's reaction had been just as I'd expected. Perhaps, though, somewhere deep down, I'd hoped that they would prove me wrong.

CHAPTER FOURTEEN

Gabriele

Lira and I walked together from the tube to the theatre. She was her usual chatty self and seemed to have recovered from whatever had upset her earlier; her eyes definitely looked far less bloodshot than they had been an hour ago. If she wanted to talk about it, I would listen, but she had assured me that she wanted to focus on the show, and I respected her decision, and would have made the same one myself.

Except for Carlos, I did not think anyone felt quite as invested in tonight's success as the two of us, although of course, the entire cast and crew hoped that *Slow Burn* would get amazing press coverage. Theatre critics were notoriously hard to please – sometimes it felt as though they were *trying* to tear you down, purposely looking to find things wrong with the production: sloppy directing, a running time too long for its own good, over-indulgent routines and so on. But if the reviews were *good*, we could expect a huge surge in ticket sales for the remainder of the run, and I hoped that this would likely translate across to our European tour, too.

'What are you thinking about?' asked Lira, as we navigated the backstreets behind Leicester Square.

'You really want to know?' I asked.

'Course I do,' she said. 'I can practically see your brain ticking over. It's good to talk, you know.'

I gave her a look. 'Really? Only I thought we didn't do that?'

When I'd found her crying earlier, I had been genuinely concerned. I still had no idea what had prompted it; it could have been anything from a relationship break-up – I had not heard her mention a boyfriend, but that did not mean she did not have one – to family problems, to fears about tonight. In my fantasy, she had never found anyone special, either, after our night together in Paris. Although, of course, I really had no idea. And there had been that kiss the other night – she had not kissed me like she had a boyfriend, but I could not rule out the possibility completely.

'I appreciated you asking if I wanted to talk earlier,' she said, a little guarded. 'But I don't find sharing my problems helpful. Particularly with the show on my mind. I had this feeling that if I started talking about it, the tears would just come flooding out and then I'd be exhausted and puffy-eyed for what should be one of the most exciting nights of my life.'

I nodded, completely understanding. It was always easier, in my opinion, to bury things rather than deal with them. One day, when I had time, I would go and sit on a beach somewhere – Bali, maybe, or some remote Caribbean island – and I would let myself think about my life and what I'd achieved, what had gone wrong and what had gone right. But it suited me much better not to address anything much at the moment because I was scared of what might happen if I did.

'Anyway, we were talking about you,' she insisted.

I laughed. 'Fine. It was nothing huge. I was worrying that my name is not enough of a pull for people in the U.K. In Italy it is different.'

'You're a celebrity there,' she said.

I shrugged. 'A little. I get recognized in the street, I can get tables at the best restaurants. Here in London, I could be anybody. Carlos is probably more well known than I am.'

'So the two of you together is the appeal,' she said. 'And the five-star reviews we'll get tonight, obviously.'

She grinned at me.

'You think?' I asked.

'I'm manifesting.'

I frowned playfully. 'Manifesting? What is that?'

'I really don't think you'd be into it.'

We reached the theatre and I held the backstage door open for her. 'Do you profess to know everything I am into, Lira?'

As she brushed past me through the door, something

sparked between us; a feeling I could only describe as a gut-punch, but in a good way. I was suddenly acutely aware that she knew *some* of the things I was into – in bed, it had been as though we knew exactly what to do to please each other.

Every night lately, when I went to bed, I fantasized about Lira up on stage in that red, ruffled dress she had worn when I had first noticed her across the hotel bar in Paris. But older now, wiser, and more sure of herself than she had been then. I was desperate to explore every inch of her body all over again, but that was typical of me – I always wanted what I could not have. And Carlos would kill me if we complicated things by getting romantically involved.

But, if I were being honest with myself, it was because I knew that one night with Lira would never be enough – it had not been then, and it definitely would not be now.

As we walked along the corridors backstage, I thought she might have been thinking about our connection too, because suddenly her cheeks were redder than they had been before, and she could not properly look me in the eye.

'We must focus on the show,' said Lira earnestly. 'That's all that matters, right?'

'Right,' I said, convincing myself as much as her.

'And I know how much *Slow Burn* means to you, too. I won't let you down.'

'Of course you will not, that I am sure of,' I said, stopping outside of my dressing room.

Lira carried on walking, glancing at me over her shoulder.

'See you later,' I called to her before opening my door and going inside.

At around 5.30, after Daniella had led us through the warm-up on stage, Carlos gathered us all together for a pep talk. The air was thick with anticipation – in ninety minutes' time, the audience would begin filing into the auditorium. In two hours' time, the first piece of music would be piped through the speakers and we would be waiting at the side of the stage, ready to begin. It did not feel possible that, just three weeks ago, I had had no idea who my leading female dancer would be, and now here we were, with the dances I loved performing most being the duets I had with Lira.

'I want to express my gratitude to you all,' said Carlos, 'for your hard work and dedication these past few weeks. As you know, our schedule was *very* tight, and without your complete and utter focus, we would not be performing a show of this calibre tonight.'

The cast murmured their appreciation, a few clapped half-heartedly. Everyone was nervous, everyone felt the weight of responsibility. I was on stage for all but ten minutes of the running time, which was entirely taken up with costume changes. If I did not dance at my best, it would affect things for everyone.

I kept my eyes directly on Carlos, not wanting anything – i.e. Lira – to throw me off. If the first time I properly looked at her tonight was when we were on stage together, that would be the best thing. I would retreat to my dressing room after this and then I would harness all my pent-up energy into my performance.

'I hope you all have family and friends coming again tonight to cheer you on,' said Carlos.

I glanced furtively around me – there were lots of nods and 'yesses'. I did not dare look to see if Lira was nodding away, too. Was I the only person who did not have somebody coming to watch them, to support them, specifically; somebody who would tell me I was wonderful no matter what? Sure, I could tell myself it was because I was Italian, because my friends and family were over there, not in London. Yes, that was the reason. When we took to the stage in Florence, people would come to see me, and by then my performance would be perfect: I would make my mother and father proud.

After Carlos had finished speaking, I headed directly for my dressing room. If somebody stopped me to say good luck, I said the same back to them, but I did not want to engage. Annoyingly, however, Daniella seemed determined to talk.

'Good luck tonight,' she said. 'You know you'll be brilliant, right?'

'Thank you. I hope so,' I replied.

'If you fancy relaxing afterwards, let me know,' she said. 'We can have our own private press night celebration.'

She winked at me. I forced myself to smile, because I did not want her to feel bad, but really? Did she think sex was on my mind, at such an important moment for my career? And honestly, even if it had been, it would not have been Daniella I would have been daydreaming about having it with.

'We will have cast drinks,' I said, as gently as I could manage. 'And then I will be heading home to get some sleep. The last few days have really taken it out of me.'

Luckily, we had reached my dressing room and I pushed open the door, shutting it behind me with another cursory smile at Daniella. When the time was right, I would have to explain to her that I was not interested in her romantically, nor was I interested in anyone else. For all the attitude she gave about us being casual, about it being sex and nothing more, I sensed she had feelings for me. I supposed I was flattered in a way, but it only served to hammer home how completely incapable I was of taking things further, of having an actual relationship.

One day, perhaps, I would work out why that was. I knew it was not because I did not enjoy being with the women I slept with – being with *somebody*, full stop – but because I had this need to keep an *emotional* distance that I could not quite explain. My father had repeatedly told me that dancing was for girls. The kids at school had teased me relentlessly for doing ballroom dancing lessons instead of football. Sometimes, I wondered if this was my way of showing everyone just how much of a red-blooded alpha male I could be.

As if she could somehow sense my thinking, my mother called. I nearly did not pick up, I should be preparing for the show, but she was probably calling to wish me luck and it felt mean to let it ring out.

'*Ciao*, Mama,' I said, putting my feet up on the dressing table and letting myself relax. I had a little while until I had to be on stage, and speaking to my mother might be good for me. At least it would stop me worrying about not having any friends who wanted to come and watch me perform in the biggest show of my career.

'Is now a good time?' asked Mama, sounding more subdued than usual. Something was wrong.

'What's happened?' I demanded to know, sliding my feet back onto the floor, sitting up straight. 'Is it Papa?'

There were a couple of beats of silence. It was Papa, then, and whatever it was my mother was about to tell me was not going to be good.

'He had a fall,' she said. 'Out in the vineyard.'

I swallowed hard. '*Cazzo*. Is he okay?'

'He's been checked over by a doctor. Apparently, he needs to ease up – they say he's been working too hard.'

'Right,' I said. I knew where this was leading.

'Can you come home, Gabriele? Just for a night or two? A day, even, to give him a little time to recover?'

I was about to go out on stage – there was no way I could make decisions like this right now.

'Mama, I'm about to perform. Can this wait until later?'

My mother went quiet for a second or two. 'We wouldn't ask you to come if it wasn't necessary. We know how important this show is to you, but we need you here, Gabriele.'

'What did the doctor say, exactly?' I asked. 'Is there something else, something you are not telling me?'

My mother sighed. 'It is not for me to say.'

'You called me! The least you can do is give me all the facts. If it is an emergency and I need to come home, I will have to put measures in place. Get the understudy to take over. Is that what you want, Mama? Is that what you need me to do?'

I thought I probably sounded more frustrated than I meant to. And it was selfish of me to be thinking about myself at a time like this. But I could not help hoping that there would be some other way. If Papa was going to get better, then surely he could find temporary help for the farm? Did I really need to give up on this role, this show? *My* show.

'Gabriele, we have let you follow your own path all of these years. Papa never wanted you to dance, you know that. He could have forced you to work on the farm years ago.'

'Forced me?' I said, confused. 'And how would he have done that, exactly?'

'Do not speak aggressively to me,' said my mother. 'I won't have it.'

'This is my life, Mama. My choices. Why are you holding my dancing career over me? I didn't realize I had to choose between my job and my family – I thought it was possible to have both.'

'It was, for as long as we could. But now we need you. It's what any son would do.'

'You sound just like Papa!' I said, raising my voice again and putting my head in my hands. Why could they not understand that their demands had been unreasonable? Living in rural Tuscany, running a farm, I would never have been happy. And I disputed the idea that it was what all sons would do – most of the dancers I had met over the years thought only of themselves and their careers, and I had always been envious of their freedom. My parents were wonderful in lots of ways. I just did not agree with them on this one – admittedly very big – thing.

'It's time, Gabriele. Time to put your family first. I'm sorry, I know the timing is bad, but your father is getting sick – he wouldn't want me to say this, but that is how it is. And he needs you. We both do. And we would like you to come home to run the farm with us as soon as *Slow Burn* has completed its run.'

I let this sink in. The realization that this was it, the moment I had been dreading and hoping would never come, but knowing deep down that it would. It was looking increasingly likely that this was going to be my last tour.

The entire cast were in costume, made up and waiting in the wings. Mama's phone call had thrown me, but I had put it to the back of my mind for the show. Our only brief tonight was to do what we did best: entertain people; transport them to another place for an hour and a half and ease their worries away. If we were engaging enough, they would be thinking only about what was on stage and not about the difficult things that were going on in their own lives. I wanted them to be completely captivated, and I had every confidence that we – particularly Lira and I – could do that for them.

The stage manager gave the five-minute call. I stole a glance at the auditorium through a gap in the curtains. Carlos had been right, it was packed, and there was an air of excitement, the anticipation of being one of the first to see a show that would soon be talked about in newspapers and online, and if it proved to be a sell-out, they would be pleased that they had taken a risk on booking tickets. If we played it right, they would be the first to tell everyone at work about us, to buy tickets for their in-laws, to gush about it to their friends. Word of mouth could not be ignored – if we wanted the show to be a success, we needed people all over the country to be talking about us.

I felt a shift in energy as the house lights went down. I knew I said I would not, but I snuck a quick glance at Lira, and she must have had the same idea, because her big brown eyes, shining even in the semi-darkness, met mine.

She nodded.

I nodded back.

We did not need words. We knew what we had to do. And there was no going back now.

Out on stage, I let the audience drive me, my fears waning as I glided across the floor, spinning Lira, lifting her, finding the spotlight, performing moves that I knew were daring and thrilling to watch. The audience were enraptured, and broke out into applause and cheers after each and every number. We were doing it. They loved it; it was working. I pushed myself even harder, made every step even more perfect, because I wanted that for them, I wanted them to come away feeling the emotion that I was feeling with Lira in my arms.

It was only as I pulled her out of our final position at the end of our Argentine tango that I let myself look at her as anything other than a dance partner. It was not true to say that she could have been anyone before that – it had almost entirely been about the particular spark that we generated together. But as we stood at the front of the stage to take our first bow, and the audience were on their feet, I took her hand and linked my fingers through hers. When I glanced across at her, she was beaming, enjoying the moment, just as I was. And I felt proud of her for deciding to say yes to performing again; for even showing up to that audition after years away from competing. And if this was my last tour, I was happy that my very last professional dance on stage would be with her.

Carlos had instructed us to go straight to the bar after the show, where he would likely want to introduce us to some of the influential guests he had invited this evening: producers, tour managers, agents and journalists. A glass of champagne was pressed into my hands and I lost sight of Lira as Carlos took me by the arm, congratulating me in my ear.

'That was magnificent, Gabriele. We will have the press eating out of our hands.'

As I met person after person, all of them on a high and exceptionally complimentary about the show, I found myself dropping Lira's name into the conversation. It felt only right that her performance should be equally as lauded as mine.

Lira James is a protégé of Carlos Torres.

Lira James is a former world champion who has been out of the industry for a little while and now she has come back with a bang.

Lira James is the most phenomenal dancer I've ever worked with.

I kept catching Lira's eye as she worked the room, hanging mainly with Luca, but occasionally Carlos would pull her across to talk to a producer or a particularly influential member of the press. I wondered what she was saying about me. Was she as complimentary about my dancing as I had been about hers? I guessed I would find out when the reviews came out.

When we finally had a moment alone together, I wanted to keep hold of it.

'Come to my dressing room,' I said to her on a whim.

She nodded, following me to my room, stepping inside after me. When I turned, it was like she had been frozen to the spot; as though she was unsure about being here in this room with me. I was not sure, either, given our track record for being alone together, but I decided for her, reaching past her to press the door shut. She looked at me, her face shiny from the exertion of the last couple of hours, her eyes bright and animated, as though maybe she had never had a night as wonderful as this.

Physically, we were close. Closer than we had been for a while, if you did not include the dancing; if you did not include that night at her studio.

She pressed her back against the door, although her eyes never left mine. Before I could stop myself or think better of it, my mouth was on hers. She responded quickly, deeply. It felt . . . like nothing I had ever experienced. Her lips were so fucking pillowy and satin soft, like I could just fall into them and never come back out. A moan coursed through my body; I could not hold it in. She must know now how much I wanted her.

'Lira,' I said, enjoying the way her name bounced around my mouth, kissing her neck, running my tongue all the way up to her earlobe. She arched her back away from the door. She wanted me too.

Good. A relief.

I found her mouth again because it was just too delicious not to. She parted her lips and I slid my tongue inside. Jesus, it felt so good. Everything about me felt more alive than it ever had; every cell inside of me was begging for more. Whatever it was she was doing to me, I needed her to keep doing it.

Suddenly she put her hands on my chest, pushing me lightly away.

'We shouldn't—'

I hesitated. Nodded. 'I know,' I said.

There were a few painful moments of longing before I plunged my mouth onto hers again. It was no good; I could not keep away. I was frantic with longing. Threading my fingers through hers, I pinned them above her head as she ground against me.

Of course we should not do this. It was a terrible idea, especially after the conversation I had just had with my mother. Much like our first meeting, there would be a definite ending to whatever this was. I would be in Italy after the tour had ended, most likely, and Lira would be beginning a new chapter of her life elsewhere.

And yet, still I wanted her.

I let her arms drop, sliding my hands into her hair, gasping with pleasure as my fingers became tangled in her soft curls. For the show, she had worn her hair slicked off her face and held in place with a shiny bun, but now strands of it were breaking loose and I buried my face in it, breathing in the scent of her. I moaned again, completely involuntarily, and this time I did not care how loud I was, or who might hear us. She cried out, too, seemingly not caring either.

I pulled her towards me. Effortlessly, she wrapped her legs around my waist. I carried her across to the dressing table, gently placing her down on the edge of it. Removing one hand from her body, I swept all my things off the table, sending everything clattering onto the floor.

She was still wearing her final costume, a red satin

dress that clung to every curve. I eased the thin pieces of fabric off her shoulders. She found the zip herself, reaching behind her back, letting the dress fall forward to reveal a black lacy bra that barely contained the full, round breasts I had thought about repeatedly over the years. I unclipped her bra, wanting it out of the way, throwing it to one side, and then I ran my thumb over one nipple and then the other.

She threw her head back, laughing with delight. How lucky I was to have found her again when I had thought that one night was all I would ever have.

I was so caught up in how beautiful Lira looked half-naked, the baby-soft skin of her back pressed flat against my mirror, that it took me a moment or two to register the knock on my door. And Carlos's voice outside in the corridor.

'Gabriele? Are you in there? There is somebody you must meet!'

Lira looked at me with fear in her eyes – she knew as well as I did that Carlos would not be happy to find us together. With no words needed, we instantly began scrabbling to get dressed, to right ourselves, to put on the clothes that had been peeled off and flung aside. She put the back of her hand against her cheeks, hoping, presumably, to calm the flushed skin there.

I ran my thumb under her chin, desperately wanting to kiss her again but knowing I could not.

'Rain check?' I whispered.

She nodded, an unreadable smile forming on her full lips as I sighed, straightened myself up and headed for the door.

CHAPTER FIFTEEN

Lira

Two days later, it was unusually quiet in the house when I woke and padded downstairs for breakfast. Mum and Dad had left for their trip, their ship setting sail from Southampton and heading for sunnier climes.

We'd only spoken once since our argument at the studio, and the conversation had been stilted and tense, not helped by the fact they were rushing to finish their packing, and I was obviously anxious about my performance. I hadn't wanted to admit it to myself, but the truth was, I'd sort of expected Sedi to make the effort to come and watch the show instead of wasting the ticket I'd put aside for her at the box office. Sure, she had a temper, and was definitely one to storm off and sulk on occasion. But we'd always been close despite our differences, one of which was that usually

I avoided conflict at all costs while she waded right into the middle of it, all guns blazing. Nolo was more like me in that regard, although even she wouldn't shy away from speaking her mind when she had to. I wasn't sure where this need to be perfect all the time had come from – was it something my parents had done differently with me, or was it just part of my personality, something I would have to work hard to change?

Whenever we'd fallen out in the past, always over something relatively small, I'd been the one to approach Sedi; to say sorry first. But I hadn't done that yet because, well, I didn't think I needed to. What exactly would I be saying sorry for? Okay, I definitely could have told them earlier, when it first happened, the night Carlos had returned to the studio and asked me to audition. But wasn't I allowed to keep *anything* to myself? I'd never imagined it would go this far, and hadn't thought in a million years that I'd be cast, so I hadn't exactly felt like broadcasting it to my entire family. Also, I knew their reaction would have put me off – they'd have been keen to remind me that it had been years since I'd set foot on a proper stage, and that it took time and practice to be a professional dancer, neither of which I had in their opinion. They were right – I definitely didn't have the time, what with running the family business for them 24/7.

I made myself a coffee and some breakfast, threw open the French doors and took a seat on our little patio, looking out over the garden, relishing the peace and quiet of having the place to myself.

It was a lovely home, and of course I felt a hundred percent comfortable here; it was where I'd spent almost all of my life. But I didn't own this house, just like I didn't own the studio. I craved having something that was actually mine and only mine; something that nobody else had any say over, that wasn't in some way linked to any other members of my family.

What I was going to do about this realization I had no idea, but even recognizing it was a start.

After breakfast, I walked down to the local newsagent's and bought one copy of every newspaper they had in stock. Carlos had told me that, as it was Thursday, most of the reviews would come out today. It nearly killed me, but I didn't look at them until I got home, scared of what I might find.

What if they were terrible? What if they raved about Gabriele – as they would, I was sure – but were disappointed by his less-talented female lead? What then? My family would have an I-told-you-so field day. And I would be left wondering why I'd tipped everything on its head for nothing.

Back at the house, I stalled even longer. I made a cafetière of coffee. I emptied the dishwasher. And finally, when I started clearing out the tins cupboard, a job I usually avoided at all costs, I knew enough was enough. I was going to have to look and face the consequences of whatever these journalists had to say. After all, even if they'd hated it, it didn't mean everyone who came to see it would feel the same way. Although, could we really hope for packed auditoriums if it was panned across the board?

I laid the papers out on the breakfast bar, deciding to get one of the harshest critics out of the way first. I was familiar with their scathing reviews of books, restaurants, TV shows and anything else they could turn their somewhat vicious pen to. Nervously, I flicked through the pages one by one until I reached the theatre reviews column. There, in glorious technicolour, was a photograph of myself and Gabriele at the end of our rumba. He was standing behind me, one arm in the air, the other across my stomach. My hands were over his hand, holding him close, our last step before he spun me around and we ended the dance in an almost-passionate clinch. The headline read:

SLOW BURN IS A SEXY TRIUMPH

I swallowed hard. That was good, wasn't it? I skimmed through the rest of the review, still half expecting them to highlight me as the show's weak link. I only got one mention, but they'd called me a relative newcomer and an exquisite dancer, so that was okay. I could breathe again. Although there were still seven more newspapers to go.

I was busy reading our sixth glowing review when my phone started burning up. The first message was from Diane, one of the freelance dancers who'd been helping me at the studio.

WAAAAAHHHH! You kept that quiet. So proud of you!

My old dance partner, Tomas, had also reached out. We'd kept in touch over the last decade or so – he'd been devasted when I'd had to break up our partnership, but he knew my parents well and eventually accepted the fact that family responsibility weighed heavily on me. Unlike Gabriele, he understood that I wasn't free to fully pursue whatever I wanted to, or go wherever I wanted. He'd gone on to find another dance partner and was still performing and competing across the world. I thought we'd probably never forget each other, particularly our last heady win in Paris. He had four words to say:

You've still got it!

I smiled to myself. I did, didn't I? The comments spoke for themselves: I was a dancer, not a dance *teacher*. Or, at least, I was both. Not prepared to let my sisters make me feel bad anymore, I texted them both, already deciding that I wouldn't take no for an answer.

Family Zoom. Midnight U.K. time, 7pm New York time. I'll send a link.

It wasn't unusual for us to chat so late. We might usually have tried to do it a little earlier in the evening, but Nolo often had rehearsals all day, and with the time difference it tended to mean a late call time our end. Plus, I had a show tonight.

Anyway, I knew for a fact that Sedi was never in bed before 1am, so there should be no problem. I put my phone in my bag, determined not to spend all day wondering if they'd read it, wondering what their response would be. Surely they couldn't hate me so much that they were going to refuse to speak to me?

I had to keep reminding myself that I had done *nothing* wrong.

I felt a shot of nerves as I walked backstage to the dressing room at 6pm. I had no idea where the land was going to lie with Gabriele after what had happened in his dressing room on press night, and I'd purposely rushed off straight after the performance yesterday because I was a coward, and I was one hundred percent avoiding having a conversation with him about it.

The only saving grace was that we hadn't actually had sex – thank God Carlos had interrupted us. Even if the nearly-sex had been just as amazing as I knew it would be. Because here I was, making the exact same mistakes I'd made over a decade ago. I'd seen the way he garnered looks wherever he went; the way all the dancers checked him out, even though he barely gave most of them the time of day. And now I was one of them, one of the many who had fallen victim to his *considerable* charms. If I slept with him one day, he'd probably move onto somebody else the next, and I'd have to spend the remainder of the run pretending I wasn't bothered. Luca might think it was all bravado, but I certainly wasn't convinced, and I wasn't sure that Gabriele could do anything *to* convince me.

As I passed his dressing room, I had the idea that maybe I'd be more mature about this than I had been when I was nineteen and would try to talk to him about it. Shut it down. Name it for what it was – a moment of passion, brought on by the high of coming off stage. It wouldn't be repeated, I was pretty sure we'd be on the same page on that. I paused and rapped my knuckles on his door before I could change my mind.

The door swung open and Daniella stood in the doorway.

'Oh,' I said. 'Hi.'

'Hello,' she said, making me feel like an unwanted interruption.

My eyes were drawn to Gabriele, who I could see over her shoulder. He was sitting at his dressing table, not yet in costume, wearing a white T-shirt and blue jeans, his hair pulled back into a messy bun, his eyes burning into me.

'I'll leave you to it,' I said, already backing away.

'I was just leaving,' said Daniella with a smile that felt all kinds of insincere. 'He's all yours.'

I nodded, standing aside to let her pass. This had now become a bigger thing than I intended it to be. A quick conversation about how, sure, we'd fumbled our way around his dressing room the night before last, but let's draw a line under it and go back to being professional dance partners, had now taken on a different significance. Because was he still seeing Daniella? And if he was, did she know what had happened between us? It could put the whole show in jeopardy if we all fell out, and I'd feel awful about it if I'd hurt her feelings, even if she did act like Gabriele was her property.

'Hi,' I said, finally addressing him.

'Are you coming in?' he asked, nodding at the door.

It felt too dangerous to go inside and close the door again, the memories already coming flooding back: the way the mirror had steamed up, how ice-cold it felt against my back, the franticness of it all.

I skulked in the doorway instead, feeling safer there. Except, then I realized that anyone walking past would hear what I had to say and that would be mortifying, so I stepped lightly inside, closing the door behind me, but keeping as much distance between myself and Gabriele as I could.

I sincerely wished he didn't look quite so hot *all* of the time. How could a man make a simple white T-shirt look like *that*? I could practically see the muscles rippling underneath it; could just imagine the taut, golden-brown skin I'd find if I just lifted the hem and pulled it right off.

'Are you finally ready to talk about press night, then?' he asked, swivelling around so that he was full-on facing me. There was no escaping his gaze now.

'Well, obviously it was a mistake,' I said.

'Obviously,' he said with smirk.

This man was infuriating. It was like he could see right through the fake nonchalant vibes that I was trying to give off. He knew I wanted to sleep with him, it was probably seeping out of every part of me. And sure, if there was nothing at stake, I'd probably just walk across the room and straddle him on the spot.

'I can't mess up this show,' I said.

He nodded. 'The reviews were good. Did you see?'

'Yes. They loved you.'

'They loved us *both*,' he said.

I dug my fingernails into the door behind me. Was it hot in here? At this rate the mirror would be steamed up all over again.

'We're going on tour in a few days,' I said.

'And visiting some of the most romantic cities in the world,' he said, teasing me.

'There's nothing romantic about what we did the other night, Gabriele,' I said.

He raised his eyebrows at me. 'Then what would you call it?'

Fuck. What would I call it?

'I call it getting carried away. I call it a high from being out on stage and you being in the right place at the right time.'

'So you would have kissed anybody like that, is that what you are saying, Lira?'

'Not anyone,' I said. 'But if I'd been thinking straight, I also wouldn't have kissed *you*.'

I tried to remember to breathe. I couldn't read Gabriele's expression, but surely we were on the same page with this.

'Message received,' he said, never taking his eyes off me.

'Good,' I said. 'Glad that's all sorted.'

As I turned to leave, he called after me.

'Lira?'

I turned to look at him over my shoulder. 'Yes?'

'You do know that one day we are going to have to talk about Paris?'

My heart sank. 'I tried that once and you said it would be a waste of time. You couldn't see what good it would do,' I said. Was it weird I'd remembered our conversation word for word?

'I changed my mind,' he replied.

Fuck. Really?

Since I didn't have any comeback to that, I turned and left the room, my whole body fizzing with God knows what as I walked to the shared dressing room. The first person I saw was Daniella, of course. The two of them were making my head spin.

From now on I would keep my distance from both of them and let them get on with whatever it was they had going on.

Six hours later, I was back home and sitting at the kitchen counter with my laptop open in front of me. I'd taken off my stage make-up and had changed into my favourite sweat pants and top, which was made of the most deliciously cosy peach felt fabric. I'd poured myself a glass of wine to celebrate the success of our performance, even if I was drinking entirely alone; even if it felt a bit crap not to have anyone to celebrate with. I was about to speak to my sisters and I wasn't convinced they'd even ask me how it went. How sad was that? Especially in a family of dancers. Was putting myself first really such a crime?

I started the Zoom call, downing a huge mouthful of wine before the two of them joined, although I knew that nothing was going to make this any easier. We had a WhatsApp group called *Sisters Are Doin' It For Themselves* – Sedi had come up with the name – and usually we were pinging messages back and forth all day, and sometimes all night. But the group had been strangely silent of late, with my messages going mostly unread, leaving me wondering whether they were having private chats elsewhere without me.

The screen pinged to life as Nolo joined the call – it was a running joke in our family that she was always early, I was to-the-minute on time and Sedi was perennially late. Since it was only early evening in New York, Nolo was still dressed like the epitome of an off-duty ballet dancer. I imagined she'd walked home from her rehearsal space on the Lower East Side and hadn't long stepped through the door of her cool but grimy Brownstone walk-up.

'It's good to see you,' I said, leaning closer to the screen.

'You, too,' said Nolo.

Okay, this was a good start, although I supposed she hadn't actually been there to experience the full horror of the row at the studio. Clearly she'd been told what had happened, and I wondered what she thought. Whatever it was, I suspected she wouldn't hold back from telling me.

'How did rehearsals go today?' I asked her, stalling for time until Sedi made an appearance.

She shrugged. 'Pretty well. It's tough doing back-to-back shows. There's talk of us getting a proper break at some point, but probably not until after the summer.'

'Hopefully you can come home for a bit, then? It's been ages since we've seen you properly.'

I craved spending more time with my youngest sister, who had moved to the US when I was twenty-one. She'd lived with a family friend initially, attending classes at the dance academy for a year until she was chosen to join the principal company at seventeen. I'd been to New York a few times to visit and I loved the place, but it was expensive to get there, and much as I loved travelling, it had always been difficult to get more than a few days away from the studio.

'Maybe,' said Nolo non-committally.

Sedi finally joined the call. She was in her pyjamas like me, but still looking as striking as ever with a full face of make-up and her gorgeous afro hair worn in a natural style.

'Sorry I'm late,' said Sedi, not looking as though she was sorry in the slightest.

'I was just telling Nolo how much we miss her,' I said.

'Hardly,' scoffed Nolo. 'Mum and Dad are never at home, anyway, and you'll be off on tour again soon, Sedi. It'll only be you at home,' she said, looking pointedly at me.

'Probably. Although you never know, do you?' I said, suddenly irked by the assumption that things would go straight back to normal after *Slow Burn* had finished its run. That I'd be back managing the studio where, in their eyes, I belonged, all notion of performing forgotten. They'd probably been talking amongst themselves about how maybe I just needed to get it out of my system so that, afterwards, everything could return to its rightful place.

'What do you mean "probably"?' asked Sedi.

'Oh, so you are speaking to me, then?' I said. 'Only I haven't heard from you for days.'

'I've been busy,' she snapped.

'Too busy to come and see me perform?'

Sedi shifted uncomfortably in her seat. 'Look, I tried to make it, but I'd already made plans I couldn't get out of.'

'It's fine,' I said. 'I'm not sure why I expected anything different.'

I'd lost count of the number of times I'd happily travelled to see my sisters perform, and my mum on occasion, too. If I was in their position, I would have dropped almost anything to show my support.

I took another sip of wine, buying myself some time. I could already feel things getting heated and that hadn't been my intention when I'd suggested a chat.

'Look,' I said, getting to the point of the call. 'I asked us to meet tonight because I hate that we've all fallen out. Let's talk it out. And why don't we start with you two telling me exactly why all of this has upset you so much?'

Sedi rolled her eyes. 'Do you have to be so dramatic, Lira?'

'I don't even know why I'm getting pulled in to all of this, anyway,' complained Nolo. 'What can I do about any of it from over here?'

I bit my lip, trying to be gentle with them, because if I went in hard, they'd only get defensive and we'd end up worse off than we'd been before the call.

'That's kind of my point,' I said. 'Since I agreed to help Mum and Dad run the studio, it feels as though you've all carried on regardless while my hopes and dreams have been pushed to the side. Both of you have done exactly what you wanted to do. You've moved halfway across the world, you've made a home wherever you feel like it, and you've had the freedom to audition for something without having to think about a million other things before you said yes.'

'You're the one who said you were happy to be a dance teacher. Mum said you'd realized the professional dance world wasn't for you,' insisted Sedi.

'You know how hard I found it – *still* find it – to say no to Mum and Dad. How persuasive they can be, especially with me.'

'You're too weak-willed,' said Nolo. 'I know you probably think we're selfish or something, but at least we're not putting other people's needs in front of our own all the time. Why shouldn't we go after what we want?'

'Fair point,' I said, 'which is why I decided – when the opportunity unexpectedly arose – to do the same thing myself. How could I not have done?'

Sedi sighed. 'I think what bothers me is that it all feels

so deceitful. Creeping around, pretending you had GP appointments when actually you had auditions. It leaves a nasty taste in my mouth.'

I nodded. 'And I'm sorry. I definitely should have been honest with you both from the beginning. It was just that it felt like such a huge thing. Something I was very likely to fuck up. I'd convinced myself that it was best not to say anything until I was sure Carlos Torres had meant what he said – that he wouldn't instantly regret hiring me and fire me on the spot in front of the entire cast.'

'That's ridiculous. You're a beautiful dancer and you know it,' said Nolo.

'But I don't know it, not really. Choreographing at the studio is hardly pushing me to my limit, is it? I had no idea if I'd be able to keep up with Gabriele, and it was obvious he was looking for something very specific, and that it had been Carlos not him who had wanted to hire me. I had a lot to prove, and part of me wanted to focus on that without also having to deal with talking about it to all of you when I didn't know what kind of reception I'd get.'

'We could have helped you if you'd asked,' said Sedi, resting her chin in the palm of her hand. 'It's okay to have doubts, you know, and that's what sisters are for – to champion each other. To give each other strength and encouragement.'

I believed the same thing myself until all of this – where had Sedi's strength and encouragement been on press night?

'Sedi's right,' said Nolo. 'You've spent years looking after us, but sometimes it feels as though you won't let either of us in. Maybe we'd like to see you mess up sometimes – it would make us feel better about ourselves, instead of having this perfect and always-together older sister to have to compete with.'

'I didn't realize we were competing,' I said quietly, knowing deep down that they had a point. To me, asking for help meant revealing a weakness, but what Sedi and Nolo were saying was that it would actually show strength of character to admit that everything wasn't wonderful all of the time.

'Well, you wouldn't, because in Mum and Dad's eyes, you're always number one. Imagine what it's like for us, desperately trying to live up to the high expectations you've set for us all,' said Sedi.

I swallowed hard. I'd had no idea they felt like this, nor had I ever imagined that they thought I'd had it easy compared to them.

'Maybe we all wanted what the others had, instead of appreciating what we *did* have,' I said quietly.

'Maybe,' said Sedi.

Nolo leaned closer to the screen. 'Does it feel right what you're doing, Lira?'

I didn't have to think about it for long; the answer was right there on the tip of my tongue.

'One hundred percent right. It's what I'm meant to do, I know that now, just like it's what you two are meant to do. And now it's my turn to make something of myself, and I don't know what that means for us, or for the studio.'

'Mum and Dad have already said they expect me to

do more for the business if you decide to carry on with this,' said Sedi, looking less than impressed. 'Maybe they shouldn't have opened the business in the first place if they didn't have any interest in actually running it.'

'Now you know how I feel; how I've always felt.'

'I'm going on tour with Barbed Wire soon, though. I'll be on the other side of the world,' said Sedi. 'I'm going to tell them that unfortunately I won't be available to give couples with two left feet wedding dance lessons!'

'Well then we'll have to find another way to make it work,' I said, refusing to back down.

'Talking of Barbed Wire, have you met Tate Fellows yet?' asked Nolo, changing the subject completely, no doubt before either of us could ask what *her* contribution to the running of the studio might be.

Tate Fellows was the lead singer of Barbed Wire, who were currently the biggest rock band in the world. A loud, American, slightly unhinged – in my opinion – man with tattoos covering at least seventy percent of his body. He was cute, I supposed, if you liked that kind of thing, but boy did he know it. He was photographed with a new model or actress practically every week.

'I met him at the final casting, yeah,' said Sedi, casually.

'What's he like?' gasped Nolo, clearly finding this line of conversation a whole lot more engaging than my dance career and the running of James Jive Studio.

'He's okay,' said Sedi, shrugging.

'Gorgeous, though, I bet?' said Nolo.

'*Full* of it,' declared Sedi.

'Anyway,' I said, wanting to bring the Tate Fellows-fest to an end. Although I'd lost momentum now, and until I actually got another dancing gig, there probably wasn't much use in me pushing my point. 'I'm going to go. I'll be at the studio in the morning and then straight to the theatre late afternoon. It'll be a long day.'

'Fine. I need my bed, anyway,' said Sedi.

I hesitated. 'I'm glad we had this conversation.'

'I'm not,' said Nolo miserably.

In for a penny, in for a pound, I decided to leave them a parting shot.

'Oh, and I know I'm supposed to be looking after you while Mum and Dad are away, but I reckon you're old enough to fend for yourselves, don't you? You know where I am if you need me.'

Then I cut the call and closed my laptop, proud of myself for opening up about some of the things that had been festering in my head for years and that, until now, I'd never had the guts to say.

CHAPTER SIXTEEN

Gabriele

I lifted my face to the roof of the theatre, letting the light rain down on me, the applause ringing pleasingly in my ears. The audience was on its feet, clapping and whooping and whistling for more. It was the last night of our London run and I thought that it might have been our best performance to date. Everyone in the cast had been energized by the excellent press reviews – we knew every ticket had been sold and that, already, people were calling for more London performances later in the year; a longer run. Carlos had even hinted he was in talks about a national tour. I was trying not to think about the fact that the show might have to go on without me.

Needless to say, I had not shared this possibility with a single person. What good would it do to talk about it; to burden other people with my family issues? Perhaps, deep down, I was hoping that a miracle would happen, and that my father's health would drastically improve and that he would insist on running the business himself for the foreseeable future. It was stupid of me to dream such a dream, but there it was, fluttering hopefully away in the back of my mind.

The company was travelling to Spain at the weekend — first to Madrid and then on to Barcelona, then to Porto and Lisbon. And then the final run of shows would be in my home country, something I knew would feel spectacular on every level: Venice, Milan, Rome and finally Florence. My parents would come to the Florence show, if my father was well enough. I would scroll through my contacts to see who else I could invite. And no doubt there would be the *Bring the Heat* fans hanging around backstage, asking me to sign autographs for them. I was well known in Italy in a way that only being on television could manifest, and I fully intended to enjoy it while it lasted.

With one more bow, I led a beaming Lira off stage. These days she dropped my hand the second we moved beyond the curtain and out of the audience's sight. It was like she could not wait to stop touching me. I knew this was my fault, because I had not tried to kiss her again. In fact, I had been actively avoiding being alone with her. That moment in my dressing room had been incredible, and it was what I thought of now when I lay in bed, feeling as lonely as ever and wishing Lira was lying next to me. I wanted to fold into her curves again, to rest my head on her chest, to have her stroke my hair and whisper in my ear like I imagined she might. Because Lira did something to me that no other woman had ever done: she penetrated the protective shell I had built around myself and made me wonder if I was capable of having a romantic relationship after all. But we could not be together, and that was that. The timing was always wrong for us, and I had to accept that perhaps the closeness to her I craved was not meant to be.

Two days later, the entire cast was safely housed in a slick, modern hotel in central Madrid. Right across from the building, on a bustling shopping street, was the theatre we would be performing in for four nights straight. Every seat had been sold, apparently, which was hardly surprising given the Latin origins of the show and the excellent re-views we had garnered in London.

We had a performance that evening, but I had decided to take a walk around the city and take advantage of the few hours I had free first. One thing about Italy I missed when I was in London was the weather, and this June af-ternoon in Madrid was reminiscent of home, on account of the hot sun, the sort that baked the hairs on your arms and licked the back of your neck. I would explore the Malasaña neighbourhood we were staying in, perhaps stop for some refreshment in one of the coffee shops on Plaza del 2 de Mayo. Enjoy some time to myself before meeting up with everybody mid-afternoon for a quick lighting check. That was the thing about being on tour – it sounded glamorous, but you barely got to see any of the places you were performing in.

The weather warmed me from the inside out the second I stepped out onto the pavement. I turned left on a whim and then left again, weaving my way off the busy main road and into a side street that felt shady and quiet in comparison. I was keeping half an eye out for somewhere to grab a drink – perhaps something cold and over ice rather than coffee – when I spotted Lira in front of me.

I recognized her straight away. She was wearing a yellow summer dress and sandals and her hair was pulled back into a loose ponytail at the nape of her neck, her sculpted shoulders perfectly framing her dark curls on either side.

I would recognize the dimensions of her body anywhere – the way her waist nipped in exactly where it should, the slim, muscular legs that only a dancer or an athlete would possess.

She was taking a photo of something up ahead. I hesitated for a moment or two, wondering what to do. Should I turn back, pretend I hadn't seen her? But why would I do that? We had to dance together that night; it would be strange – and rude – not to acknowledge her. And not only that, now that I had seen her, I could not un-see her, and despite myself, I wanted to talk to her again, because it had been days now and, annoyingly, I missed her.

I upped my pace. As long as she didn't move, I was going to be standing next to her in approximately two seconds flat and then I would have no choice but to speak to her. I instinctively glanced at my reflection in a shop window. I was wearing linen trousers, because I did not do shorts, not in the middle of the city, and a simple cotton T-shirt with a short-sleeved shirt worn over it. My hair was tied back in a bun because it was too hot to have it hanging loose around my neck.

I was parallel with Lira now and wondered how long it would take her to notice me standing there. I cleared my throat loudly. She fumbled around with her phone and glanced across at me, a little startled.

'Oh, it's you,' she said, seemingly relieved.

'You thought there was a stranger staring at you for no reason?' I asked, laughing lightly.

I liked that she had relaxed when she had seen me – it was a definite improvement from the way she used to recoil when we first started rehearsing together. Perhaps being away from home was good for her. She looked great – relaxed, happy to be here. Happy-ish to see me.

'Have you ever been here before?' I asked her, taking in my surroundings, too. I had been to Madrid a couple of times, but I had never had time to get a proper feel for the city. From what I could tell, I liked the vibe very much – it reminded me a little of Milan, except sunnier and with even more tourists.

She shook her head. 'It's hard to travel. With the studio. But I love exploring new places when I get the chance. Taking photos, trying new foods, all of that. It's one of the things I can't quite believe about this tour – that I get to experience three different countries in the space of five weeks.'

I smiled. Her enthusiasm was infectious. And she was right, of course. This job we were doing was pretty spectacular when you thought about it – even if we were staying in very basic three-star hotels, which would not usually be my choice.

We fell into step beside each other, meandering slowly along the street. For the first time in ages, I started to properly look around me, looking up at the beautiful buildings we were passing, which were painted in tantalizing shades of tomato red, sky blue, palest pink and sunshine yellow, and flanked with wrought-iron balconies housing tropical plants and mini palm trees. I breathed in the sweet smell of sugar, no doubt from the tempting-looking bakery we had just passed, suddenly letting myself enjoy the local atmosphere in a way I had failed to do on my previous visits here. It felt as though I was seeing the city for the first time, through Lira's less-travelled eyes.

'Look, there is a flamenco show in town tonight,' I said, pointing to a sandwich board outside what looked like an art gallery. 'It is something I have always wanted to see live in Spain, but have never found the time to.'

Lira nodded enthusiastically. 'We should get some people together after the show, maybe? I'd love to see it, too.'

'Sure,' I said, furiously pushing the sensation that I should never have mentioned flamenco to the back of my mind. What happened to spending as little time together as possible? Even if there were other cast members there, I already knew that standing together in some sexy, hot, basement bar with sultry guitar music and one of the most sensuous dances in the world being performed right in front of our eyes would be a very bad idea.

'Do you have time for a drink?' I asked her. 'I was going to try to find a café.'

It had rolled off my tongue before I could think better of it. My God, what had happened to me? All my resolve to stay away from Lira because of what was happening with my family seemed to have flown out of the window the second we touched down in Madrid. Perhaps the sun could be blamed, or the fact I felt less anxious now I knew how successful the show was proving to be. And anyway, the truth was, it had been the same in London – I simply could not make the best decisions for myself when I was around Lira James. And I had no idea what I was supposed to do about it, other than avoid her completely, which clearly was impossible.

She looked down at the ground and then back up at me, perhaps having the exact same reservations herself. When our eyes connected, I felt a sensation I had no control over; it was how I felt with her on the dance floor, a sort of longing I could not turn away from. I realized I really wanted her to come for a drink with me. And that I did not want to spend yet another afternoon alone killing time before the show.

'Okay,' she said. 'Why not?'

'Great,' I replied, desperately trying to mask the chaos in my head from being in such close proximity to her.

Earlier, I had passed a bar carved into what looked like a cave, and so I led us there. The sun put me in the mood for a glass of sparkling Cava, but I knew that I could not drink alcohol until after my performance – I was strict about that. I needed to conserve all of my energy for tonight, and daytime drinking risked leaving me feeling sluggish. Lira must have felt the same way, because we both ordered cappuccinos.

'I am extremely tempted by the churros,' I admitted to Lira, as a plate of the sizzling donuts was whisked past us and delivered to the table of the two women next to us.

Lira groaned. 'God, me too. It's taking all my strength not to say "to hell with it" and order them!'

I laughed.

'Sometimes the life of a dancer is tough,' I said.

She nodded. 'Not that I've really felt like a proper dancer, not since I was a teenager. This is definitely an adjustment.'

'Why did you give it up?' I asked, settling back into my seat, enjoying the fact that I had Lira all to myself for, at the very least, as long as it took us to finish our coffees. I would be sure to make mine last as long as possible. In Spain, like in Italy, such things – hanging out in a café, drinking good coffee with friends – should be savoured, not rushed.

Lira put her elbows on the table between us, resting her chin on the backs of her hands.

'You really want to know?'

'I *really* want to know.'

She shook her head, a little embarrassed, perhaps. I waited. Because I couldn't imagine what would make a dancer as talented as her give it all up to work in a studio. I presumed it was something to do with her family, and if anyone knew about familial responsibility – or at least how to avoid it – it was me.

'So I'm the oldest of three sisters,' she told me. 'Although, I think you know that.'

She looked at me with a hint of a smile. She knew, on that first day of rehearsals, that I had remembered this fact about her. Now it was my turn to be embarrassed.

'I have a vague memory of it,' I said, trying to play it cool, although it was a little late for that.

'They're dancers, too,' continued Lira, thankfully letting me off the hook. 'And my mum – she was South African Latin world champion. Twice.'

'Incredible. What is her name?' I asked, intrigued.

'Amahle James?'

'The most famous Black dancer of her generation?' I exclaimed, shocked. 'She was an amazing performer, so ahead of her time. I never knew she was your mother!'

Lira smiled and shrugged. 'How would you? We've never properly talked about our families, have we?'

I was taken back by her directness. My instinct was to move the conversation back into safer waters, but there was something about her willingness to be honest with me that made me feel as though I owed her the same thing.

As though she might even understand. I had always been reluctant to be vulnerable in front of others, but what if it helped? What if hearing somebody else's opinion on my predicament could actually be useful?

'We have not. But it is not too late to start,' I said quietly. 'Please, carry on. I want to hear about your mother, about how this impacted your own career. Was she hard on you when it came to dancing?'

Lira thought about it.

'In a way. When she sees me perform, or any of my sisters for that matter, she doesn't hold back. She tells us everything we could have done better, and you have to do something exceptional to get a compliment. Deep down, though, we know she's proud of us. But she was always so busy with her own career that she didn't have a lot of time to get to know what made us tick; what we really wanted from life. It was all dance, dance, dance. And as the oldest girl, there was this expectation, steeped in tradition, I suppose, that I should prioritize my family, and what *they* needed.'

'Which was . . . ?' I asked, thinking how achingly familiar this all sounded.

'They'd been planning to open the studio for a couple of years and the original idea was that all of us would run it together. Take turns, do a few lessons each. My mother was the big-name pull and she wanted to be very present initially. But then she started getting more and more opportunities – she was a judge on a big TV show in South Africa, then she and my dad ran the entertainment on one of the big cruise ships, bringing in dancers, choreographing onboard shows, that kind of thing. They pretty quickly realized that opening a studio on top of that had been somewhat ambitious of them.'

Our coffees were delivered to the table, large ceramic mugs topped with creamy froth and a leaf carved into each fluffy topping.

'This looks delicious,' I said.

Lira dipped her finger in the froth and licked it, groaning with delight. I dug my fingernails into my thigh, wondering how this innocent act had suddenly made me feel like doing a whole host of decidedly *less* innocent things to her. I cleared my throat, trying to focus. It was good to talk. And it did not always have to lead to sex; there were other ways to connect with people. Or, at least, this was how I felt when I was with Lira.

'Continue,' I said. 'The studio?'

'Ah,' she said. 'So one night, when I'd just turned nineteen, my parents sat me down and told me that they would like me to help them with the business full-time. They said that maybe I wasn't cut out for an uncertain career like dance, that I'd had my time competing – to be fair, they didn't know my partner Tomas and I were about to *win* the World Championships. They told me that a dance career was tough; that I was too level-headed for it and had skills that could be better utilized helping the family business grow. Apparently, they'd noticed how patient and kind I was on the odd occasion they'd even *seen* me teach a routine to somebody, and suggested that, once the championships were over, I should come straight back to Castlebury and take over the management of James Jive.'

'*What*?' I said, baffled. 'Even though they knew how talented you were?'

'I suppose so, yes.'

'What did you say? You told them no, *si*? Surely, Lira.'

She looked at me with sadness in her eyes. 'I'd always had this need to please my parents. In a busy house like ours, with two very loud and demanding sisters, it felt like the only way I could be noticed. By complying and never getting into trouble. I was my parents' favourite and I felt compelled to keep it that way. I asked them whether I could do the two things at the same time – perhaps as the business grew we could employ more staff and then I'd have some time to go off and do other things. Dance myself. Perhaps my sisters could help once they got a bit older – they were only sixteen and fourteen at that point.'

'You suggested a compromise,' I said. Although it was a big one, one I would never have agreed to if my parents had asked when *I* was just nineteen. 'Did they support this idea?'

'Half-heartedly. But then, whenever I did ask for time off or suggested we employ another teacher, they'd brush me away, say we'd talk about it later. Which, of course, we never did.'

I nodded, trying to understand. Why hadn't she put up more of a fight?

'And this happened when you were nineteen. Was that . . . ?'

'When we met in Paris? Yes.'

I let this sink in. That had been her last competition. The end of her dancing career, until Carlos found her and gave her another chance at the thing she had wanted for herself all along.

What a waste of talent.

I felt angry with her parents. I supposed they must have had their reasons, but to me, as an outsider, it seemed that they were thinking only of themselves and not what was best for their eldest daughter. Parents were supposed to give things up for their children, weren't they, not the other way around?

'That Argentine tango we danced in the hotel?' she said. 'That was my last dance with a professional partner. Until now, obviously.'

It had felt as important to her as it had to me, then. More so, even. I reached across the table and took her hand. If I had thought it through, I might not have done it, but I had reached for it without thinking and I did not regret it. She squeezed my hand back.

'Why did you leave that night?' I asked, the question that I had been dying to ask since she had walked into Pineapple Studios a few weeks before. Why had she run away?

'I had a flight to catch,' she said.

'And you could not have told me?'

She removed her hand from mine, sitting back in her seat, the connection we had had a second ago gone completely. It was my fault, perhaps, but I needed to know the truth. I needed some closure because I had been going over it in my head ever since and it still never made any sense.

'That evening marked the end of my old life and the beginning of my new one. And that night with you was the most spectacular ending. But everything was about to change forever, and I knew you couldn't be part of that, that you wouldn't want to be. You belonged in the world of dance and hotels in Paris and elite competitions. You had a bright future ahead of you. That part of my life was over – I knew we'd have nothing in common once I was back in Castlebury working as a dance teacher.'

'How do you know?' I said. 'You never gave me the chance to tell you how I felt. What I wanted.'

'If that night meant so much to you, why didn't you try to find me?' she asked, her eyes flashing with indignation.

'I did not know anything about you, other than your name! And even that wasn't right, was it, *Li*?'

'I'm sure you could have asked around,' she said.

She was right. And, of course, it had crossed my mind.

'The truth is, nobody had ever walked out on me before,' I said. 'I did not know how to react. I assumed it meant you were not interested and that I would simply have to get over it.'

'It was all about your ego, then?' she asked, narrowing her eyes in confusion.

I didn't think so. It was more that I thought she must have been so disappointed by the whole event that she had sneaked out while I was asleep without so much as a peck on the cheek to say goodbye. And yet, I had been sure that the short time we had had together had been special. That passion we had, the way our bodies had so effortlessly fused together, had been real. I had been sure of it then, and I was sure of it now.

Lira finished her coffee and began rooting in her bag for some money.

'I should go,' she said.

'Put your purse away. I will get these,' I said, a little more tersely than I had intended.

It was just that I did not want her to go. I wanted to sit and talk more, and now I had chased her away. Perhaps it was a mistake to have been quite so truthful about what had been going on in my head that night.

She stood up.

'See you at the theatre later,' she said.

I nodded, unable to find the words I wanted to say, so choosing to say nothing at all. What was the point when I knew that, after this show, our lives would be going in completely different directions yet again. She was just discovering herself – and I hoped that she would be at the height of her career after the success of *Slow Burn*. I was sure choreographers would be queueing up to work with her. And I would be in Italy, with my parents, on the farm.

It was happening all over again, except this time in reverse.

My eyes followed Lira as she walked out of the coffee shop, swivelling her hips to move past the too-close-together tables, hoisting her bag over her shoulder. She stepped outside, the sun throwing her shadow onto the pavement, pausing for a moment or two and then turning left, back in the direction of the hotel.

My melancholy mood was soon interrupted by the buzz of my phone in my pocket. I took it out, glancing at the screen. I had a message from my mother.

Anxious now, I opened it up. She had been contacting me a lot lately, pressuring me for an answer about my plans. I had explained that I must see out the tour and then I would come home to be with them both and look after the business, at least for a while. Was that not enough?

I glanced down at the message, which made my heart race so hard I was sure other people could see it beating through the fabric of my shirt.

I'm worried about your father. He has looked very tired the last few days and his breathing sounds different. He's breathless a lot. What should I do, Gabi?

It was like the words were swimming in front of my eyes. I could not bear the idea that something bad would happen to him while our relationship felt so distant. I had always hoped that, one day, we would be close again, like we had been when I was very young, before I had started dancing.

At first, he had half-heartedly entertained the idea of ballroom lessons, blaming my mother and my grandmother for introducing me to such a 'girly' pastime, but certain I would soon grow out of it and decide that playing football and working with him at the vineyard were much more appealing. But, of course, that never happened and, as time went on, I talked to him less and less about my life, and he snapped at me more and more whenever I mentioned dancing. I had always imagined, though, that somehow we would find a way to embrace our differences, to tell each other that we loved each other deeply despite of them. But what if I did not get the chance?

You must take him to the doctor again, Mama.
Immediately. Make the appointment now.

I watched as she received the message and began typing a reply.

He will not go. He says he is fine, he has had enough of being poked and prodded. You know how he is.

My father was stubborn – my mother joked that I was too much like him, which was why, most of the time, we did not see eye to eye. But when it came to his health, he was particularly hard to deal with, preferring to bury his head in the sand instead of facing the possibility that something could be wrong.

I messaged my mother again.

Then I don't know what to say. But you need to get him checked out, Mama.

I pushed my phone back into my pocket, my head swirling with fear. Why was he refusing to listen to Mama's advice? Could he not go and get himself looked at, for her, for *me*? Or did he like the idea of us worrying about him? Did he like the idea that he was now consuming all of my thoughts when I was supposed to be stepping out on stage in just a few short hours?

I stood up, needing some fresh air. Mama was probably overreacting. Perhaps it was nothing. And I had a show to focus on.

CHAPTER SEVENTEEN
Lira

Slow Burn had been well-received in Spain. In fact, I wondered why we hadn't performed more dates here given that Carlos was pretty much a national treasure. After a four-night run in Madrid, we had arrived in Barcelona for our final three nights in the country and it was a sell-out. Most of the cast were having lunch together at a bar on the beach to celebrate. I'd never been to Barcelona before – in fact, I'd barely been anywhere outside of the UK, come to think of it – and I was loving everything about it. The beach bars were modern and trendy, with cool, ambient dance music playing out of speakers and a perfect view of the vast sandy beach.

'Who is up for sangria in a cosy little bar after the performance later?' asked Daniella, throwing her arm around Gabriele's shoulders.

She had, of course, commandeered a seat next to him, and now and again her eyes had flickered to mine, her eyebrows arched as if to dare me to protest. I refused to get pulled into competing for a man I didn't even want. Well, that wasn't strictly true. A man I absolutely *shouldn't* want.

'I'm in, if everyone else is,' said Luca, catching my eye.

'Gabriele, are you up for it, my love?' Daniella asked, pulling him close to her possessively.

Perhaps I was only seeing what I wanted to see, but he didn't exactly seem happy at her sudden display of affection. In fact, he looked positively pissed off about it.

'I'll be getting an early night,' he growled.

'Boo. Party pooper,' she teased, pouting.

I thought she must have got the hint, though, because she swiftly removed her arm and began gossiping with Abi, the dancer sitting to the other side of her.

I caught Gabriele's eye. For some reason, since our little heart-to-heart in Madrid a couple of days ago, I'd found it easier to look at him without my whole face burning up. Everything that had been left unsaid between us had now *been* said – there were no more secrets. We'd had our chance and we'd blown it, and now life had moved on. Neither of us were in a position to commit to any kind of relationship and I, for one, wanted to focus on myself, without any distractions. I had stuff with my family to sort out, my career to think about. Gabriele was far too complicated for me to want to add an affair with him into the mix, too. Then again, who had said anything about an affair? I didn't think two, albeit *spectacular*, kisses constituted that.

When my phone rang, I was surprised to see my mum calling and quickly excused myself, imagining her mid-ocean, leaning glamorously on the railings, the wind in her hair.

'Back in a sec,' I said to nobody in particular, squeezing past Carlos's knees and walking out onto the sand.

I thought that looking out at the water might keep me measured, whatever it was that my mum might be calling about. I realized how sad it was that I saw her name come up on my screen and assumed I'd upset her again. It never used to be like this, but that was back then when I agreed to anything she asked.

'Mum!' I said, bracing myself. 'How's the cruise?'

A breeze licked against my face and I closed my eyes for a second or two, letting calm wash over me. It would be fine. This was my mum: she loved me, she wanted the best for me – even if what I wanted was proving temporarily inconvenient. Eventually, she'd come around.

'Very nice. We're docking in Crete tonight,' she said.

'Lovely. Enjoy all that delicious Greek food,' I said, mentally putting the country on my ever-increasing list of places that I wanted to visit.

'And where are you, may I ask?' she said. 'I was expecting you to update me on your plans for the studio and the house while you go off on your tour.'

'I sent you a message last week!' I insisted, irritated. She was already having a go at me and we'd been on the phone for less than thirty seconds.

'Oh. Well the Wi-Fi on board is terrible. Perhaps your message has been delayed,' she said, sounding huffy that she was having to backtrack.

'Maybe. So Sedi's friend, Jess, is house-sitting for us,' I explained, keeping my voice as calm as I could manage. No point having a row when we were thousands of miles away from each other. 'She's in London for a couple of months working on a show and needed somewhere to live, so it seemed like the perfect solution, and it saved her paying extortionate rent elsewhere. She'll look after the place for us in exchange for free bed and board.'

'Is she trustworthy, Lira? Have you met this girl?'

'Once,' I said. 'She seemed nice. But I guess we're going to have to trust Sedi's judgement on this one, aren't we?'

Mum scoffed. 'It's not like she always chooses the most desirable friends.'

Sedi had befriended a group of girls at school who Mum had had a pathological dislike of. They were 'it' girls, the popular crowd, and they were okay individually, or in small doses, but as a group they were pretty toxic. Even Sedi had eventually seen sense and barely spoke to any of them again once she left town to go to dance college.

'She's fine, Mum. In her mid-twenties, seems very sensible.'

Mum tutted, clearly not entirely appeased. It sometimes seemed like she wanted it both ways – to relinquish control to me so that she could go out and enjoy her own life, and to control the decisions I made in her absence.

'I'll make contact with both Sedi and Nolo whenever I can,' I reluctantly reassured her. Since our Zoom call I'd barely reached out to them, and honestly, I didn't see why I should. If Mum was that worried about her adult children, she could surely call them herself.

'And as I said in my message, the studio is all in hand. I've emailed my clients personally to let them know I'm away and that they'll have a stand-in teacher for five weeks, plus I'm on hand 24/7 to answer any questions. Everyone seems happy.'

I could practically hear Mum bristling on the other end of the line.

'Mum? Are you still there?' I asked.

'Yes, yes, I'm here.'

There was an awkward silence, during which I glanced back over my shoulder, catching Gabriele's eye. I quickly swung back around to face the ocean.

'I saw the reviews for your show,' said Mum, sounding hesitant.

'Did you?' I asked, keeping it light. I had no idea where she was going with this.

'When the Wi-Fi came back on again. I looked them up.'

I felt a shot of pride – she'd cared enough to find out how the show was doing. Maybe, secretly, she was prouder of me than she'd been making out.

'It sounds as though you are dancing very well, Lira,' said Mum. 'Well done.'

I braced myself as I waited for the punchline, because there was bound to be a 'but' involved. *But* you belong in the dance studio. *But* you are not a dancer anymore. *But* you've let us all down. When no 'but' came, I was forced to cobble together a response.

'Thanks, Mum. I hope so,' I replied. 'I'm enjoying every single second of being on that stage.'

Mum was quiet for a few seconds. For once, I'd refrained from telling her what I thought she'd want to hear and expressed what I truly felt instead. But was it too much too soon?

'This Gabriele Riccitelli, he is very good. Very talented. Extremely handsome. Have you danced with him before?' asked Mum.

'No, not really. Never professionally.'

'And are you? Keeping it strictly professional?'

'Yes,' I lied. 'Of course.'

Me and Mum never talked about men or relationships or love. There was never really time and there had never been anything of note for me to say. Was I really going to tell her about my arrangement with Jack – which reminded me, I owed him a message to tell him I was away – or that I'd been fantasizing for years about Gabriele, a man I'd met once? It would be mortifying. She'd think I was mad. There was no way I could explain that, while we *mostly* danced together, we'd almost had sex in his dressing room.

'I know men like this, Lira. If you're serious about dancing again, don't get involved. That would be my advice.

He thinks only of himself, I can see it in his eyes. He will hurt you.'

I squirmed. One minute Mum spoke to me like I was a naïve young child who was going to make the biggest mistake of her life, and the next she expected me to run the entire James family while she cruised around the world. Which was it to be? Which version of me did she want?

'I'm not going to get involved with Gabriele Riccitelli, Mum,' I said, shutting the conversation down. I looked over my shoulder at the group laughing and talking together in the bar. I was sure I could see Gabriele watching me again. Somehow, I could always feel it when his eyes were on me.

That evening's show took place at a very grand theatre in the El Poble-sec area of the city, the theatreland of Barcelona. I noticed the Spanish crowd were much livelier than the Brits, with a jovial, slightly more unpredictable atmosphere in the auditorium, which was uplifting and in-fectious. For some of the more upbeat numbers – the samba, the salsa – a large portion of the audience even jumped to their feet, gyrating their own hips to the music, their arms raised above their heads with delight, their bodies twisting in time to the music. I liked to see how much joy we were bringing them; that maybe we were helping even just one person in the audience feel better that day.

Afterwards, we all left the theatre together as a cast, with some going on for drinks or paella. Luca's parents had flown out to watch, so he quickly introduced them to Gabriele and I and asked if we wanted to join them for dinner. Both of us declined – I had some studio admin to catch up on and planned to head back to the hotel. Earlier, Julia, one of the teachers holding the fort, had emailed me with a couple of queries and it was important to be responsive – and *quickly* – so that she didn't feel like she had to muddle through on her own. I wondered why Gabriele was so reluctant to socialize with the others – he seemed like he had the weight of the world on his shoulders lately, and I didn't think it could be the pressure of the show, since in that regard, things couldn't be going better.

I smiled at them all, and briefly at Gabriele, before heading in the direction of the Gothic Quarter and our hotel. A few minutes in, I stopped to take a photo of a stunning, floodlit church and, on a whim, posted it on the 'Sisters Are Doin' It For Themselves' WhatsApp group. These days, it was hit and miss as to whether anyone would respond, a situation I was going to need to do something about when I was back in the UK.

Was it just the change in me my family couldn't get their head around? Or was it that they felt as though I was disrupting their lives as well as mine? Trying not to overthink, I let myself enjoy the sensation of walking in central Barcelona at night. During the day, the cobbled streets teemed with tourists and locals going in and out of the high-end shops and hotels in this part of the city, and it might be shaded, for the most part, due to the narrow streets and stone buildings, but I found it humid and airless, and definitely not meant for the thousands of people that flocked there. But tonight it felt different. A cool breeze ruffled the back of my neck and, except for the odd tourist taking the long way back to their own hotel, the streets carving their way off the main drag were quieter and emptier than I'd ever seen them.

'What do you make of Barcelona. A good crowd, no?'

Startled, I turned to see that Gabriele had fallen into step beside me.

'Sorry. I seem to have a habit of creeping up on you,' he said.

I laughed. 'My fault, I was in a world of my own. And yes, the audience were great tonight. Talk about getting into it!'

'Wait until you meet the Italian crowd. This is *nothing*!' he said with amusement.

We walked in silence for a beat or two, before I plucked up the courage to ask.

'Is everything okay?' I said.

'Why, have I been even more of a recluse than usual?' he teased.

I considered how to put my thoughts into words, and whether now was even the right time to do it. He didn't seem the most attuned to the effect he had on other people, or how his own attitude or mood might be obvious to others. He was who he was, it seemed, and he wasn't afraid to show it. I liked that about him.

'You've been a bit distant since we arrived in Spain.

Since we had that coffee in Madrid. I wondered if it was something I said. Is it about Paris?'

He shook his head lightly. 'Of course not. It has nothing to do with you, Lira.'

I felt a shot of embarrassment. As if I could impact his mood like that.

'So tell me what's bothering you,' I said gently. 'Is there anything I could help with?'

Over the past few days, he had definitely seemed more withdrawn, and it wasn't just his usual borderline sexy brooding; it was something more, I could tell. And it hit me then that maybe I cared about him more than I was letting myself believe, otherwise I wouldn't have noticed his subtle change of mood in the first place.

Gabriele rubbed the back of his neck, slowing his pace, as though he couldn't walk and think at the same time. 'You know how you told me you feel a responsibility to your family? To run the studio for them; to be the person they can rely on while everyone else is scattered around the world doing their own thing?'

'Yes,' I said, wondering where this was going.

Of course I knew. I felt it every minute of every day, especially while I was out of the country. If something happened at the studio while I was away, my parents would never forgive me, although, for the first time, I was beginning to realize that I'd probably, eventually, be able to forgive myself. I couldn't be there all of the time, and it was my prerogative to take a break every now and again, no matter what it was for. If nobody was prepared to step up to help me manage James Jive, then it was also on them if things didn't go exactly to plan.

'I have something very much like that going on. With my father,' said Gabriele, his voice sounding different. Strained, quieter. Like it was difficult for him to admit any of this to himself, let alone to me.

'Tell me about it,' I said, softly, so as not to scare him off.

'My papa, Enzo, is Italian, in case you did not know that already. My mother is from Argentina. They met while he was on a work trip to Buenos Aires and fell instantly in love. My mother moved to Italy with him almost immediately and they have lived there ever since, in Tuscany, where I was born. That was thirty-five years ago now, and they are still very much in love, although sometimes you would not know it from the way they disagree about absolutely everything. Loudly!'

I smiled. I could imagine it very well. In our house, it was my mum and Sedi who were the most volatile and explosive, with the rest of us trying our hardest to stay out of conflict as much as we could. We'd given up trying to help them smooth things over and had learned that they just needed to get it out of their systems. Also loudly. They always got over it eventually.

'It all sounds very romantic,' I said, imagining meeting my future husband on the streets of Argentina, with tango music hanging in the air and dancing on every corner.

He nodded. 'And until now they have been very happy together, living on my father's farm in Tuscany.'

'Farm?' I said. 'As in animals?'

Gabriele shook his head, laughing. 'No, not animals. Olives. And grapes. My father makes wine.'

'Ah,' I said. 'Hence the work trip to Argentina.'

'His business used to take him all over the world, but these days he cannot travel so easily. He gets tired. Working so many hours puts a huge strain on him now, and although he loves the farm, it is a lot for one person to cope with, especially now he is nearly seventy years old.'

I was beginning to realize that Gabriele and I might be more similar than I'd imagined. The businesses of dancing and wine might not have much common ground, but a family business was a family business and I could guess at what Gabriele was about to tell me next.

'Does your father want you to help him with the farm?'

Gabriele looked at me with a grim expression. 'He has always wanted that. And the expectation was that I would begin working at the vineyard as soon as I had finished school. But by then I had fallen in love with dance and I knew I was very good at it and that it was what I wanted to do with my life. My father has never let me forget how much I let him down, and now things are becoming even more difficult. He is getting older. My mother is worried about his health, and a few days ago she called to tell me he had fallen over outside, but of course he refuses to see a doctor, because he is stubborn. Or maybe scared, I do not know. And I feel this . . . obligation to step in and help, even if I am not quite ready to give all of this up.'

I took all of this in. 'So we're the same, in a way,' I ventured. 'Because the question is, do we follow our own dreams and accept that we're going to have to let our families down, or do we do what's expected of us and sacrifice what we want for them?'

'Until now, I have been okay with letting them down. My father has never wanted me to dance. In fact I think he finds it an embarrassment. When his friends ask what his son does, he does not want to have to say he is a dancer. It is not masculine in his eyes, especially in rural Tuscany. This shifted a little when I was on TV in Italy. My mother would tell everybody she came into contact with and my father did not protest as much as usual. But he did not say he was proud of what I had achieved. He still thinks I should be working on the land, getting my hands dirty, as he likes to call it.'

'That must be hard for you,' I said.

Gabriele groaned. 'At least you have done as your parents asked. You *have* been a good daughter; you sacrificed everything for them. But me ... I have simply run away from the problem. I have not done a single thing to help my father with his vineyard and farm. And if he has made himself ill working himself to the bone, then surely it is my fault?'

I stopped suddenly, grabbing Gabriele's arm gently.

'No, Gabriele, it's not your fault. Your father is a grown man who can make his own decisions. If he can't cope with the business on his own, he should hire more staff, or employ somebody to run the business for him. It doesn't have to be you. Surely, he must see what a talent you have and that it can't be wasted?'

Gabriele looked deep into my eyes, as though he couldn't believe that he was telling me all of this, and that I was listening and wanting to help.

'He has never seen me dance, not for years. He refuses to come.'

I was shocked. Although, was I, when not one member of my own family had made the effort to see me dance in London either, or had even shown remorse that they couldn't find the time to come? And, in a way, I'd normalized situations like this, because my family were the people I spent the most time with and I didn't have a vast well of experience of other people's families to pull from. I'd told myself that lots of people had the exact same issues I did and that many people, of course, had it much, much worse.

'What about your mother?' I asked, as we turned into a particularly narrow side street. I looked up as we walked under an ornate archway, taking in the beautiful, enclosed walkway above our heads, which seemed to lead from a building on one side of the road to one on the other. I wondered what its history was and made a mental note to look it up in my guidebook when I got back to my room.

'She supports me,' he said softly. 'But at the same time, she is worried about my father. I do not know how she would cope if something happened to him. He is her whole life.'

'She has you,' I said. 'You are her life, too.'

And then Gabriele reached out and put his hands on my shoulders, running his smooth hands along the lengths of my arms.

'It feels good to talk to someone about this,' he said softly. 'Thank you for listening. I have a tendency to keep things inside, but with you . . . I don't know. You make it easy to speak the truth about how I feel.'

His stare seemed to penetrate deep inside me.

Slowly, my hands went to his waist, almost of their own accord, as though they had a mind of their own. I slipped my arms around him, pulling him closer to me. I knew what it felt like to face sacrificing everything you'd ever dreamed of to please your family. And it was worse for Gabriele; he was an only child – at least I could convince myself that my sisters would be there to help out if I wasn't, even if that wasn't quite the reality of how our family functioned. I wanted to hold him, to let him know that everything would be all right, that he wasn't the terrible person he probably sometimes thought he was.

As we backed into the shadows, Gabriele gripped me tighter and tighter, pressing his forehead against mine, guiding me into a doorway, hiding us from any fellow tourists who might decide to wander past. He moved his hands to my face, cupping my jaw, looking into my eyes as though he was wrestling with a decision. I knew what it was, because I felt it, too. Only this morning I'd promised my mum that there was nothing happening between Gabriele and I, but I'd been lying to her, and lying to myself.

'Here we are again . . .' I whispered.

He ran the tip of his tongue across my lips, parting them. I let him do what he wanted, closing my eyes, letting my body react, acutely aware of every single delicious sensation as he kissed me harder, deeper, losing myself in the warmth of his mouth. My body shuddered as he ran his palms under the hem of my dress, stroking my inner thighs with his thumbs. He made me feel so beautiful, so desired, and it had always been that way between us. Under his gaze, his touch, I felt like the best version of myself, completely uninhibited, free to express anything that came into my mind in that moment.

'Not here,' I said, knowing that kissing him wasn't going to be enough, not tonight.

He hesitated, kissed me once more and then he nodded and took my hand.

Back at the hotel, we stumbled out of the lift.

'Come to my room,' he said. 'It is closer.'

He had the key to his room ready, tapping it hard against the pad as I wrapped my arms around him from behind, burying my face in his back.

'Hurry,' I said.

He slammed the key onto the pad again. 'Why do hotel keys refuse to work for me?!' he growled in frustration.

I prised it out of his hand and tried it myself; the handle turned first time.

'You have the magic touch,' he said, falling inside the room and pulling me with him.

Before I could think or even speak, he took a step towards me, his lips crashing into mine. All that mattered was being here with him and surrendering myself to the sensations that were coursing through my veins now that we were finally alone, our tongues slipping effortlessly and deliciously in and out of each other's mouths. He lifted me up again, like he had that night in his dressing room, cupping me underneath as I wrapped my legs around his waist, carrying me the few steps to the bed. I grabbed a fistful of his hair, tugging it gently as he lowered me onto the mattress, easing himself on top of me.

'What are you doing to me, Lira?' he asked, running his finger from my chin, down the centre of me, until it was between my legs again, where I wanted it most. I moaned with pleasure, grappling with the zip of his trousers, desperate to push them off his hips, making him help me when they weren't coming off fast enough. Once he'd removed them, he kneeled half-naked in front of me and peeled off my own underwear, flinging it across the room.

'How are you so beautiful?' he asked, sliding back up onto the bed and lowering himself on top of me, our lips almost touching.

I gasped with pleasure as his groin made contact with mine.

'Yes . . .' I moaned softly.

I could feel how hard he was and it thrilled me to know how much I turned him on, just as he did me. There was no doubt that he wanted me as much as I wanted him, and it gave me the sort of power I'd never felt in bed before – the power to let go, to do whatever came naturally.

'Take off my dress,' I commanded him,

He did as he was told, sliding the crepe silk fabric over my head. I was wearing only my bra now, and within seconds he'd pushed it aside, revealing my breasts, his mouth dipping to take first one then the other nipple in his mouth.

'This feels so good,' I said, reaching behind me and un-clipping my bra myself so that I was completely and utterly exposed to him, so that he could see every inch of my body. I shivered at the thought of what he might do with it.

Palming my breasts, he raised his head, his eyes burning into me as we looked at each other, deeply connected. In his hand he held a condom. I had no idea where it had come from and I didn't care. My bones felt like they were turning to liquid as he tore it open. The second it was on, he was between my legs, hard, insistent, guiding himself inside me. Closing my eyes, I let my knees fall open, crying out instinctively, feeling as though I could scream and it wouldn't be enough of a release.

'Jesus,' he said, as my body began to move to his rhythm, his breath coming in ragged bursts. 'Jesus, Lira.'

*

Afterwards, we lay in bed, wrapped up in each other's arms. For the first time since seeing Gabriele again, I felt relaxed enough to let myself drift off to sleep, enjoying the rise and fall of his smooth chest underneath my cheek. The room felt warm and heady, the sounds of Barcelona floating through the open window, delicious smells from the restaurant across the street lingering in the air. Somewhere there was music, too – flamenco – and I couldn't help thinking that there was nowhere else I'd rather be at this precise moment in time, and nobody I would rather be with.

My relaxed state was soon interrupted by the trill of my phone.

I groaned.

'Ignore it,' said Gabriele, his fingertips making circular patterns on my back in a deliciously comforting rhythm.

'It might be my parents,' I said.

'So what? Call them back.'

'Or the studio,' I said.

He was right, of course, there was nothing to stop me ignoring either. But this was me we were talking about, and learning how *not* to be at everyone's beck and call was going to take some more work. Plus, I was completely paranoid that the whole place was going to be burned to the ground while I was away, and every time the phone rang I assumed it was one of the teachers telling me the fire brigade were on their way.

I inched my hand across to the bedside table and to my phone.

'Sorry,' I said to Gabriele, rolling off him and onto my back. 'I know I'm pathetic.'

'I never said that,' he said, watching me with a smile.

I glanced at the screen. Shit. It was Julie, one of the teachers from the studio. What was happening?

I answered the call, feeling as though my heart was stuck in my throat, and hoping this was a total overreaction to what could be a call about many different things, none of which involved flash flooding or armed robbery.

'Hello?' I said, trying not to sound as though I was in the grip of panic. 'What's up?'

I knew to at least *try* to play it cool.

I slipped my legs inside the duvet, feeling weird about taking a work call completely naked.

'It's Julie. Sorry to call so late, but I wasn't sure what time you'd be back from the theatre.'

Julie had been working at the studio off and on almost as long as I had. She was one of our most trusted employees and my mother had been vaguely appeased when I told her I'd put Julie in charge in my absence. We all knew she'd do a good job, and the clients loved her.

'Everything okay?' I asked.

I glanced across at Gabriele, who was scrolling through his phone now, too. As if sensing me watching him, he turned to face me, propping himself up on one elbow and grinning at me in a way that would have been extremely sexy if I wasn't about to have an anxiety attack about the studio. I looked away again – I couldn't focus with him looking at me, and this was important.

'Yes, don't panic, it's nothing urgent,' said Julie. 'Is this a good time?'

'Sure,' I said. Julie wasn't to know.

I took a few deep breaths. It was okay. Something was happening, but it didn't sound as though there was a threat to life.

'I thought you'd want to know that a few of your clients are talking about leaving and going elsewhere for lessons. They miss you, and some of them aren't convinced you'll come back. They said they'd signed up because they wanted *you* to teach them, not one of us,' said Julie.

'Right,' I said. God. Really? 'Can you ping their names over and I'll send them a personal email. Reassure them that I'll be back in a few weeks' time and that normal service will resume?'

Julie was silent for a few seconds. 'Will it, though? Only, I thought you might have caught the performing bug. Everyone's raving about you in the press – I bet if you got an agent now, they'd be getting you seen for anything you wanted.'

My heart began to thump in my chest again, but with a different type of adrenaline this time. It wasn't about whether the studio had suffered some sort of catastrophic incident, but about whether Julie was right. I hadn't allowed myself to seriously consider whether I wanted to go straight back to the studio. And sure, I'd told my sisters that I wanted to keep dancing, but I had no idea how that would look, or if it would even be possible. And although I knew the show was going brilliantly, I'd always assumed that had far more to do with Carlos and Gabriele than me.

'I assumed I'd come back and pick up right where I left off in some capacity,' I said to Julie, deciding honesty was the best policy, with her at least. It's not like she would mind either way. 'But maybe you're right. Maybe this is a sign I need to change things up completely, do something different with my life.'

But how was I going to stop our clients leaving in droves? My parents would kill me if the membership rate started to drop. We relied on those monthly direct debits to keep the money rolling in – rent in Castlebury might not be at London levels, but it was still extortionate, and the electricity bill was through the roof. Dad had tried to blame it on the revolving glitter ball.

'Let me have a think about how to stay involved with the studio while I'm touring,' I said. 'There must be a way that I can connect more with our members. Let them know that I'm thinking about them all, that I care about the studio, and that I haven't just abandoned them to go off and dance my way around Europe.'

'Good idea. But do it fast,' advised Julie. 'And keep me posted!'

When I ended the call, Gabriele was still watching me with that intense stare of his.

'What are you looking at?' I said, laughing lightly.

'Can I not look at you?' he asked innocently.

'No, you can't,' I said, scooting down the bed so that my whole body was covered with the duvet, feeling self-conscious suddenly.

'I overheard your conversation.'

'Hardly surprising when you're lying right next to me,' I said, jokingly tutting at him.

'You need to connect more with your studio clients? Your members?' he said, running his hand under the covers.

'Mmmm,' I said, suddenly completely unable to concentrate on what was happening with the studio because Gabriele's hand had wormed its way into a position that felt achingly, devastatingly good. I pressed my hand on top of his, not wanting him to go anywhere.

'Then I have an idea,' he said mysteriously, rolling on top of me.

CHAPTER EIGHTEEN

Lira

While I stood self-consciously on stage, Gabriele had positioned himself in the front row of the theatre's auditorium, which loomed dark and empty behind him. His phone was in his hand and it was pointing towards me. There was clearly an expectation that I was going to do something, but I'd drawn a massive blank as to what.

'Social media really isn't my thing,' I whimpered pathetically, hoping that would go some way to explaining why I was currently frozen on stage like a rabbit in the headlights.

I'd been trying to get out of doing this for at least forty-five minutes, but it seemed to be having little effect – Gabriele was insistent.

'You need to reconnect with your clients, *si*? You are away on this exciting dance journey. If they feel like you are thinking about them, that you are taking them with you, giving them behind-the-scenes access to something they would not usually get to see, then they will feel special.'

He had a point, even if he had surprised me with his insight. I hadn't imagined he'd be a social media afficionado either, but when I checked out his Instagram – something I'd forced myself not to do up until that point – I was pleasantly surprised. Sure, there was indeed the odd gratuitously topless shot (and of course he looked amazing), but mostly it was videos of Gabriele breaking down a dance, teaching his thousands of followers a particular step, talking about the history of the rumba or whatever. His content was surprisingly engaging – he appeared very natural, even funny at times, and I wondered whether a career in TV presenting might beckon. Because of his usual glowering mood, or at least that's what I'd call it, I'd never have imagined he'd come across so warmly on screen.

'We don't all have hidden talents, you know,' I grumbled. 'I'm not good on camera.'

'I do not believe it. And anyway, how do you know if you have never even tried?' he reasoned.

'Let's just say I'm hazarding a guess. Come on then, let's get this over with,' I said, positioning myself in the centre of the stage. 'Is here okay?'

'Hmmm,' said Gabriele, twisting the camera first one way and then the other. 'There is not much light in here, but it will have to do. So, a reminder – we will tease this on Instagram, but only your members will have access to the full video via the James Jive newsletter. You will say something about where you are, why you are here, what kind of dances you are performing. You might want to mention me . . .'

'Oh really? I might have guessed you'd want to get in on the act!' I joked.

'I will start recording on "action",' he said, smiling to himself.

I nodded in approval, feeling a shot of nerves. I wasn't lying when I said I was terrible on camera. Sedi had been on at me for years to do more on the James Jive Instagram page. She even tried to persuade me to set up a TikTok account, but I'd drawn the line at that. She currently had twenty-five thousand followers on there, apparently, which sounded impressive, but in the case of the studio, I didn't think the majority of our clientele would even be on TikTok, since it was mostly made up of couples in their thirties, busy mums and senior citizens. I thought I had a better chance with Instagram, and I posted the odd thing – perhaps if we had a new teacher, or a new class, or photos from one of our events. But I'd always made sure that I didn't appear in any of the shots, even if Sedi had tried to persuade me that I was the 'face of James Jive'. I'd called her bluff and said that she should shoot some footage at the studio for herself, put it out there to her thousands of TikTok followers, and she'd half-heartedly agreed, but to date it had never happened and I knew better than to bother pushing it.

'And . . . action!' yelled Gabriele.

I looked at the camera, which I could barely see because of the darkness and the fact it was a tiny, black, slimline phone, but even so, looking at a piece of tech equipment was definitely preferable to looking into Gabriele's eyes, which were altogether distracting, so I went with it.

'Hello, everyone. It's me, Lira, from James Jive. I hope you're all well and I'm so sorry I haven't been around for the last few weeks. As some of you may have heard, I had the opportunity to join a new dance show called *Slow Burn*. We started the run in the West End and now I'm in Spain, would you believe? Here I am at the *Teatre Apolo* in Barcelona. It's four hours before showtime and my dance partner, Gabriele Riccitelli, and I have arrived early to run through the four duets we have in the show. We thought it might be fun to take you along with us . . .'

I smiled at what I thought was the camera and waited for Gabriele to stop recording.

'And . . . cut!' he said.

He put his phone down and looked at me with suspicion.

'I thought you said you were not good on camera?'

I walked closer to the edge of the stage. 'Actually, it wasn't as bad as I thought, once I got going. I just pictured my clients and imagined chatting to them at home in the studio. It took the pressure off.'

He nodded, impressed.

'So, now let me set up the camera and we will show them a few steps from each of our dances. Something they can copy and do at home,' said Gabriele.

I frowned. 'Do you really think they'd be interested?'

'Yes,' he said, putting his phone in his pocket and leaping up the steps onto the stage. 'These reels I do on Instagram get the most views. People like to be taught something. And there is the thrill of being shown a step by a professional dancer. They will like it, I promise you.'

'They might be thrilled to see you, that's true,' I said. 'In fact, chuck me your phone. I want you to introduce yourself, too.'

He shrugged, handing me his phone. 'Sure.'

I took a few steps back, framing Gabriele so that the camera caught a glimpse of the stage and the auditorium behind. I thought some of the studio's female clients might enjoy seeing exactly who I had been dancing with since they saw me last!

'Just open the top button of your shirt for me?' I suggested cheekily.

Gabriele laughed and did as he was told. 'Just one button?'

'Yes!' I said, holding my hand out to stop him before he got carried away. 'Action!'

He looked at the camera, making sure his smouldering good looks translated onto the screen. My clients would be watching this on their phones or laptops back in Castlebury, so he needed to go big. And he definitely did.

'I am Gabriele Riccitelli,' he said, as though he was talking to a group of fans live in the room. He was so natural, I wondered whether he'd had professional training. 'Today,

I will be performing in the show *Slow Burn* with your very own teacher, Lira James, as my partner for four spectacular duets. We do the rumba, a classic American smooth, a fun and energetic salsa and a very intense Argentine tango together. The Argentine tango is a favourite of both Lira's and mine, perhaps because I was taught how to dance by my grandmother, who is from Buenos Aires. I learned the heart of the dance from the very best – the locals who dance it daily on the street. And today, we will teach you a very short routine to do at home. When we return to England, Lira and I would love to see what you have all come up with.'

He gave the camera – my clients – a dazzling smile and I stopped the recording.

'Wow,' I said, blown away. 'You're going to have them eating out of your hand. I'm pretty sure they won't be leaving now. Did you mean it?'

'Mean what?' he asked, clearly pleased with himself as he walked towards me, grabbing me around the waist.

For a second, I was self-conscious, worried that another cast member might arrive early and see us. But then I thought: so what if they did? We weren't doing anything wrong, and even though I'd tried to convince myself that getting involved with Gabriele would be unprofessional, the reality was it happened all the time on tour. Luca had said the same thing. People got close. People hooked up. And part of the reason for telling myself that it would be frowned upon by the rest of the company was that it gave me an extra layer of defence, another reason not to go there. And the more reasons I had, the more likely I would be to stick to the vow I'd made to myself: *do not fall for Gabriele all over again.* Last night had been perfect, and it seemed as though Gabriele felt the same, but then there was his track record. He'd clearly hurt Daniella in the past – was I setting myself up to be left heartbroken all over again, too? Even my mum had warned me off him. Was I crazy to get involved?

'Did you mean it about coming to the studio to see my members dance? They'd love to see you in person; a bona fide TV star. One of the best Latin dancers in the world,' I said.

'They already have one of the best Latin dancers in the world as their teacher. They should be very happy already.'

I laughed. 'I'm not sure they see me that way. You, on the other hand ...'

He put the palms of his hands on the small of my back, pulling me closer. If I'd imagined my life a month ago, before any of this happened, I'd never in a million years have thought I'd be standing on a huge, opulent stage in Barcelona, under the switched-off lights, the smell of drapes and dust in the air, in the arms of the man I'd literally dreamed about for the last thirteen years.

'I will come. Of course I will come,' he whispered, stroking his thumb tenderly across my cheek.

'Still up for recording a few steps of the Argentine tango?' I asked, thinking it would be safer to get back to business before I declared undying love for him on the spot.

He nodded. 'Let me set up the camera and we will begin.'

Because I'd arrived at the theatre so early, I'd finished my hair and make-up well in advance, leaving me time to find a quiet corner to upload the videos, along with a blog-style message to all the members on our database. I promised I'd give them regular check-ins from each city we were visiting, and asked them to let me know if they enjoyed learning the dance steps that Gabriele and I had demonstrated. I also promised to organize a gala evening when I returned, at which Gabriele would watch them perform the steps we had taught them. I had no idea how any of this was going to go down – I imagined they'd like it. My clients were generally fascinated by *Strictly*, and if they didn't know who Gabriele was before, they would likely look him up, and the fact he'd been on the Italian version would be a huge pull. Plus, our events always went down well. Usually, my mum would swan in looking fabulous in something long and sparkling. Occasionally, Sedi came, but it wasn't like she helped me serve drinks or anything, preferring instead to circle the room talking about her own exciting adventures to anyone who would listen.

I pressed 'send' on my members-only newsletter and posted an Instagram reel of Gabriele and I dancing, suggesting people come and join our James Jive family if they wanted to see more. I'd check in with Julie and the others in a few days to see if anyone had mentioned it and, in the meantime, I'd try to think of other ways to keep our clients engaged while I was away.

When my phone rang, making me jump because it was still in my hand, I was surprised to see it was my mum. Strange; we'd only spoken the day before.

'Hey, Mum,' I said, my voice a little breathless. I tried not to let my mind wander to the worst-case scenario. Like was Dad okay? Was *she*?

'Can you hear me, Lira?' shrieked Mum, talking far louder than was necessary, probably because she was standing out on the ship's deck or something. At least she sounded fairly upbeat. Dad mustn't have fallen overboard or anything.

'Loud and clear,' I said, with emphasis on the 'loud'. I leaned my back against the dressing-room mirror, relieved that nothing appeared to be wrong. 'What's up?'

'There is a Spanish couple on board and they somehow managed to get hold of a copy of *El País* when we docked in Crete. There are pictures of you all over it!' said Mum.

'Me?' I said, confused. 'You mean a review for the show in Madrid?'

'Yes! Five stars they've given it. But not only that, they are raving about you, Lira. They are saying you are an undiscovered talent, that you have great things ahead.'

I let this sink in. The British press had been kind, but it had been Gabriele they had focused on, and of course Carlos had a mention. There had been the odd grainy picture of Gabriele and me in hold, but that had been it. If you didn't read the caption in tiny print underneath, you'd never have known it was me.

'Seriously?' I said, taken aback, wondering how I could get hold of a copy for myself. 'Can you take a photo of it and send it to me?'

'I'll ask your dad to do it, you know I can't do texting.'

I smiled to myself. Mum was not the most tech-savvy person and I didn't blame her for refusing to learn. I thought life might be a whole lot simpler if you weren't in constant communication with people via WhatsApp and social media, anyway. I quite liked the idea of living your life completely oblivious to what everyone else was doing, and even what they thought of what *you* were doing. My mum had always been very good at putting herself first, and I didn't mean that in a negative way, not entirely. I admired her for it, in fact, and wished that I'd inherited more of her extroverted personality and less of my dad's more reserved one. Because people who spoke out and said what they wanted *got* what they wanted, generally, didn't they? And the rest of us scuttled along behind them, picking up the scraps, taking the jobs they didn't want and doing the tasks they didn't have time for.

'I never realized you still had this talent, Lira. Of course I remember how beautifully you danced when you were young. How elegant you looked, how you brought so much of yourself to each dance. But it has been so long now – how have you fallen right back into it, so much so that you are impressing some of the harshest theatre critics in the world?'

I was lost for words for a second. Was my mum complimenting me? Saying actual, really nice things?

'Thanks, Mum. I guess it's a lot to do with the choreography. With my dance partner, Gabriele. Maybe it's about our connection. Perhaps I couldn't have done this with anyone else.'

'That I don't believe,' said Mum. 'You have something special, Lira. And . . . I'm sorry.'

This conversation was taking a turn I'd never in a million years have expected. My mum – tough, no-nonsense, slightly emotionally averse Mum – actually sounded choked up. Had she just *apologized*?

'I'm sorry for assuming that you didn't mind giving everything up to run James Jive. And I'll admit it, it made my life easier. I had my own career to pursue and I wasn't ready to give it up. But what about you? What have I done to you?'

I heard my mum sniff.

'Mum, are you *crying*?'

'Only a little,' she said. 'And I don't want you feeling sorry for me. I deserve all the guilt I'm feeling right now.'

I was touched. And thrown.

'Look, Mum, it's not all your fault. I could have said no. If I'd had the guts to stand up for myself, I could have told you there and then instead of waiting until I was into my thirties and it was almost too late. I'll have a couple of years of performing at best, and then I'll be back running the studio. We can make it work, can't we?'

She sniffed again, harder this time. 'I promise you, Lira, we will make it work.'

And for the first time ever, I believed her. And it didn't matter that usually when she said 'we' would do something, what she really meant was that *I* would need to do something. I truly believed that she'd suddenly got it; that seeing a review of my dancing in black and white in a national newspaper – that I struggled to understand how she'd even managed to read, given she didn't speak a word of Spanish – had made her realize that working in a dance studio wasn't the only thing I wanted to do with my life. Perhaps this was always meant to be my time to shine – a few years later than anticipated, but better late than never.

'And listen,' said Mum, 'I've been talking about you to the cruise company. They're doing a special press event in Dubai in the autumn and they want you and Gabriele to appear. An all-expenses-paid trip. Plus a fee, of course. Would you be interested?'

I was shocked. Shocked that somebody else would pay to see me dance; that they didn't just want Gabriele. And Dubai? I'd heard so much about it, but it was the kind of place I didn't think I'd ever go to just for fun – I had principles, after all – but if it was work, well, why not?

'I'll speak to Gabriele. But it sounds good. Thanks, Mum.'

When I put the phone down, I noticed a message from Jack. I hadn't thought about him for ages. Sure, I didn't have the connection with Jack that I had with Gabriele, that unexplainable thing that made me feel giddy every time he looked at me, but Jack was sweet and gorgeous and kind, and sexy in his own way.

Are you back yet? Missing our PT sessions . . .

I smiled at our special code. I didn't think the joke would ever get old. Although, one day, I might actually want some *real* personal training sessions with him, and then how would I differentiate between the two? I sent a message back.

Still away! Message you soon.

I pushed the thought that I might never contact him again from my mind. When my normal life resumed, I might very well be craving the excitement of a sexy tryst on Jack's desk at the gym, however cold the thought of it not being Gabriele left me right at this moment.

An hour before curtain-up I was in the dressing room I was sharing with Daniella and another dancer, Astrid, touching up my make-up and spraying about a can-full of hairspray onto my bun so that there was no chance of it coming loose during one of the costume changes.

'Evening,' said Daniella, setting up next to me.

'Hey,' I said, casually.

Things still felt a little frosty between us and I didn't

quite know why. I knew she'd been Gabriele's dance partner for years, and that she'd wanted the lead in the show, so
I supposed that was enough for her to resent me from the
off. And she was milking her role as dance captain, using
the power it gave her to pull people up on their sloppy steps.
She'd criticized one of my lifts the other day and Gabriele
had told her I was doing it one hundred percent accurately,
and that since she didn't know the steps as well as he and I
did, she should probably keep her opinions to herself. But
there was clearly another layer on top of professional jealousy – I'd felt *that* from most of the other girls – but with
Daniella it was different. I suspected Gabriele had still been
seeing her at the beginning of the run, certainly during
rehearsals. I tried to ask him about it, to make sure I wasn't
stepping on anyone's toes, but whenever I broached the
subject he shut me down immediately, insisting there was
nothing going on between them. I didn't own Gabriele; he
could sleep with whomever he wanted. He didn't owe me
a single thing. And yet, it felt as though we were getting
closer and closer. Could I really let that happen if he was
also getting closer with other women? Was I saying, then,
that I wanted Gabriele all to myself?

'Do anything interesting today?' asked Daniella, brushing
copious amounts of bronzer onto her face and décolletage.

I busied myself slicking on another coat of mascara.

'Not much,' I said. 'I recorded some bits and bobs for
James Jive's social media pages. You know the studio I run?'

Daniella stifled a smirk. 'Sure, I remember.'

Every time I started to feel bad about potentially stepping on her toes with Gabriele, she went and did something that made me lose empathy for her all over again.

'You think it's funny, don't you?' I asked, for once not wanting to let her get away with her bad behaviour. 'That I have to teach dance rather than just perform. You find it strange.'

'I never said any such thing,' she said, giving me a baffled, gaslight-y look, as though I was a bit mad for suggesting it. 'I mean, it's not something *I* could do, that's all. I think if you're a dancer, you're drawn to the stage like a moth to a flame. Nothing would ever get in the way of that for me.'

I nodded, as though in agreement. 'Well, I'm glad you're in a position to do exactly what you want with your life. Not all of us are so lucky,' I replied.

I put my mascara away and pulled out my concealer, dabbing some onto one of my fingertips and applying it to all the areas of my face that needed smoothing out.

'I noticed Gabriele has been helping you with your socials stuff,' said Daniella, leaning into the mirror to apply her eyeliner. 'Seems like you two are spending more and more time together.'

I shrugged. 'He's good at that kind of thing. He offered to help, no big deal.'

'But you've been seeing each other, right?'

I tried to focus on finishing my make-up, but she was putting me on edge and my hand was shaking a little. I had no idea why she had this effect on me, but she reminded me of some of the girls at school – the mean girls, the bullies who had tried to intimidate me and my friends, a group of equally quiet and studious people, who I still saw for dinner and drinks now and again. I realized that Daniella was like a grown-up version of one of those girls, and I seemed to have regressed into the teenaged version of myself. I would not let myself be walked all over, not anymore.

'I don't think that's any of your business,' I said, sounding arsier than I'd intended. Better to overplay it than under, probably. At least this way she'd get the message that I wasn't a total pushover.

'Oh, it's not,' she said, her tone changing slightly. Was it my imagination or was she the tiniest bit thrown by my pushback? That was the thing with bullies, or at least that was what they told you, wasn't it – if you got them on their own, they lost most of their power. 'I just don't want to see you get hurt, that's all,' she said, obviously lying.

I almost smirked this time, but I wasn't going to lower myself to her standards. But honestly, as if she cared about my feelings. This was entirely, one hundred percent about her.

'Thanks for your concern, but I can look after myself,' I said.

'You know he's been sleeping with me as well, though, right? And probably a couple of other women, too. Have you seen the contacts in his phone? He has hook-up after hook-up listed and, because of who he is, the way he looks, he can pick any of them to come over whenever he chooses.'

I swallowed hard. Contacts? Hook-ups? Obviously, I'd never seen inside his phone, and now I was annoyingly intrigued. Because there was something off about having a list of women you picked from at random whenever you happened to feel horny, and it made me slightly sick to think that I might be one of these women. There was no way that I was going to let Daniella see it, but she'd got to me.

'You really like him, don't you?' said Daniella.

Our eyes met in the mirror.

'And so do you,' I said, softening my tone.

I was all for supporting other women, usually, so maybe I needed to find some sympathy for Daniella here, even if she was going about things all the wrong way. This was happening because she had feelings for Gabriele, plain and simple. And I, better than anyone, understood how that felt.

'Maybe we should both tell him where to go,' said Daniella. 'It would serve him right.'

I smiled tightly. 'Maybe. But whatever happens, please let's not argue over it anymore,' I said.

'Agreed,' said Daniella, unzipping her make-up bag with a flourish.

For the next five minutes, we finished getting ready in silence, but not the sort of angry, resentful silence we'd experienced before. I was glad we'd finally addressed the issue between us. And I wondered whether I'd been taking my anger out on her when, deep down, it was myself I was angry with, for letting myself get caught up in the whirlwind that was Gabriele Riccitelli all over again.

CHAPTER NINETEEN

Lira

Just when I didn't think European cities could get any more stunning after three nights in laid-back, colourful Porto, we arrived in Lisbon for a five-night run. The sun had been shining and the skies were a clear electric blue as we'd stepped off the plane that afternoon, and although we were needed for a light check later that day, we weren't actually performing until the following evening, so I fully intended to make the most of every single minute I had spare. Guidebook in hand, I left my hotel room almost as soon as I'd checked in and bumped straight into . . . Gabriele.

'Hi,' I said, pausing reluctantly, suddenly wishing I hadn't worn the tiny, flippy mini dress that I was pretty sure had been shrunk in the hotel laundry in Barcelona, because I did not remember it being *this* short.

'Fancy meeting you here,' said Gabriele, who somehow looked cool and polished and not like he'd stepped off a plane an hour ago. His eyes skimmed briefly over my body, which sent a not-unpleasant fizzing sensation running through me. I took a deep breath to calm myself, even if what I really wanted to do was fly into his arms and have him kiss me wildly right there in the hotel corridor.

'Thought I'd go and take some photos of the city for the James Jive socials,' I stuttered eventually.

Julie's warning about our members not being happy about my absence had been weighing heavily on my mind and I was aware I needed to keep up the momentum when it came to making our clients feel connected to me and the rest of the James family, even if hardly any of us were actually in the country and – in the case of my siblings, at least – the studio was the furthest thing from their minds.

'Then I have the perfect location,' said Gabriele, leaning easily against the wall.

'Have you now?' I asked a little flirtatiously. I could do with a little local knowledge.

'I am planning to buy the original and best custard tarts in Portugal. Believe me when I say this place would make a spectacular photo for your social media. Come, I will show you.'

He pushed off the wall and started down the corridor. I hesitated for a second, not because I didn't want to go with him, but because I was thrown by the easiness between us. We hadn't had sex again since that night in Barcelona – the cast had tended to hang out together in Porto and there hadn't been time to be alone together, even if we'd wanted to be.

We walked along the banks of the River Tagus, glittering and powerful, and, according to my guidebook, at its widest here in Lisbon after starting over six hundred miles away in Spain and now about to spill out into the Atlantic Ocean. I reckoned this explained why I felt like I was on the coast – the River Thames this was not. In fact, it was giving me San Francisco vibes and, referring to my guidebook again, the stunning orange suspension bridge leading from Lisbon to an area called Almada had partly been modelled on the Golden Gate Bridge.

'I take it you've been to Lisbon before, then?' I said, glancing across at Gabriele, who had expensive-looking sunglasses on and was sporting a soft white cotton shirt that rippled in the gentle breeze.

'Many times,' he said, 'although when I come to a different city to perform, I often do not see much more than the hotel and the theatre. Perhaps I will get to see some cafés and restaurants, but that is it. Being with you is making me feel that I should get out and explore more,' he said with a shrug.

'I guess when you travel so much, it loses that magical appeal.'

'I am not sure it does, or should. There is always more to discover.'

I nodded, thinking briefly to how it could have been the

same for me if I'd continued on a similar trajectory after winning the World Championships all those years ago. How different things would have been, how well travelled I'd be by now, too.

'How's everything with your dad?' I asked gently.

I'd picked up that Gabriele rarely talked about his family. When we were together as a company, the other dancers would share funny stories about their childhoods, or perhaps a parent or a school friend or a sibling would be coming in to watch a particular show and we'd all be introduced to them afterwards. I knew very little about Gabriele's background, other than what he'd revealed to me that night in Barcelona, and to my knowledge nobody he knew had been to see any of our shows. I felt a small comfort at not being alone in that, although I also wouldn't wish it on anyone.

Gabriele sighed. 'Not great. He is still refusing to see a doctor. And he will not listen to my mother. She has spoken to his staff, has asked them to take on a little more of the workload to secretly ease what my father has to do, and they have agreed, of course, because they are worried too.'

'Maybe you could get through to him?' I suggested. 'You'll see him when we get to Italy, won't you? Perhaps if you tell him how upset it's making you all—'

Gabriele laughed hollowly. 'If he will not listen to my mother, there is zero chance he will listen to me. We are not close in that way, not anymore. Feelings and concerns are not something we discuss, as a family.'

257

'That's normal, I reckon,' I said. 'It's the same for me. I don't think I've had an in-depth conversation about feelings with my parents ever.'

'But you have your sisters . . .'

'Yes,' I said, suddenly craving how close Sedi, Nolo and I had been before *Slow Burn* came along. I hoped it would get back to normal eventually, but I thought that maybe it would take me a while to get over everything that had happened. I'd known my parents would be unhappy, but I'd honestly thought Sedi and Nolo would have had my back no matter what, especially since they were more than capable of standing up to our parents about their own stuff. I'd honestly thought they'd have come around quickly, excited to see their big sister having the kind of career they'd enjoyed themselves.

I took a photo of the bridge and pinged it to the WhatsApp group. Things might be a little off between us all, but I didn't want the distance to get any wider, and I'd always been the one to pull the three of us together. Sedi immediately sent a heart emoji back. Nolo, in New York, would still be sleeping.

'So this is one of the places I wanted to show you,' said Gabriele, sweeping his arm out towards some kind of fortress sitting in a small bay, several metres from the shore. 'The Belém Tower. It makes a beautiful picture, no?'

I flicked to the relevant page in my guidebook and read it out to him.

'The Belém Tower, a UNESCO World Heritage Site,

is one of Lisbon's most striking monuments. In 1514, King João II led a project to defend Lisbon from enemy ships, a plan that included the building of the Belém Tower.'

'I had no idea it was so old,' said Gabriele, looking surprised. 'We can climb up to the top, I think, but look, the queues . . .'

The line to get in was about a hundred people deep and I was pretty sure that the view from ground level was almost as lovely. I began snapping away, adding in a couple of videos, panning from one side of the tower across to the bridge on the other, accidentally getting a bemused Gabriele in shot. I loved the way he smiled so naturally at the lens, how he never seemed fazed by having a camera pointed at his face.

In front of us was a small beach, where clear and shallow water from the river washed onto a sandy shore with the tower as its backdrop. Gabriele saw me watching people kicking off their shoes and wading in.

'Come,' he said, bending to slip off his loafers and promptly rolling up the hem of his trousers. 'We must go in.'

'What?' I said, laughing.

'We must paddle. I have always wanted to, but I felt like a fool on my own. But now you are here,' he said, standing up with a satisfied smile and holding out his hand. 'Ready?'

I nodded and took his hand, feeling safe and looked after the instant his fingers closed around mine. Kicking off my sandals, I dipped a toe in the water, grimacing.

'It's freezing!' I exclaimed.

Gabriele laughed. 'This is the Atlantic Ocean, you must be brave. Come, let us go deeper.'

Together we waded further out so that the water soon came up to my knees.

'Your trousers are already soaked,' I warned him, looking down, thinking he'd be irritated, but he just laughed it off.

'Then there is nothing for it,' he said. 'I am going to have to soak you, too.'

He dropped my hand to bend and scoop up palmfuls of water before throwing it all over me, breaking out into a deep rumble of a laugh that I'd never heard from him before. Shocked for a second and gasping at the sharp coldness of the water on my face and arms, I barely hesitated before dipping my own hand into the Tagus and splashing him right back.

Our clothes dried off in the sun during the fifteen minutes or so it took us to walk to the infamous Pastéis de Belém, the former monastery and home of the Portuguese egg tart – *pastel de nata* – that I'd been dying to try ever since I'd heard we were coming to Portugal. According to every single travel guide ever, the tarts at Belém were the original and the best.

As we stood in the – *long*! – queue to be served, Gabriele and I chatted easily about, well, custard tarts, mainly, but also about how he thought the show was going, what he thought I should do next – he wanted to introduce me to his agent – and also what he was most looking forward to about returning to Italy in a few days' time. I teased him that he wanted to be asked for autographs again, that was what he was most excited about, but he denied it vehemently, insisting it was the food. And seeing his mama, who he told me had booked tickets for herself and his dad for the last night of our run in Florence.

I took a photo of the monastery and then a selfie of both of us grinning madly in front of it and posted it straight onto the James Jive Instagram account, with a caption about arriving in Lisbon and heading straight for custard tarts. Then I clicked on the red heart at the top of the page and nearly dropped my phone clean out of my hand when I saw that the teaser reel I'd posted of Gabriele and me running through an Argentine tango routine in Barcelona now had 625 likes and seventy-nine comments. This was unheard of for the James Jive account, which could usually expect about ten reactions – at most! – to any given post. I flicked through the brief messages underneath, which were mostly from studio members congratulating me and saying they wished they'd known about the show when it was in London, and how they couldn't wait to practice the steps Gabriele and I had demonstrated. The @jamesjivestudio account even had seventy-five new followers, which potentially meant several new clients. Gabriele was on to something here! I showed him, my mouth open in slightly exaggerated shock.

'I told you,' he said smugly. 'Followers adore this kind of content.'

'Hmmm,' I said, reluctant to tell him he was right, because I knew he liked to be, and therefore I didn't feel like giving him the satisfaction.

Soon it was our turn in the queue and Gabriele bought us two tarts each, which I thought was a little excessive until we found a spot at a table and I tasted them.

'Oh. My. God,' I said, pausing my munching for effect.

They were unbelievably good – flaky yet crunchy pastry, soft wobbly custard, caramelized sugar on top; they might just be the most delicious thing I'd tasted in my entire life. Gabriele wasn't holding back, either.

'These things are addictive,' he enthused, in between mouthfuls.

'I think I'm in love with custard tarts,' I said dreamily, already wondering whether it would be too much to go back to the counter to buy a box of them to take back to my room.

We didn't speak properly again until we'd finished eating, the silence peppered only by loud chewing and moans of delight. With four tarts polished off between us, I wiped my mouth with a napkin and dusted pastry flakes off the front of my dress.

'Wow,' I said.

Gabriele smiled.

'It is nice to have someone to share these things with,' he said.

I'd never seen him as light and happy as he'd been this morning, a playful side to him appearing that I'd never known existed. We either seemed to be tearing each other's clothes off or putting our hearts and souls into a performance. Seeing this different aspect of him made me wonder why he didn't show people these parts of him more often.

'I never knew you were capable of such jollity,' I said, winking at him to prove I was joking.

He shrugged. 'There is much you do not know about me.'

'Is there now?' I said, challenging him to tell me – or show me – exactly what.

'Maybe one day you will find out.'

'That sounds like a promise.'

'Okay, I promise that one day you will know me better than you do now. That you will realize there is more to me than you think there is. That you will discover I am not always so serious.'

'And that you're not always on the verge of a bad mood?'

He raised his eyebrows and I thought maybe I'd pushed it too far. But then I thought, so what? It was true.

'For that very uncalled-for comment, Lira James, I instruct you to eat one more custard tart,' he said, pushing back his chair and heading back to the counter.

CHAPTER TWENTY

Gabriele

I had been to Lisbon several times before, but had seemingly avoided most of the typically touristy things. I had certainly never walked up to the Castelo de São Jorge. I had noticed it from afar, its huge, fairytale-like structure towering over the higgledy-piggledy houses of the Alfama district, but I had never made the time to go up and see it properly.

It had been Lira who suggested we walk up here, the afternoon before our first show in the city. My instinct had been to say no. I did not know why at the time, but upon further analysis I realized it was because I was scared of what spending more time alone with her might mean for us.

Yesterday had been one of the most special times I had experienced on tour ever, which was worrying to say the least. Being alone with Lira in bed was one thing – sure, it was amazing, but I had amazing sex with lots of women – but wanting to go for long walks uphill in the sun and talk about things other than dance . . . that was not normal, not for me.

'This area is gorgeous!' enthused Lira, striding ahead, seemingly enthralled by the winding streets and the colourful tuk-tuks jostling for space, and the quaint little shops selling everything from bottles of port and custard tarts, to bath oils made with local herbs and flowers. I watched her, smiling to myself. She looked lovely today, in a simple outfit of jeans and a T-shirt worn with flat sandals, her hair piled in a bun on her head. I was in my trusty linen trousers again, which the hotel had kindly laundered for me after yesterday's impromptu paddle.

'I think the entrance is up here,' she said, turning to me, her face sparkling with anticipation.

I nodded, following her, wondering for about the hundredth time whether this was a good idea. I was already enjoying myself far too much, and could I really relax into it when I knew that it would be impossible for us to be together after the tour had finished? Could I risk falling for her, knowing I was very likely to lose her all over again?

The castle was even more impressive close up. Its cobbled surroundings had a laid-back, chic atmosphere I had not expected. There were little huts selling food and wine, and I almost broke my no-drinking-before-a-performance rule and bought us both a glass of the local cherry liqueur, Ginja.

'Don't even think about it,' warned Lira, who had seen me eyeing it up.

'Spoilsport,' I joked.

I grabbed us a cappuccino each instead and then joined Lira, who was leaning against the castle walls, taking in the view. Below us, the rooftops of one of the oldest parts of the city tumbled down towards the Tagus, a sea of terracotta tiles and washing lines reaching from one apartment to another. On the other side of the bay, green mountains loomed out of the water. I breathed it all in, the scent of churros from a stall behind me wafting into my nostrils, a soft breeze licking the back of my neck, Lira's arm pressing tantalizingly against mine. It could not have been more perfect if it had tried.

'I never knew Portugal was so beautiful,' said Lira. 'And then we went to Porto and, obviously, it was absolutely stunning, and now this. My mind is blown!'

'You have caught the travel bug,' I declared.

'Why the hell haven't I put myself out there and explored the world properly before?' she said, impassioned, suddenly.

'You still have time to do all of those things, Lira. There is no rush,' I reassured her.

'I do, don't I? I don't have to go back to my hotel and book myself a flight to New Zealand or anything like that. All in good time.'

I glanced across at her. God, her skin was perfect. I wanted to run my thumb across her cheek right now, pull her into me, kiss her hard on that plump, pink mouth, but I owed it to Lira to have my head straight before I started promising her things I might not be able to come good on. And, of course, there was the fact I didn't know for sure what *she* wanted. I felt something when she looked at me – it *seemed* like she liked me for who I really was, bad bits and all – but until we actually had that conversation, there was a chance that this closeness between us could all be in my head.

'Why do I want to kiss you every time I look at you?' she said, suddenly.

I laughed, my breath catching in my throat. She *did* feel the same way. I watched a blush creep into her cheeks and, without overthinking it, I put my hands on her face, pulling her close.

'I like hearing you say that,' I whispered.

'What exactly is it that you want from me?' she asked. 'Because it's really difficult to tell what you're thinking; whether the feelings I have when I'm with you are reciprocated or not. Whether you have this kind of connection with everyone.'

'Everyone?'

'Other women. Daniella, for example.'

It took all of my strength not to pull away, because that was what I always did when I came up against something that felt difficult emotionally; when something required me to dig deep, to make myself vulnerable. Of course I wanted to dodge her question, to shut it down. Tough question? Ignore it. Hope it went away. Although they never did, of course. Everything caught up with you in the end.

'You know my history with Daniella. And it is not like it is between us.'

'She said something happened recently. Since, you know . . . *we've* been spending time together,' said Lira.

She was the one to pull away from me this time, looking out over the castle's walls at the city below. I wanted to touch her again. It felt easier to be honest when I was, but I could see that she was grappling with something, too, and if she needed space, I would give it to her. I wondered whether Daniella was purposely trying to cause trouble, perhaps realizing that what I felt for Lira was special, because if I could feel it so strongly, I was sure that other people must be able to see it, too.

'Anyway, we can both sleep with whoever we like, right?' she said.

'Can we?' I replied, hating the idea of her being with somebody other than me, although of course I had no right to feel this way. 'And just so you know, there has been nothing with Daniella for a long while.'

Lira took a moment, seemingly taking it all in. 'She said you're incapable of having an actual relationship. That you have a list of women you call whenever you're in the mood for sex.'

I rubbed at my brow, realizing how bad that must sound. And, honestly, it felt bad, too, and quite often I had gone to delete every single contact in my phone so that I would not be tempted to reach for them whenever I felt lonely.

'I am not quite as callous as that makes me sound,' I said,

feeling ashamed that this was how people saw me. How did Daniella even know? Had she been through my phone? 'Lately, I have not enjoyed meeting women just for that. It feels . . . pointless. We both know nothing is ever going to come of it, other than the obvious. And afterwards, when they leave, I don't feel all that great.'

'Not great how?'

'Alone. Like my life is one big, gaping hole of nothingness.'

Lira looked as though this was not what she had expected me to say. I had never admitted how lonely I felt to anyone, ever. I had never told a single person that the only time I felt truly happy was when I was on stage performing. And how sad it was that my happiness was entirely tied up with my role as a dancer. That my job – one of the most insecure, fragile, volatile careers you could choose – was the only good thing I had going for me.

'Then why have you never been in a relationship? And I'm not sure I can really talk here, because I haven't either. And I get it – I get what you mean about feeling alone. I feel the same way, even if I don't have a huge list of men to contact when I feel like having some company,' said Lira.

'No?'

'Well, I do have *one* person. Jack. My personal trainer.'

I felt a shot of jealousy, which I had no right to feel.

'Classic,' I said, trying to laugh it off.

'I'm nothing if not a cliché,' she said, half-smiling.

I relaxed a little. We were talking about us, about feelings, sex, love, and sure, it was a little awkward, but it was definitely not unbearable. And now Lira had started talking, it was like she could not seem to stop, which gave me a small reprieve from having to say more. One step at a time.

'Maybe we're both too scared to actually feel something for somebody,' said Lira, slowly, as though she was choosing her words carefully. 'To risk getting hurt. I can only speak for myself, but I like to be in control of my emotions. My whole life, really. I like to know that I'm good at something, and to feel safe and secure in what I'm doing. But then Carlos came along, and the show and you, and it shook everything up. And now, I'm just not sure. Because nothing has ever felt as thrilling as these last few weeks on tour with you. And how am I going to go back to my real life knowing how good this felt?'

I cupped her face in my hands, needing her to know I understood, that I felt the same way. I did not want to go back to feeling alone any more than she did.

'I have missed you, Lira,' I said, resting my forehead against hers, closing my eyes because it felt easier to be truthful that way. 'Over the last thirteen years, I have thought about you so often; about the night we shared. There was something about you leaving that tore my heart into pieces, and I can assure you that it was not just my ego taking a bashing, it was because I could not stand the thought of losing you when I had only just met you. Crazy, when you think about it. We were so young. It was one night. And yet, I can still remember every detail of it.'

She wrapped her arms tightly around me so that there was no space between us at all.

'Do you think it's fate that brought us back together all these years later?' she said.

'I do not know,' I admitted. 'But we are not the people we were then. We were young and impulsive and we had not learned how to have difficult conversations yet. But look, here we are, having one.'

She nodded. 'And that feels like a good start, doesn't it?'

We held hands on the way back to the hotel. It was downhill all the way, and we chatted about lots of different things, one of us pointing out a beautiful building or an interesting display in a shop window as we passed it, or the facades of a building decorated with beautiful blue and yellow ceramic tiles. The sky above our heads was clear and bright, and with Lira's hand in mine I felt like a different person altogether, a world away from the guy who had spent his birthday completely alone, with nobody except his parents so much as acknowledging it.

Our hotel was on a pretty side street and no words were needed as we stepped inside the foyer and took the stairs up to my room. It was cool and dark inside, since it overlooked a shady courtyard rather than the bustling street at the front of the building, and quiet except for the hum of the air-conditioning unit.

The housekeeper had been – the bed was perfectly made, smooth and inviting. The muslin curtain billowed in the breeze from an open window; on the street down below, a tram rattled past.

'If I'd told you that I was leaving that night, why I had to go – about the studio, that I was giving up dancing – what would you have said?' Lira asked me, her face serious.

It felt important for her to know, but on the other hand, how could I be sure? How could I transport myself back to that place and imagine what my twenty-two-year-old self would have said or done?

'I think I would have told you to stay. To miss your flight. To say no to your parents. That you were too talented a dancer to give it up.'

She bit her lip. 'Would you?'

'I cannot know for definite,' I said, taking both of her hands, pulling her towards me, wanting her to relax. 'I was not the same person I am now. I would have been thinking selfishly. I would not necessarily have considered what was best for you.'

Anyway, the past was the past. Why did it matter so much what we did or did not say to each other then? We were here *now*. We had the second chance I had always craved.

I burrowed my face into her neck, breathing in the scent of her, her perfume that smelled like bitter orange and cloves, the hair product she used that lingered on my skin whenever she had been near me. I tilted her chin so that her eyes met mine.

'Let us enjoy this for what it is. It is impossible to know

what will come, to predict what will happen in the future,' I said.

She ran her hand underneath my shirt, sending shivers shooting up and down my spine. It was like she was opening herself up to me, I could feel it happening in real time. Then she took my hand and led me to the bed, laying down and pulling me on top of her, our fingers entwined above her head. She smiled at me.

'This feels different,' she said.

I nodded. 'I know.'

I was not sure if she meant different from the last time we had slept together, or different from being with anybody else, but either way I was in agreement. 'Except that this time you have far too many clothes on,' I teased.

I began to unbutton her jeans with a focused intensity, needing to run my hands over the silky soft skin I knew was beneath them. I tried to ease them down her body, but they would not come easily and I was becoming increasingly impatient.

'I am going to have rip these right off you,' I groaned as she wriggled beneath me, trying get them down, too. 'Do not worry, I will buy you new ones.'

She half-laughed, half-gasped as I gave one huge yank and they finally slid down her legs. She kicked them off over her feet, revealing a delicate white lace underwear set that sent my body temperature soaring on the spot.

'I wore these especially for you,' she whispered, as I flipped her on top of me, caressing her thighs as she straddled me, groaning at the glorious sight of her mostly naked body.

'Such a shame you have to take them off, too,' I said, helping her out of them, dragging off the remainder of my own clothes. Our breath was fast and ragged, the need between us becoming almost unbearable.

I had never been this turned on in my life.

The second she had slipped a condom onto me, her hands deft and warm, I guided her into place, crying out with pleasure as I moved effortlessly inside of her. I knew that I could never, ever get enough of this, no matter how many lazy afternoons in bed we might spend together.

Afterwards, she lay in my arms and I stroked her hair as her breathing softened and stilled. It was all so idyllic that I was beyond irritated when my phone rang, shattering the comfortable silence we had been languishing in. I wished I had turned the thing off, but I had heard it now, and I could not un-hear it. It's just that I had never realized being with someone after sex could feel so good. That staying with them, keeping the connection alive, holding them, letting them stroke their hand up and down your stomach so delicately. It instantly made me feel as though I was less alone in the world.

Reluctantly, I reached out my hand, sliding my phone off the bedside table and glancing at the screen. It was my mother calling. I could hardly speak to her now, butt naked and with Lira splayed across my chest. I let it ring out.

But within seconds she was ringing me again and I knew, instinctively, that something was wrong. I eased Lira gently off me.

'Sorry,' I whispered. 'I should take this.'

I sat up, swinging my legs off the side of the bed, simultaneously answering my phone. For some reason, I felt the need to get up, to pace around the hotel room.

'Hey, Mama,' I said.

For a few seconds, all I could hear was Mama's breathing. Heavy, laboured.

'Mama, what is wrong?' I demanded to know.

'It's your father,' she said. 'He's in the hospital, I'm here with him now. They say he's had a heart attack, Gabriele.'

She dissolved into tears; big, wracking sobs that I was almost sure Lira would be able to hear. I looked over my shoulder and, sure enough, she was watching me with a look of concern in her eyes.

'Mama, it will be okay,' I said, keeping my voice low and reassuring, even if I knew that what I was about to say could well be a lie. 'He will be fine. He is in the best place. The doctors are with him now. They will fix this.'

'He was out in the vineyard,' sobbed Mama. 'I was at home, preparing dinner. He would have been finishing up, about to head home. I heard shouting outside and when I looked out of the window I saw him, crumpled on the ground. Gio was screaming for help.'

Gio worked on the farm with Papa; he had been with us

275

for years. It must have been a shock for him, too, to have seen Papa like that.

I heard Mama talking to someone in the background. From what I could make out, it was a doctor, asking her to come somewhere.

'I have to go,' said my mother, sounding calmer, although perhaps it was that she had no tears left. 'The doctor wants to speak to me.'

'Call me straight afterwards,' I said. 'I want to know exactly what he said. If you need me to, I can get on a flight tonight.'

'What about the show?' sniffed Mama.

'There is an understudy, Mama,' I said as she ended the call.

I could not bear to look at Lira at first, although another part of me wanted to throw myself into her arms and let her hold me and comfort me. But that was not how I handled things. Although, how did one handle a parent being seriously ill? It had never happened to me before. For all Papa's ailments and poor health, I had never expected anything anywhere near as terrible as this – not yet, not this soon.

Suddenly, Lira was standing next to me, slipping her arms around me.

'What happened?' she asked. 'What's wrong?'

I swallowed hard, her care for me making me feel like crying, something I had not done for many years and had no intention of indulging in now. I would remain positive, expect the best. My father would make a full recovery. I had to believe he would, because the alternative was too awful to contemplate.

'My father had a heart attack,' I said. My voice sounded weak and strained, I could hear it myself, so I knew that Lira would pick up on it too.

She held me tighter.

'I'm so sorry,' she said.

I gently removed her hands from around me. It was not that I was unappreciative of her being here, but I could not be emotional in front of other people; it just was not in my DNA.

'I should go,' said Lira, picking up on the cues.

I turned to face her, trying to be kind, to not leave her feeling rejected or as though I did not appreciate what she was trying to do. I touched her face lightly.

'I think I need to be alone for a moment or two. If that is okay,' I said.

She nodded, immediately beginning to get dressed, gathering up her things that were strewn around the room.

'Of course,' she said, sounding flustered.

I had hurt her feelings, but I could not think about that now. I felt almost robotic, as though my brain was shutting down to protect itself, and that it was not sending the right signals to the right places.

I watched her leave, closing the door behind her, feeling wretched about a whole host of things. I sat on the edge of my bed and only then did I let the tears fall.

Please let Papa be okay, I said to nobody in particular. Because who was going to help me now? I was entirely help-less, at the mercy of the gods, and the hope I had pretended to have a few minutes ago was nowhere to be seen.

CHAPTER TWENTY-ONE

Lira

Gabriele wasn't himself on stage that night, although the audience would never have known. He danced each step perfectly, executed each lift with skill and confidence, and to the naked eye, our chemistry on stage was as sizzling as it had ever been. But there was something in the way he held me that wasn't the same. I couldn't put my finger on it, exactly, but it was like he was touching me, holding me, spinning me because he had to, not because he wanted to, or because he was so caught up in the moment, in our dance, that it flowed organically from one movement to another, which was how it usually felt. And when he looked at me, his eyes weren't sparkling, flirtatious; they were deadened, as though his mind was elsewhere entirely, which, naturally, it would be.

We still got a standing ovation. He still held my hand as we took our bow. He still smiled and waved at the audience who were enraptured by his good looks and his phenomenal dancing. But as soon as he was able, he dropped my hand and walked ahead of me, going into his dressing room and shutting the door behind him.

'What's up with Gabriele?' asked Daniella, falling into step beside me.

It wasn't my place to say. 'Not sure,' I replied.

I went to the dressing room I was sharing with a few of the other girls and removed my stage make-up, combed out my hair and changed into jeans and a light sweater, because the temperature dropped a little in Lisbon at night. I wasn't sure what to do – whether to leave Gabriele alone or to knock on his door and see if he was okay.

Daniella and Luca had already left for drinks in Bairro Alto, trying their best to persuade me to join them. Daniella had teased me about not coming anywhere unless Gabriele was there. I'd laughed it off because maybe it was true, but all I could think about was him and how he was doing after the news about his dad. I knew he had a complicated relationship with him, a dynamic that sounded even more challenging than the one I had with my parents. At least I didn't think they were disappointed in me; they were just a little unobservant and caught up in their own needs and wants, but I could forgive them that in a heartbeat.

After hanging around aimlessly for a bit, still undecided, I picked up my bag and headed out of the room, taking my time as I walked along the corridor, which was quiet now, subdued and dark. I stopped outside Gabriele's dressing room, wondering whether I would be able to hear something if he was still inside. He could be back at the hotel already, for all I knew, and I'd have been skulking around outside his door for nothing. But then I couldn't bear to think of him being all alone in there either, struggling with whatever was going on with his dad.

I tentatively knocked on his door. No answer. I put my ear to the door, checking to see if there was any sign that he was inside, although he clearly didn't want to talk to anybody even if he was. I tried once more.

'Who is it?' I heard him say.

His voice sounded strange – muffled, subdued – but perhaps that was just because there was a wooden door between us.

'It's Lira,' I said, elevating my voice as much as I could, without drawing too much attention to myself. I wasn't sure who would still be within earshot – some of the production team would most likely be hanging around, clearing the stage, setting it for the following night's performance.

The door swung open and Gabriele was standing there. I could tell immediately that something terrible had happened.

He took a step back, letting me in. I closed the door behind me, my eyes searching his face, which looked drawn and grey in a way it hadn't out on stage. The same dead eyes, but now even more vacant than before, as though he'd heard something that his brain wasn't equipped to deal with.

'What's happened?' I asked.

He tried to speak, but had to stop to clear his throat. Whatever it was, he was finding it difficult to say. I braced myself for the worst.

'My father died an hour ago,' he said.

Without thinking about it, I walked the few steps to him and wrapped my arms around him. At first he felt rigid beneath my hold, frozen almost, but slowly his muscles began to soften and he folded into me, resting his head in the gap between my cheek and my shoulder.

'I'm so sorry,' I said, my throat tight with my own tears. 'I'm so sorry, Gabriele.'

It was the natural course of things, to lose a parent when you were a certain age. But Gabriele was too young; his father been taken too soon and so suddenly. How could life be so unfair?

In the absence of anything useful to say – because what was there? What could possibly help? – I stroked his back, letting him hold me, letting him know that I wasn't going to let him go, not until he wanted me to.

When he eventually pulled away, I held his face in my hands. His eyes still had a slightly haunted look about them. It must have been such a shock for him, to come off stage and to have heard that.

'Sit down,' I said, ushering him into a chair, slightly worried that he might just crumple into a heap on the floor if he didn't. He did as I suggested, leaning forwards, covering his face with his hands. 'Can I get you something?' I asked gently. 'Some water? Something stronger?'

He shook his head. 'I do not need anything.'

I crouched down next to him. 'How's your mum doing?'

He groaned. 'As badly as you can imagine. My father was the love of her life. She has never so much as looked at another man. He was her everything and now he is gone, snuffed out like a flame. One minute she was watching him out in the vineyards, the next the doctors were telling her he was unresponsive, that there was no hope. She had not wanted to tell me how ill he was before I went out on stage, but in the time it took for us to perform our show, he slipped away.'

His voice broke and my heart went out to him. I clutched his hands in mine, feeling like sobbing myself, but desperately trying to hold it together. This wasn't about me, it was about him and his family, and I was determined to do whatever I could to help him get through this. Where did one even start when something this huge happened?

In the back of my mind, I had a vague thought about the show. There was no way Gabriele could carry on now. But that would have to wait; it didn't matter. We would cancel shows if we had to. What mattered was making sure he was okay, that he had everything he needed to get through this.

'What do you want to do?' I asked. 'Shall we walk back to the hotel together? You can lie down. I'll bring you something to eat.'

He shook his head. 'I could not swallow a single thing.'

I stood up, looking around the room. Gabriele was neat and precise in all areas of his life, it seemed. Whereas the dressing room I shared with the other girls was chaotic, a mess of make-up and hairspray and costumes flung haphazardly on rails, Gabriele's things were hung neatly with equal space between them. Only a handful of products were lined up on his dressing table. A book – its title in Italian – lay next to them.

'Shall I pack up your stuff?' I asked, searching for a bag to put them in.

'Leave them,' he said. 'I will not need any of this for the moment.'

He stood up as though it was an extreme effort to even move, pulling his coat over the costume he wore for our final Argentine tango. This in itself showed he wasn't thinking straight, because changing into something more comfortable was the first thing he did every night.

'We can go,' he said, abandoning his dressing room, leaving it as a stark reminder of how everything had been better before he walked out on stage that night, and that everything had taken a terrible turn for the worse by the time he got back.

I walked him back to his hotel room because I wasn't sure what else to do and I didn't want to leave him. I wanted desperately to hold his hand, but he was even harder to read than usual and I couldn't even begin to imagine how I'd feel if it was me in his position, and therefore

I didn't presume to know what was best. Perhaps I'd want to be alone, too.

At the door to his room, he fumbled for his key, patting down his jeans, checking all of his pockets.

'I can't remember where I . . .' he said, eventually finding it in his back pocket.

He buzzed himself in.

I stood on the threshold, unsure whether to follow him inside.

'Will you be all right?' I asked from the safety of the doorway, watching as he slumped on the bed, as though every ounce of energy had been zapped out of him. He slipped off his shoes without using his hands and lay back on the bed, staring up at the ceiling.

'I will have to be,' he said.

I shuffled awkwardly from one foot to the other.

'Shall I stay with you or . . . ?'

'You go. Have a nice evening.'

'Gabriele,' I said. 'I'm not going to have a nice evening. Not when you've had news like this. Let me stay with you. Let me look after you. I know there's nothing I can do to make any of this better, but let me be with you while you go through it.'

He didn't move, nor did he say anything. Unsure whether it was the right thing to do or whether I'd be overstepping some kind of invisible line that seemed to be constantly shifting between the two of us, I slipped off my shoes and my coat, leaving them by the door. And then I walked over to the bed and I lay down next to him, flat on my back so that I was looking up at the ceiling, too. And then I reached out and took his hand.

After a few moments, he squeezed it, pulling me into him, shifting his body so that I was lying on his chest, wrapping his arms around me. I stayed there, closing my eyes, listening to the rise and fall of his breath, just wanting to be there for whatever he needed me to be there for.

'My mother wants me to fly straight home to Italy,' he said eventually, his voice piercing the silence.

'Of course she does,' I said. 'She needs you.'

'But the tour . . .' he said, letting his words drift off. He didn't need to say more. I knew how he must feel. *Slow Burn* was *his* show; he was carrying the entire thing. Getting up and leaving it in somebody else's hands was never going to be easy, no matter the circumstances.

'We'll make it work. It's what understudies are for: moments like this. It can't be helped and the show will be the least of all our worries,' I assured him.

He sighed and my heart broke for him, because not performing would be another loss: his father and now the show he had helped create, that he loved being a part of.

'I do not want the show to fall to pieces because I am not there,' he said, his voice barely a whisper. 'I want it to be a success, for Carlos, but also for you. And Luca might be my understudy, but I do not think he is good enough to take my place. He is a solid dancer, he will be able to pick the steps up easily enough, and I know you have taught him most of the routines already, but I have seen you dance with him in the group salsa number and there is no chemistry there. No connection.'

I ran my hand across his stomach, wanting to soothe him, wishing he would stop worrying about things he couldn't control. The producers would work out what to do; Gabriele just needed to get himself on a plane and travel to be with his family.

'I'll make it work,' I said. 'Please don't focus on the show. It's more important that you worry about your mother and the farm, and allow yourself time to grieve your dad.'

I thought he might push me away at that point, become defensive, but instead he held me tighter, and I did the same to him, wanting him to know that I would match him step for step; however much of me he needed, he could take.

'I feel like I am going crazy,' he said, running his fingers through my hair. 'My head will not let me think about Papa or the fact that I will never see him again, that maybe I let him down, that he probably died resenting me, thinking me useless, unhelpful. Wondering if I loved him enough. I cannot think about all of that because it is too much, too painful. I must focus on what I can control – the show. I can make sure I do what is best for you; it will give me something positive to think about.'

'Okay,' I said, propping myself up on one elbow, looking into Gabriele's eyes. Because who was I to say he should do one thing or another?

'In a second, I will call Carlos. Tell him what has

happened. That he must tell Daniella to call Luca into the theatre first thing tomorrow morning for a run-through with you.'

I nodded. Carlos had not joined us for this leg of the tour, as was usual for choreographers, instead leaving us in the capable hands of his dance captain and second in command, Daniella. He had been planning to fly out for the final shows in Florence, but I wondered what would happen now, if it would be necessary for him to change his plans.

Gabriele rolled on top of me, bracing himself on his arms so that he didn't squash me.

'I want you to be okay, Lira. I want this success for you.'

I cupped his face in my hands. 'I can't believe you're thinking about me at a time like this. This is all about you. Tell me how you're feeling. Talk to me.'

'I will,' he said, nodding, and I could see in his eyes that there was so much going on in his head right now that he probably couldn't even begin to articulate it. 'But I cannot do it tonight. But when I can, I will. And you will be the only person I will tell my innermost thoughts to. Would that be okay? Could you bear it?'

'Of course I could,' I said, unbelievably touched that he felt able to open up to me when I knew he found it almost impossible to do that with anyone. 'You can tell me anything. It won't be too much for me, I promise. You can say anything that comes into your head, but only when you're ready. You can also be silent and say absolutely nothing because, honestly, I get that too.'

He hung his head before rolling off me completely.

'I think I will go take a shower. Will you wait for me?'

'I'm not going anywhere,' I said, watching him pull off his costume wearily as he disappeared into the bathroom, closing the door behind him.

For the first fifteen minutes or so, I assumed he was finding the shower soothing. That it was helping ease the pain of everything, although I didn't know how it could, not tonight. But as time ticked on, I began to worry.

I sat up, propelling myself to the end of the bed and pushing myself to my feet. Creeping over to the bathroom door, I called his name, quietly the first time, more loudly the second.

'Gabriele? Gabi? Are you okay in there?'

There was no answer, and just as I was panicking about either having to break down the door or call reception to ask them to do it for me, the door unlocked from the inside.

Gabriele was wet from the shower, a towel around his waist. Behind him, the room was backlit and steamy. I didn't notice it at first, but then I saw that he'd been crying. It must have hit him in the shower. He'd probably been in shock before. I rushed to him, wrapping my arms around him, not caring that he was sopping wet and that I was now, too. He let himself cry harder, sobbing softly into my shoulder.

'I did not even get to say goodbye,' he said.

'I know,' I said, wishing there was something I could say to make things better for him, just a little bit.

'How am I going to live with the guilt of what I have done?' he said, gasping for air in between sobs. 'I let him down time and time again. I am not like you; I was not a good son. I refused to put my family before what *I* wanted.'

'And that's okay,' I said, stroking him, desperate for him not to blame himself. 'That's what you *should* do. I was wrong; you were right. Your dad would have admired you for that. I bet he was so proud of what you'd achieved, even if he didn't say it.'

And as I held him tighter, wondering how we'd got so close, never wanting to lose what we had in that moment, even if it had come at the most devastating of times, I realized that all I wanted was for him to be happy again, whatever that looked like.

'Thank you,' he said, coming up for air.

I nodded. 'I'm here. Any time you want me.'

CHAPTER TWENTY-TWO

Lira

I stayed with Gabriele all night, just holding him. At one point, I must have fallen asleep, but I had the feeling that he'd barely closed his eyes at all. As we walked to the theatre together the following morning, I thought he looked worse than he had the night before, if that was even possible.

'Did you get any sleep at all?' I asked, as we waited for a bright yellow tram to pass before crossing the street.

'Maybe an hour,' he said. 'I had another message from my mother. She wants me to let people know – extended family, Papa's friends – so I spent all night working out exactly what I was going to say to everyone. Later I will need to make some calls.'

I squeezed his hand in sympathy. 'And you booked a ticket home?'

'Yes. I leave for Florence on the 5pm flight.'

When we arrived in the auditorium, Daniella was already on stage, talking Luca through the steps for the salsa that Gabriele and I usually danced together. As dance captain, it was her role to step in and take charge, and I imagined she would have been revelling in the authority it gave her under less awful circumstances. I swallowed sharply, suddenly thrown by the realization that I might never dance with Gabriele again, certainly not on this stage, possibly not at all, and the thought took my breath away. I reminded myself that this was not about me. That it was selfish to even consider myself at a time like this.

Daniella ran over to hug Gabriele and Luca patted him awkwardly on the back.

'Sorry about your dad,' he said to Gabriele.

Gabriele grunted in response. He probably didn't trust himself to speak.

'Okay, we have work to do,' said Daniella, clapping her hands together. Lira, Luca, up on stage. Let's start with that salsa I just showed you, Luca.'

I did as I was told, putting on my Latin shoes, getting up on the stage. There was no music as we marked out the steps, and I corrected Luca here and there, but Gabriele had been right: he had learned the steps remarkably well already. If only it was as simple as that, because I felt clunky in his arms. I couldn't explain it – when I danced with Gabriele I felt light and beautiful and capable of anything. Dancing with Luca was hard work. When he looked into my eyes, I felt nothing, and when he put his hands on my waist, it was as though he was going through the motions, as though if he could have got out of touching me, he would have done. Why was it so difficult? Out of everyone in the cast other than Gabriele, I was probably closest to him. I'd confided in him, we'd gossiped together, I really liked him and hoped we'd stay in touch. So why couldn't we generate the chemistry we needed for this dance?

I swallowed my unease and carried on, trying to smile, trying to look as though it was okay, because Gabriele was watching with a frown on his face and I didn't want him to worry. I didn't want him to know that suddenly I was dreading tonight, having to perform the steps I'd previously loved, with someone who just appeared to be going through the mechanics of it all instead of really feeling it, like I knew both Gabriele and I did, night after night.

'Let's try with the music,' said Daniella, also looking concerned.

Luca and I took our places on stage.

'Am I doing okay?' Luca whispered to me.

'Sure,' I said, smiling reassuringly. 'And relax. I know it's hard, you're probably still trying to remember the steps. But let's focus on our connection this time. Let's really go for it.'

'I don't know what's wrong with me. This is supposed

to be what I wanted, a chance to take the spotlight, and there's nobody I'd rather dance with than you. It's just I feel so bad for Gabriele. And I know I'm not going to be able to recreate what the two of you have together.'

'You don't need to. Our dances will be different, but they'll be just as good,' I said, praying I was right.

'Five, six, seven, eight!' yelled Daniella.

As Luca and I moved around the dance floor, trying to generate the heat and fun the salsa required, I gave myself a talking-to – I had to pull this together. We'd all worked so hard on this show, it couldn't fail now, and if we flunked the duets, I'd feel as though it was all my fault as the less experienced dancer. There was no doubt that Luca was a beautiful performer, so all we needed to do was find the connection and everything would be fine. It might not *feel* fine, but it would probably look it, and that would have to be good enough, given what had happened.

At the end of the dance, Daniella and Gabriele were both on their feet, whispering urgently to each other. Neither of them seemed happy, especially Gabriele, who kept raking his fingers through his hair and gesticulating with his hands. Shit, had it really been that bad? I mean, it had *felt* bad, but I was sure I'd done enough to make it *look* good.

'Come down here, please, both of you,' barked Daniella.

Okay, clearly not.

'Was that any better?' asked Luca hopefully.

Gabriele rounded on him immediately. 'No, Luca, it is still not working. The two of you have zero chemistry.

None! It was like two wooden planks had been forced to dance together.'

'Gabriele, be kind,' said Daniella, hiding a smirk.

I felt my skin begin to flush – I'd never seen Gabriele like this, not with other dancers, not with me. Planks of wood? I knew it hadn't been *that* bad.

'It was our first run-through,' said Luca, clearly panicking. 'We can work on it.'

'I expect you to be able to make a dance look sexy,' said Gabriele, raising his voice. 'But the way you performed it, you are going to have a bored audience leaving in droves during the interval!'

I dug my thumbnail into the palm of my hand to stop myself from reacting. I was supposed to be a professional dancer now, one who could take criticism and negative feedback. It was just that it was Gabriele doing the criticizing. And also because I knew he was right.

'So what do you suggest?' I asked, trying to keep my voice steady. This wasn't the real Gabriele; he was grieving, stressed. 'How can we fix this?'

'This is what we need to work out,' said Daniella. 'Steps we can work on, but a lack of spark is more difficult to work with.'

'Lira, what about your old dance partner? The one you won the World Championships with?' asked Gabriele.

'Tomas?' I asked, wondering why he was bringing *him* up.

Tomas and I had had that brief exchange when he saw I'd made the cast of *Slow Burn*, but I could count the number of times we'd spoken to each other recently on one hand. Sedi and Nolo used to tease me that he'd been in love with me, but it wasn't that – at least, I didn't think it was. And I'd felt terrible, because when my parents asked me to run the studio, they hadn't given a second thought to the impact that their decision would have on Tomas's future.

'He is still dancing. I saw he was in something in Brazil,' said Gabriele, warming to his subject. 'But I think the show was about to finish. Would he be free? The two of you work well together, yes?'

'We used to.'

'But you could slip back into it, right? Can you call him? Ask him if he can step in and do the Italian leg of the tour with you?'

'Um . . .'

'Please, Lira. It is the best solution.'

I looked at Daniella, who nodded in agreement. And then I looked at poor Luca, who was looking tired and humiliated and as though he wished the ground would open up and swallow him whole.

'If that's what you want,' I said, standing up, fishing my phone out of my bag. 'Let me speak to him.'

CHAPTER TWENTY-THREE

Lira

Venice was even more beautiful than I'd imagined from the photos I'd seen, especially in the early morning sunlight, which gave it a misty, ethereal feel. We were sitting at a table outside a little café, with the most perfect view of the Doge's Palace, and the iconic Grand Canal churning majestically in front of it. Or, at least, it would have been perfect if it was Gabriele sitting opposite me rather than Tomas. Gabriele had been on my mind almost every minute of every day, except for those brief moments on stage, when I'd managed to lose myself in the music and focus on my performance.

I smiled at Tomas. None of this was his fault, and I was grateful to him for stepping in. Luckily for us, he was in between shows and had a month off, and two weeks of travelling through Italy performing in a hit show to guaranteed sell-out audiences had fallen into his lap like a gift. Carlos and the producers had taken some convincing, but then again, Gabriele was very persuasive, and I think they felt so bad for him that they finally agreed to fly Tomas over and have him try out with me. As Italy was Gabriele's home country, his appearance in the show had been the main draw, and they'd been worried that the audience wouldn't be happy with a replacement. But luckily the advance reviews from London, Spain and Portugal had been so positive that the Italian theatres hadn't cancelled, and any returned tickets had been swiftly snapped up. Tomas had joined us for the final few days of the Lisbon run, with him and I working on our routines during the day. Despite him having only five days to learn all of the duets – Luca had agreed to step into Gabriele's role in the group numbers – everything seemed to be working out pretty well, although we were both apprehensive for our first performance together.

'Can we run through the Argentine tango a couple of times before tonight?' asked Tomas, stirring sugar into his double espresso. 'I'm still struggling with that second set of *boleos* into the *colgada*.'

'Yeah, that's tricky. We struggled with that at first, too,' I admitted.

Thankfully, Tomas and I had fallen right back into the way we'd always danced. It wasn't what I had with Gabriele, but it was good enough, and ten times better than it had been with Luca.

'I remember seeing you and Gabriele dancing the

Argentine tango in Paris,' said Tomas with a half-smile. 'I was sitting at the hotel bar and desperately wanted to ask you to dance, but that wasn't the done thing, was it, to dance with your own partner? But you looked so pretty sitting there, and I saw you swaying your shoulders to the music. You were wearing a red dress, if I remember rightly. I was on my feet about to come over when I saw Gabriele swoop in.'

'You saw that?' I asked, feeling my cheeks redden. It had been a moment I'd played over and over in my mind, one that had felt much too intimate for anyone else to have witnessed. But now here was Tomas, telling me he'd been watching us the whole time.

He nodded. 'I sat back down on my stool, feeling utterly dejected, and that only got worse when I saw how good you looked together; how your chemistry was raw and instant. I was insanely jealous.'

I laughed lightly, hoping he was joking.

'I'm serious,' he insisted. 'I was in love with you, if you hadn't realized.'

Aaaargh. My sisters had been right all along. How could I have missed the signs? But, then, Tomas had been like the brother I'd never had. We'd danced together since we were eleven years old, since boys and love and sex were the very last things on my mind. He was handsome in his own way, but his boyish good looks and dimples had never appealed to me. Even if Gabriele hadn't been there, nothing would ever have happened with Tomas.

'I never knew,' I said, touching his arm lightly, not

wanting him to feel embarrassed. Years had passed; he'd have got over it long ago. 'All those raging hormones flying around, I'm surprised we weren't all in love with each other.'

'Are you in love with *him*, then? Gabriele?' asked Tomas.

I nearly choked on my coffee.

'We lost touch that night. I hadn't seen him for thirteen years until very recently.'

'And yet I can see it in your eyes,' said Tomas. 'When you talk about him, when you were teaching me the steps you'd danced with him.'

'I'm worried about him, not in love with him,' I said, trying to convince myself at the same time.

It couldn't be love. Could it? Although I had nothing to compare it to, because I'd never been in love with *anyone*. Was that sad, at thirty-two years old, never to have ex-perienced a feeling like that? And yes, Gabriele and I had messaged each other several times a day since he left to go home to Tuscany, and that felt new and different, for us at least. But it wasn't necessarily love I was feeling.

'Don't close yourself off to it, that's all I'm saying,' said Tomas. 'I could see something special between the two of you, even then. And look at the reviews you've had! We're great together, but we'd never get the reaction you two do when you take to the stage.'

I tried to shrug it off.

'We're a great partnership. *On* the stage.'

Then I downed the rest of my cappuccino and stood up, needing to not be under Tomas's scrutiny any longer, because he was making me think about things I had been doing an excellent job of avoiding until now.

That night on stage, I tried to enjoy the experience for what it was – a gorgeous venue, the Teatro Goldoni, which looked like a wedding cake if you were on the inside of it, and an enthusiastic crowd. Tomas was confident in the steps and the music was as rousing as ever. The cast were just as enthusiastic, but there was something missing. As Tomas twirled and swung and spun me around the stage, I still wasn't quite feeling it. Sure, I was faking it, very well – I wasn't even sure the audience could tell the difference, although judging by the slightly less exuberant standing ovation at the end, perhaps they could. But I wasn't enjoying things in the same way. And it wasn't anything to do with Tomas; it had to do with me, and how I felt inside. Which meant that there was something special about dancing with Gabriele, and I was beginning to understand that it wasn't just about the connection we shared on stage, but about the one we'd begun to forge off of it.

My hotel room had a gorgeous view of the Rialto Bridge, which I tried to show to Sedi and Nolo on screen before throwing myself on the bed and sticking my laptop right in front of my face. I was too tired to chat, really, but Nolo had suggested we meet, and it had been the first time they'd reached out to me in weeks, not to mention the first time they'd spontaneously organized a Zoom themselves, ever. I'd worried that if I'd said no this time, it would be ages before we all got together again. Which admittedly was confirmation that I still struggled with boundaries – if one of those two had been as exhausted as I felt right now, they'd have cancelled our call in a heartbeat. And, as usual, Sedi had been ten minutes late, meaning I had even less energy to talk by the time her face burst onto the screen.

'So I read that you're dancing with Tomas again. What happened to that Gabriele Riccitelli guy? *The Stage* just said he'd had a "family emergency"?' asked Nolo, who was sitting by the window of her apartment. She had it thrown open and I could hear the wailing of a siren and the honking of cars and taxis from the street below, the kind of sounds you imagined when you pictured New York.

'Ummm . . .' I said, trying to engage my brain, which had suddenly drifted off into a daydream about Gabriele, and everything he was going through, and his flat, emotionless voice when I'd spoken to him last.

For some bizarre reason my bottom lip started quivering, as though I was about to cry. I shuffled about, changing position, plumping up my pillows, anything to distract myself from the fact that I was about to lose it while my face was blown up on both of my sisters' computer screens. Fuck.

'Go on, then, why are you stalling? Give us the gossip,' demanded Sedi precociously.

I was going to have to talk somehow, otherwise they'd know something was up, and I didn't even know how to begin to explain.

'His father died,' I said, feeling a very inconvenient tear roll down my cheek.

I was torn – if I wiped it away, it would be obvious, so should I leave it there in the hope that they were too self-absorbed to notice? Which was always a possibility.

Of course, on this occasion, I had no such luck.

'Li, are you *crying*?' asked Nolo, peering at her screen, scrutinizing my face for clues as to what the hell was going on.

When I said I'd never cried in front of them, that was no exaggeration. Even when our grandmother – Dad's mum – died a few years ago, I sobbed only in the comfort of my own bedroom, late at night so that nobody could hear me, because I didn't want to upset my sisters, and I definitely hadn't wanted to set my mum off again. She'd been wailing for hours as it was – I was already dreading the moment when her own mother, my *ouma* in South Africa, passed away. Mum looked strong and robust from the outside, but when it came to anything related to death or illness, she fell apart completely. I always felt under pressure to keep it totally together for her.

'You are!' exclaimed Sedi, having the decency to look concerned.

I didn't think I'd given my sisters cause to worry about me, ever. They probably had no idea how to react to this mysterious turn of events.

'I'm fine, honestly,' I said, grappling around for a tissue.

I blew my nose, taking some deep, scratchy breaths,

letting air file out of pursed lips. Why did I feel so emotional at the mention of Gabriele's name? Sure, it was horribly sad what he was going through, but it wasn't like I'd known his dad. It wasn't the kind of thing that would usually reduce me to tears.

'Talk to us, Li,' said Nolo, her voice softening into a tone I'd literally never heard her use before.

Lulled into a sense of being able to lean on someone in my family for support, I thought I may as well tell them everything.

'Gabriele and I have become . . . close,' I said.

'You've shagged him. I knew it,' said Sedi, triumphantly.

'Really?' said Nolo. 'How did you know?' she asked Sedi.

'Well, have you seen him? He's gorgeous. It was obvious. Plus, the press can't stop raving about the chemistry they have on stage. You can't fabricate that stuff, not when it's powerful enough to translate to seasoned audience members and jaded reviewers.'

'Good point,' said Nolo.

'How close are we talking?' asked Sedi, who was simultaneously plaiting her hair, so that eventually it would hang in two cute braids on either side of her head.

'Nothing serious,' I said, although it *felt* serious, but I thought that said more about me than the reality of the situation. 'I've spent a few nights in his hotel room, we've been on a sort-of date in Lisbon, and yes, we've slept together and it was . . . kind of out of this world.'

Nolo gasped, as if she'd never considered that I might be capable of having wild, passionate sex with *anyone*.

'I'm insanely jealous,' she said.

'He does look like he'd be amazing in bed,' reasoned Sedi.

'So how did it happen?' asked Nolo. 'Was it one night after rehearsals?'

'Oh my God!' said Sedi, suddenly remembering something. 'He was here that night, wasn't he? When I turned up late, banging on the door, a bit drunk. I knew something was off! Your face was all flushed and the mirror was steamed up.'

'Hmmm,' I said. 'That was kind of the beginning of it. Although not quite. It started when I was nineteen. At the World Championships. Remember "G"?'

Nolo's mouth dropped open and I filled them in on everything that had happened since. On how Gabriele had looked utterly shocked and pissed off when he saw me walk into the audition room all those years later. How it had taken ages for the ice to melt between us, for us to even talk about what had happened before.

'You need to be more open, Li,' said Sedi. 'We had no idea any of this was going on. You're so closed off all the time!'

'Good to know what you really think of me,' I said, bristling.

I was only closed off because I didn't think either of them were interested in hearing about my problems. They rarely asked me what was going on in my life because they were far too busy talking about theirs. Sedi went through guys faster than the speed of light, and Nolo always seemed to have men fawning over her, hanging off her every word, but it was like she thought she was too good for any of them. I'd always felt less-than in comparison – I was rarely asked out, and although I'd enjoyed spending time with Jack, it had been painfully obvious that it wasn't likely to go anywhere.

'But that still doesn't explain why you're crying,' said Sedi, narrowing her eyes at me. 'Are you in love with him or something?'

I swallowed hard, still feeling choked up. It must be some kind of misplaced empathy for Gabriele, I supposed, but I wasn't going to be much help to him if I turned into a blubbering wreck every time I set eyes on his beautiful, mournful face.

'I don't know,' I squeaked.

'You are, and you have to tell him!' shrieked Nolo. 'Enough of this pretending not to like each other. You're going to have to put yourself out there and explain how you feel, otherwise you're risking losing him all over again.'

'How can I? His dad's just died! He's hardly going to be up for embarking on some hot new romance, is he?'

That shut them up.

'Fair enough, you might want to give him a bit of time to deal with that,' admitted Sedi.

'I do talk sense sometimes, you know,' I said.

'The fact that you're extremely sensible has never been in doubt,' said Nolo.

Perhaps it was that which gave me the strength to say what I said next; the idea that I had a reputation for being closed off and sensible. Who wanted that? It wasn't exactly sexy, was it? And sure, I might be both of those things – at times – but it wasn't all that I was.

'So on another note, I've decided I don't want to go back to running the studio full-time,' I said, my throat feeling so tight I wondered if it was about to close up completely. At least that way I wouldn't be able to speak at all; wouldn't be able to say the wrong thing and cause a row.

'Really?' said Sedi, her expression darkening.

Nolo stared at me with her eyebrows raised so high they practically disappeared into her hairline.

'Who's going to run it, then?' asked Nolo eventually, after an unbearably long and awkward silence.

I cleared my throat, keeping my cool to the best of my ability. 'I haven't had time to think it through properly yet. We need to have a family meeting at some point. I'll arrange it with Mum and Dad and let you know.'

'Maybe you should just chat to them about it first?' suggested Sedi, who I could tell was desperate to check out and get off the call so that she could pretend that none of this had anything to do with her.

'Are you worried they're going to ask you to step in and cover some of my shifts?' I asked, deciding directness was in order.

'I'd never have time for that,' said Sedi. 'This time in two weeks I'll be in Australia.'

'Seriously, guys!' I said, losing patience altogether. 'I've taken this on without complaint for all these years. I've given up on my own dreams to keep the family business afloat. Sure, I could have said no, and that's on me. But you two could also have stepped up and offered to help me out. Or even just asked me if I was okay; if I was happy doing what I was doing. Even that might have been nice!'

Nolo went to say something and then stopped. She looked upset and I should feel bad, but I didn't. Welcome to the real world, I thought. Sure, she might be resilient when it came to her career, she had to be in the ballet world. But when it came to life, to family, she was overly sensitive. If there was even the tiniest hint that somebody was criticizing her, she'd crumble, leaving the other person feeling guilty for having said anything in the first place. But I didn't feel guilty, not this time. Because she needed to hear it – in fact, she'd needed to hear it years ago.

'I think you're both quite selfish, if I'm honest,' I said, thinking in for a penny, in for a pound. 'We all have our faults, and so here I am pointing out one of yours – it's time you two start thinking about somebody other than yourselves. Because it might be cute when you're in your twenties, you might just about get away with it then, but once you hit thirty, it's really not a good look. You have a responsibility to me, to this family, to Mum and Dad.'

'What about them?' protested Sedi. 'Why do they get to swan off and do whatever they like? Aren't they selfish, too?'

'Yes. And I'll be telling them as much,' I said, doubting

it even as the words came out of my mouth. 'Perhaps not in so many words. But yeah. It's their studio, ultimately. I will officially hand my notice in and then we can take it from there.'

Sedi and Nolo stared at me in stunned silence. I bet they wished we were doing this in person so that they could join forces against the tyranny I was inflicting on them, look to each other for support, but on Zoom it was every woman for herself. You had no idea who was with you and who wasn't.

'I feel terrible,' said Sedi eventually.

I frowned – this was a different emotion from her.

'Go on,' I said.

'I can be a selfish prick at times, I'm well aware of that. You're not the first person to say it,' she said.

'Obviously,' I said. I couldn't help myself.

'And I've never given much thought to all the opportunities *I* had,' said Nolo. 'Coming to New York at such a young age. There's just so much privilege in this industry, that you forget not everyone is as lucky as you are. Not everyone gets to do what I did.'

'I didn't,' I said.

'I know,' said Nolo, grimacing. 'And it's shit, and I'm sorry.'

I nodded, tempted to let them off the hook, to say it didn't matter, that I'd been fine, anyway, without their help. But I held back. Because I wanted them to sit with this feeling, for it to really sink in. I meant it this time when I said that things needed to change. And I might not know what that looked like yet, but I would, at some point, and I was one hundred percent sure that it didn't look like running straight back to Castlebury.

CHAPTER TWENTY-FOUR

Gabriele

Once my father's funeral was over, I could start to breathe again. Everything before that had been a whirlwind of emotions – dropping out of the show, saying goodbye to the team, to Lira, especially. Returning to Italy. To my family home, but without my dad in it. To Mama, who was numb with grief and who I'd had to care for like a child since I had arrived.

I felt my responsibility very strongly now. I was the part-owner of this house, this farm, this wine business. There was no more putting it off, no easiness now about signing up for another dance show or pursuing a TV opportunity. In her current state of mind, my mother needed me more than ever, and I wanted to help her heal. And so, I had packed away all the emotions I had about my dad dying – all

311

the regret and guilt and sadness and feelings of abandonment. I stopped asking how he could leave me, how he could do this to us, why he didn't look after himself more like we'd all asked him to. And I focused on just getting through; on organizing, planning, troubleshooting and comforting Mama.

I had kept half an eye on what was happening with *Slow Burn*, but it had been too painful for me to see pictures of Lira and Tomas dancing together. The reviews were good, but not as unanimously great as they had been with Lira and me taking to the stage together. In some ways, it pleased me to know that they did not share the same sizzling chemistry that we did, but it also made me sad that this was how the show should end for her, after such an exciting start.

I felt bad for Carlos, bad for Lira, for Tomas, for how insensitive I had been with Luca, for my mother and for everyone except myself. Somehow, I did not have the headspace to think about my own place in all of this, to acknowledge how I felt. I just had to carry on for now, and to hope that, at some point, I would start to feel better again. Just as I had begun to feel hopeful about the future, about what Lira and I were beginning to build, I had been set back not a few steps, but what felt like several hundred thousand of them.

I prepared some breakfast for my mother and I, something I had been doing since I arrived in Italy nearly three weeks ago. She spent her days — and many of her nights — sitting out on the veranda, a shawl wrapped around her shoulders, staring into space. I would bring her enticing-looking food on a tray, but sometimes she would not even touch it, or she would pick at it, not managing more than a couple of mouthfuls. I tried to joke her out of it.

'Is it my cooking, Mama? Am I putting too much salt in your food? Or does it have no flavour at all?'

She tried to smile, but it never quite reached her eyes.

Lira and I had been texting regularly. She was heading down to Florence today, with a day off before the show opened in the city that was closest to my family home. It had been the performance I had been looking forward to most, and tears stabbed at the back of my eyes when I thought of the tickets I had reserved for my parents; two seats that would now remain empty, in the centre of the fifth row back, the perfect spot for my mama and papa to see me perform. In my imagination, it would have been the moment at which my father would admit he had been wrong to try to stop me dancing, that he could see now that it was what I was born to do. That he was proud of me. Now, he would never get to see me and I would never know what he might have said.

I was clearing up the breakfast things, with plans to make a start on the copious amount of emails that seemed to come through for the vineyard every hour of every day, when I heard a car pulling up outside. I sincerely hoped it was not someone else come to pay their respects. Many locals wanted to see us – well, Mama, mainly, but me, too – to tell us how sorry they were, how much they had loved my father, how dearly they would miss him. They brought us bottles of wine, which I had been working my way through worryingly quickly, and lovely home-cooked meals, although since Mama had no appetite, I had mainly polished them off myself.

When the doorbell rang, I walked down the hallway with a feeling of trepidation, because it meant I would have to make polite conversation with whoever had arrived unannounced, and would also have to overcompensate for the fact that my mother was not talking much at all. Steeling myself, I opened the door and instinctively stepped back, shocked by who was on the doorstep of my parents' house in the Tuscan hills, all the way out in the middle of nowhere. Once I had pulled myself together, I felt an altogether different sensation in my body – relief, perhaps. Happiness.

Lira was here, and my world was already infinitely better than it had been a few moments before.

'This is a surprise,' I said, thinking that was a woefully inadequate way to describe how I was feeling.

'I wanted to see how you are,' she said. 'And I was in the area, so . . .'

I laughed lightly, and she joined in. We both knew she had not been in the area; nobody ever was. This was rural Tuscany, a village in the middle of green hills and vineyards, miles and miles from the nearest station; even the closest bus stop was over a half-hour walk away.

'How did you get here?' I asked. 'I could have picked you up from the city if I had known you would like to visit.'

She shrugged. 'It was easy enough to get a taxi.'

Easy, perhaps, but also expensive. I was touched that she had made the decision to come all the way out here for me.

I suddenly realized that I had left her on the doorstep for no good reason, possibly making her think she was not welcome when she most certainly was, more than she would ever know, more than I could even admit to myself. I had not really known how I was going to get through the next few days, weeks, months, stuck here in the middle of nowhere alone with my mother, who I worried about constantly, and my thoughts and the aching hole my father had left in every single part of this house, this land.

I stood aside.

'Sorry! Come in!'

She had a large shoulder bag with her, but no luggage. With a thud of disappointment, I assumed this meant she was not planning to spend the night. Perhaps I could drive her back into Florence later – that way I could spend an extra hour with her, and some time away from the house might do me good.

Lira stepped over the threshold, looking around in what seemed like awe. It probably was impressive when you saw it for the first time. A typically Italian country house, whitewashed on the outside with bursts of lilac and pink bougainvillea hanging from baskets around the doors and windows. My parents were both keen gardeners. Papa had done the practical – the vegetables, the fruits, obviously the wine – and Mama took care of the flowers.

Inside, my mother had decorated the house in a farm-house style, making use of natural materials like wood and hessian and painting the walls in muted shades of forest green and ochre and mustard. Lira followed me into the kitchen, which opened up into a huge yet inviting space. It was the heart of the house, my mother's favourite place to be. Or at least it used to be.

'What a beautiful home,' said Lira.

She sounded breathy and unsure of herself and I wanted her to feel comfortable, so I threw caution to the wind and wrapped my arms around her, burying my face in her shoulder.

It took a few seconds for her to react. She was probably caught off guard; it was not like me to initiate touch. Sex, obviously, was different – I took the lead on that most of the time, but not this. Not the slower, sweeter stuff. That was what it felt like when she found the small of my back, running her hands up my spine, stroking me softly.

'I missed you,' I said.

I waited to regret saying it, but somehow I did not, perhaps because I refused to not say things anymore. After all, sometimes you did not get a chance to say them at all. Sometimes it was too late.

'Same,' she said. 'And I've been worried about you. Wondering how you are.'

'Have you?' I asked.

She took my head in her hands and kissed me tenderly on the lips. I had wanted to do the same thing to her, ever since

I had seen her standing on my doorstep. I hesitated, though, before kissing her back, willing myself not to overthink the fact it felt like she was the only good thing in my life right now. The last thing I wanted to become was needy, or dependent on somebody. I had never been that; I had been on my own for most of my life, or at least it had felt that way. Of course, my mother would have been there for me if I had asked, but I had never wanted her worrying about me. I saw how stressed she got about what everybody else was doing as it was – her sisters, my father, the employees they had, young men from the village who she stressed about more than ever now, since they relied on the salary they earned here at the farm.

What will they do? Who will run the vineyard now Papa is gone? Will it be you, Gabi? Please don't leave me alone with this. I don't know what to do without him.

I had placated her with soothing noises and reassurances that I was not just going to leave her, that I would be here, too, by her side, for as long as she needed me.

Throwing caution to the wind, I swung Lira around so that she was pressed up against one of the myriad worktops that my mother liked to prepare food on under normal circumstances.

'It is so good to see you,' I said, peeling off her jacket and throwing it over a nearby stool.

Underneath, she had on a strappy dress that fell just above her knees, but had tantalizing buttons all the way down the front of it. I knelt down, undoing them one by one from

317

the bottom up. She pushed her fingers through my thick hair, snagging them on my curls. It was not an unpleasant sensation as I worked to remove her dress, slowly revealing more and more of her, finally letting me see the point at which her thighs brushed lightly together at their fleshiest part. I buried my face in them, groaning at how warm and familiar they felt.

She gasped.

'Gabriele. Your mother. What if she comes in?'

I stopped, reluctantly. She had a point. I had left Mama out in the garden, but she could absolutely walk in at any moment. There was no way I would want her to meet Lira for the first time while she was in this compromising position.

Groaning with frustration, I began to do her buttons up again.

'Raincheck?' said Lira, ruffling my hair.

I stood up, running my hands over her body as I did so, dragging my mind back to reality.

'Let me introduce you to her,' I said.

I was surprised that my mother had not called out, wanting to know who was at the door. That was what she would usually have done, because she was a control freak, and she liked to be in absolutely everybody's business, but then, at the moment, I supposed she did not have the energy to project her voice even if she had wanted to, plus her throat was permanently croaky from all the crying.

I took Lira's hand and led her out into the garden. It was one of those perfect Tuscan days: a blue, cloudless sky;

temperatures warm enough to sit out wearing nothing more than a vest or a T-shirt; the smell of wine and honeysuckle in the air. Mama was curled up under the veranda. She had a book in her lap, but I would be surprised if she had read more than a few pages of it over the last few days.

I was achingly aware of Lira's hand in mine as we approached – I had not mentioned her to my mother at all. There had not been a chance before Papa, and afterwards it had not felt like the right time.

My love life felt like the least of both our worries, and yet now that Lira was here, I noted the positive effect it was having on me. I had always had relationships pinned as a problem – too much pressure, too much commitment required, *molto* hard work. But having Lira here had already made things feel just the tiniest bit lighter and less terrible, which I thought was probably all I could hope for from anyone or anything under the circumstances.

My mother looked up as we approached. I saw a brief flash of confusion on her face as she noticed that her only son was holding hands with a woman she had never even heard me talk about.

'Mama, this is Lira, my dance partner in *Slow Burn*. Lira, meet my mother, Sofia Riccitelli.'

Lira, perhaps losing her nerve under the scrutiny, dropped my hand and offered hers to my mother instead.

'It's a pleasure to meet you, Mrs Riccitelli. I'm so sorry for your loss. This must be such a difficult time for you. And for Gabriele.'

My mother shook Lira's hand, but I saw her hesitate just a second too long. I knew my mother very well and I knew when she was not happy about something; it was obvious to me in the tiny adjustments she made to her manner. And I did not think I was mistaken when I noted that she appeared to be far from delighted to meet Lira.

'Lira. What a lovely name,' said my mother.

'It's quite popular in South Africa,' said Lira. 'That's where my mother is from. Where I lived for the first few years of my life.'

My mother nodded.

'Sit, Lira,' I said. 'Can I get you a glass of cold lemonade?'

'Sure,' she said. 'That would be lovely, thanks.'

I dashed back into the kitchen, looking nervously over my shoulder, not wanting to leave them alone for too long because I did not know what my mother was capable of saying at the moment. Logically, there was no reason for her to say anything out of line – Lira had done nothing wrong. In fact, in my mind, she had done everything right. She had seen me at my worst – dismissive, tightly coiled, snappy, rude, sobbing for my father. She had seen all of those parts of me and yet still she had come for me when I needed her, when I was grieving. And I thought that I had probably given her the impression that I wanted to be alone – had convinced myself of that, even – but the truth was, having her here had already made a vast improvement to my mood. Sadly, the same could not be said for my mother's.

Glass in hand, I hot-footed it back out into the garden,

where my mother and Lira were sitting in what appeared to be an extremely awkward silence.

'Everything okay?' I asked, hastily pouring Lira a glass of lemonade.

Lira nodded and smiled. 'Just what I needed. Thank you.'

'*Parli Italiano*, Lira?' asked my mother.

Lira, getting the gist, shook her head. 'I'm afraid not. Although I would love to learn.'

She took a long sip of her lemonade, placing the glass carefully back on the table once she was done.

'Tell me about yourself, Lira,' said my mother.

I noticed that Mama's hand was shaking when she reached for her own glass of half-drunk lemonade and I made a mental note to mention it to the doctor when he called in to see her next. It worried me, because it was like she had aged ten years in one week. Was it true that somebody could die of a broken heart? Because if it was, I was seriously concerned that she would not be able to go on without my father – that she would not wish to.

'I'm one of three sisters,' said Lira, who to her credit did not seem to be intimidated by my slightly standoffish mother. I had the sense that her own mother was a force to be reckoned with, too, and they sounded similar in many ways, so perhaps she was used to dealing with interrogations like these. 'My mum, Amahle, was a ballroom and Latin dancer. In fact, she was South Africa's most famous Black dancer back in the eighties. And my dad, Michael, is British. He's more of a numbers guy.'

'And your sisters?' asked my mother.

'Both dancers,' explained Lira. 'Nolo is in New York dancing with the New York Ballet Company, and Sedi is a commercial dancer. She gets to travel all over the world with various artists when they're on tour.'

'Sounds very exciting,' said my mother. 'This must feel like the depths of hell out here in the middle of the countryside with nothing to do, and fields as far as the eye can see. You are like Gabriele; he cannot wait to get back to the city, either. Perhaps you have come to rescue him.'

For some reason, I was so tense that the coffee I was drinking hit the back of my throat and I splattered it everywhere. 'Sorry,' I said, catching my breath.

'Anything wrong, Gabi?' asked my mother all innocently, as if she had not caused me to nearly choke with her strange line of questioning and passive-aggressive comments.

'Nothing is wrong,' I said. 'Went down the wrong way, that is all.'

Lira shuffled in her seat.

'Anyway, I can't stay long. I only called in to see how Gabriele was. We were all very worried about him.'

'All?' said my mother. 'And yet you are the only one here.'

'I—'

'You do not need to answer that, Lira,' I said, throwing my mother a look.

I stood up, wanting desperately to remove Lira from this awkward conversation. It was all my fault for not having told my mother about her in the first place, and for not explaining how much she meant to me. The last thing I wanted was for Lira to go; she had only just arrived – although I would not blame her if she wanted to order the first taxi out of the village. Mind you, I did not like to tell her that Uber did not exist out here in the hills and that there was only one local taxi driver, Guiseppe, who sometimes randomly decided to take the day off. If Lira thought spending a few hours at the farm was inconvenient, she should try growing up here.

'Let us go for a walk. I will show you around the farm,' I said to Lira.

She nodded gratefully. 'I'd love to see it.'

I could feel my mother's eyes boring into us as we walked through the garden, heading for the gate leading to our plot of land comprising several acres of vineyards, the olive farm, and a barn housing huge vats of fermenting wine.

'Through there we have a little shop,' I explained to Lira. 'We have connections with some of the tour operators who work out of Florence and Siena. They bring tourists here as part of their wine-tasting tours. It is a good opportunity to tell them about our wines and sell them a few bottles each. Often they cannot carry them back to wherever they have flown in from, so instead they will order a full case to be delivered to them at home. It can be quite lucrative.'

'I bet,' said Lira. 'And after a few glasses of wine in these lovely surroundings, I bet they're ordering by the caseload!'

I shrugged noncommittally, but of course, yes, that was exactly how it was.

We walked in silence for a bit, enjoying the heat of the sun on our bare arms, the companionable silence between us easy and unthreatening.

'Apologies if my mother seems a little off,' I said. 'She is finding losing Papa very hard.'

Lira nodded. 'Of course she is. I completely understand.'

'This house here, see?' I said, pointing to a brick building to the left-hand side of one of the vineyards, 'was to be turned into a bed and breakfast. That was always my mother's dream for when my father finally retired. I have no idea what she will do now. How she is going to cope without him.'

Lira rubbed my arm gently. 'I shouldn't have just turned up like this, at such a difficult time. I don't know what I was thinking.'

I stopped, putting my hands on Lira's waist, spinning her around to face me so that she could see how serious I was.

'You coming all this way to see me, without me having to ask, is one of the nicest things anyone has ever done for me. Seeing you lifted my heart. I do not know why it had that effect on me, and I do not have the headspace to analyse it right now, but there is something about being with you that makes me very happy, Lira. And this weight that I feel I am carrying all of the time, even before my father died, is lifted from my shoulders. Because of this connection we have. The way we seem to understand what each other needs, on the dance floor and off it.'

I took her head in my hands, desperate to kiss her, to lose myself in her perfect mouth.

'Do you feel the same way?' I whispered. 'Please tell me you do.'

She nodded, just a tiny movement of her head, but it was the confirmation I needed.

'Don't leave yet,' I said. 'Please. Stay for dinner. Stay with me tonight, and tomorrow I will drive you back into Florence in plenty of time to get ready for the show.'

She had her arms wrapped tightly around me, but her face seemed more distant, like perhaps she was not sure.

'What about your mother? Are you sure she'll be okay with that?' Lira asked.

'She will come around, I promise you. We will have dinner together, all three of us, and she will see how amazing you are and then after it will be just you and me. We can sit out here, share a bottle of wine. I want to hear all about the show, about your sisters, your parents on their cruise. There are so many things I do not know about you that I want to learn.'

There was uncertainty in her eyes, I could see it simmering under the surface. The part of me that still felt like a lonely little boy assumed that it was not only my mother she was not sure about, it was me, too. But, then, when we were together, dancing, in bed, whatever, it was like she was totally with me. I did not doubt it for a second. So why was I doubting it now? Was I scared of what might happen if things became more serious between us? Because how could it ever work, with me here in Italy and Lira in England? And of course with love came loss, and this week had been a stark reminder of that. Could I really give everything of myself to someone who might leave me one day, just like my papa had? And was there any point in pursuing this when I could not imagine a way for us to be together? Or a solution to the fact that I would have to give up my career as a dancer and run my family business instead?

'Okay,' she said. 'I'll stay.'

I took one of her hands in mine and kissed the back of it, grateful and apprehensive and relieved all rolled into one.

CHAPTER TWENTY-FIVE

Lira

The atmosphere between Sofia and me hadn't improved much by the time dinner came around. Gabriele and I had spent the last couple of hours in the kitchen preparing a fresh pasta sauce, a roasted vegetable salad and an apple tart for dessert. Surprisingly, he was a very good cook and approached it in the same way he approached his dancing – there were rules, and he followed them to a tee, but then he added something unexpected on top; something extra that changed it from ordinary to spectacular.

I couldn't wait to tuck in and thought the feast we'd – mainly *he'd* – created might improve Sofia's mood, just a tiny bit. But when she joined us at the table in their open-plan dining room, she was so aggressively silent that you could have heard a pin drop. In fact, if somebody had dropped a pin, I'd have gladly dived under the table to look for it and stayed there until the meal was over and I could be alone with Gabriele again. I was going to have to try to work out what I was supposed to have done so that I could take steps to remedy it. Because this didn't feel like just grief, although of course I didn't know Sofia well enough to say, and everyone reacted differently. I just had the sense that it was me specifically she mistrusted.

She'd probably guessed there was more between Gabriele and I than we were letting on – and sure, walking out to meet her, hand in hand with her son probably hadn't been the best idea, not when emotions were so high. Perhaps she didn't think I was right for him. You only had to look at this place to realize that they were likely one of the wealthiest families in the area and she could probably tell on sight that I didn't come from that kind of affluent background.

'Where did you two first meet? At the audition for the show?' asked Sofia, serving herself a tiny plateful of pasta and salad.

I felt a pang of sadness for her and could almost visibly see the pain of losing Enzo playing out in her inability to eat.

'Actually, that is a funny story,' said Gabriele, laughing softly as he stroked my knee under the table. 'We met many years ago, in Paris. We danced the Argentine tango together – Lira was nineteen and I was twenty-two, and even then we had great chemistry.'

I smiled at Gabriele. Hopefully, he would spare his mother the remaining details of that night . . .

'And then, yes, the next time I saw her was when she walked into the audition. Carlos had discovered her working in a dance studio in a small town outside of London. It was completely random. A moment that could so easily have been missed.'

Sofia took a sip of her wine. 'Carlos found you and put you in his show? Like Cinderella?'

'There was definitely something fairytale-like about it,' I admitted. 'But I wasn't exactly sweeping floors. My family own the dance studio. I've been the manager there for thirteen years.'

'And now you want a career in dance?' asked Sofia.

'Mama . . .' warned Gabriele gently.

'It's fine,' I said to him.

It was a fair enough question, although not one I would have asked when I'd only just met someone. Perhaps the Argentinians were naturally direct.

'I know I've left it late,' I said, looking at Sofia. 'But I had family responsibilities before. As the eldest of three girls, with parents who still had successful careers in entertainment, I was expected to take the lead with the business my parents had set up. I was very compliant with what my family wanted, which now I kind of regret.'

'Oh?' said Sofia. 'You wish you had told your parents that you couldn't help them as they'd asked?'

I glanced at Gabriele.

'I think there might have been a way to compromise,' I said carefully. 'Instead of giving up on my dreams completely. Much as I loved – *love* – working in the studio and teaching other people how to dance, I've never quite got rid of the desire to be up on stage myself. So yeah, I guess Carlos did perform some magic that evening. And now I've got a chance to experience what it's like to be a professional dancer. I know there's only a small window of time, that I've only got a few years of dancing left at most, but my plan is to make the most of it.'

'You are too talented not to, Lira,' said Gabriele.

Sofia took a sip of her wine. The atmosphere was so loaded that I'd started dreading what she was going to say next. The food was delicious, but I couldn't relax enough to enjoy it.

'So what is next for you?' asked Sofia. 'More travel? Another show?'

'I'm not sure,' I answered honestly. 'I'm planning to set up some meetings with agents for when I get back to the UK and I'll take it from there.'

'And your family's studio?' asked Sofia.

'We'll make it work.'

Sofia nods. 'And what about you, Gabriele? Will you be joining Lira on another tour?'

'Mama, please,' said Gabriele. 'This is not a conversation to have in front of Lira; it is between you and me.'

'I am not blind, Gabriele. I can see that the two of you have become close. And I am happy for you, but perhaps not for myself, because I would love you to stay here and run the farm with me, but I think that's not what you want in your heart. Is it, Gabi?'

Gabriele pushed his chair back and stood up. 'Mama, please, we must change the subject. I will fetch a jug of water for us, and when I get back we will talk about something else.'

Gabriele disappeared out to the kitchen, leaving one of the interminable silences I was getting used to, the only sound being the scrape of our forks on our plates.

'I don't mean to upset you, Lira, but I am lost without Enzo, you understand? I know nothing about wine, except the tiny amount I have picked up from listening to him over the years, but I could not run the business alone now he's gone, and I am too old to learn. But Gabriele *could learn*, and I know that is what his father wanted for him. I will not force him, of course. I know how much he loves dancing. He would have to *want* to stay. And rather selfishly I'm concerned that now he has met you, he will definitely not want to live out here in the hills with his melancholy mother.'

'I understand family responsibility, Sofia,' I said, treading carefully. 'And if running the vineyard is what Gabriel needs to do, *wants* to do, then I would never try to stop him, even if I could. I'm not sure whether you've noticed, but he's quite headstrong,' I said, laughing lightly, hoping to lighten the mood. Sofia smiled tightly – it was a start, I supposed, and it was better than having her scowling at me from across the table.

'Anyway, what we have isn't serious. Not yet,' I added, to reassure her that Gabriele would not be factoring me into his decision about whether to stay or go.

Sofia looked up from her plate, surprised.

'I'm not sure that is correct, Lira,' she said.

I frowned. 'What do you mean?'

'I mean that Gabriele has never brought a woman home to meet me before. He has never sat down at a table with me and someone he is interested in romantically, not once.'

I secretly thought I understood why he hadn't, if this was the level of interrogation Sofia was likely to give every woman he brought home. And I felt a thrill that I was the first, although, in fairness, I had rocked up on his doorstep unannounced. He hadn't had much choice, had he?

'You must be special to him. For him to ask you to stay the night, to have dinner with us. It means something. I've just lost the love of my life, and I am wondering whether Gabriele has just found his.'

There was a fluttering of hope that what she was saying was true, and that Gabriele liked me as much as she seemed to think he did. When he walked back into the room, I'd never been so pleased to see anyone in my whole life. He was carrying the dessert we'd made, placing it in the centre of the table. Sofia looked at it admiringly.

'Who would like some apple tart?' asked Gabriele, looking from one of us to the other.

*

Later that evening, Sofia told us she was having an early night and Gabriele and I sat out in the garden with a glass of wine. He'd brought a speaker outside and had attached it to his phone so that soft, sexy Latin music played over our conversation. The Tuscan sky was beautiful – a bright, full moon; stars that I hadn't even known existed because, in London, and even in Castlebury, the sky was never this dark and clear.

'It's beautiful out here,' I said, tipping my head back, taking some deep, relaxing breaths.

I felt my shoulders soften now that I didn't have to watch every word I said for fear of upsetting Sofia even more than I seemed to have done already.

'I apologize again. About my mother. She is very intense sometimes, and losing Papa seems to have taken her to a whole new level. I am terrified to say anything in case I set her off.'

'I'm glad it's not just me,' I said, smiling wryly at him.

He took my hand, caressing it gently.

'I am glad you are here,' he said.

'Me too. Although I'm slightly worried I might have made things worse for you. Your mum seems to think that I have some kind of hold over you. I tried to tell her that I wouldn't be able to influence your future plans for the vineyard one way or another.'

Gabriele looked thoughtful. 'Is that really what you think? That you have not had an impact on me or my decisions at all?'

I frowned. 'Well, that's what I assumed. I mean, sure, we've enjoyed each other's company recently. But I've never let myself think beyond that.'

A hurt look crossed his face and I wondered if I'd read it all wrong. If maybe his mum had been right after all.

Gabriele looked at me. 'It's true. My priorities *have* changed over the last week or so. I could never leave my mother alone up here without Papa.'

'Of course. You have to put your family first at a time like this,' I agreed.

The opening bars of an evocative rumba emanated from the speakers. Our eyes locked together.

'I miss dancing with you,' I said. 'It's not the same with anyone else.'

He stood up, holding out his hand. 'Then shall we?'

I joined him on the lawn-cum-dance-floor, letting our bodies rock together, finding the beat. Naturally, we fell into the steps from *Slow Burn*, and this time, I let myself give in to the passion I felt for this man as he ran his hands over my hips, holding me as I fell into a backbend, my body so close to the ground that my hair tickled the grass. I came back up to meet him, eye to eye, our hips swaying in time to the music. When I kicked my leg into the air, Gabriele caught my ankle gently in his hand, supporting me as I let my body lunge to one side, knowing that he would never let me fall. Suspended in motion like that, I acknowledged how safe he made me feel, and not just while we were dancing. And it was a new feeling, because he'd always felt very *unsafe*, in that I suspected he was perfectly capable of breaking my heart.

And he still might be, but I had to change my life. Do something with it. And that meant taking risks. And being with Gabriele, for however long that might turn out to be, was one risk I was determined to let myself take.

The next morning, I was up earlier than Gabriele, and went down to the kitchen to make us both a coffee. I kept opening and shutting cupboards, looking for the potent Italian coffee I was sure Sofia must keep somewhere.

'Bottom cupboard on the right,' said Sofia, appearing in the doorway. 'It is coffee you are looking for, yes? I know Gabriele likes a cup in the morning, he has always been that way.'

I nodded. 'I'm exactly the same. Can't quite get going without it.'

I bent down to open the cupboard. I'd already looked in here, but had somehow missed it.

Sofia took a seat at the dining table, watching me as I set about making the coffee.

'Can I pour one for you?' I asked.

'That would be lovely,' said Sofia.

I tried not to show my surprise at how nice she was being. It was like the guarded, defensive, accusative woman from the night before had morphed into someone altogether less spiky overnight.

'I saw you and Gabriele out in the garden last night,' said Sofia, casually, sending me into a tailspin.

I'd thought we were alone, chatting and dancing out there. Our rumba had turned into a series of kisses interspersed with dance steps, culminating in us stumbling inside and spending all night in bed, leaving our glasses of wine undrunk and the music still on. I'd snuck out there this morning to tidy up, but what had Sofia seen? If the passion between us had looked as good as it felt, there was no way she was going to believe that there was nothing serious going on between the two of us.

'You move beautifully together,' said Sofia.

'I love dancing with him,' I admitted, bringing a pot of coffee over to the table and going back for the mugs. 'He's got a real gift. Don't you think?'

'Of course,' said Sofia. 'He's been a wonderful dancer all his life, from the moment he took his very first class aged two and a half. Enzo wasn't keen on him pursuing it at first, I'm not sure if Gabi told you.'

'A little,' I said, not wanting her to think he'd been criticizing his father.

'He was a traditional man. A career in dance wasn't – *isn't* – the usual thing out here in rural Italy. He had his opinions, and they weren't always right, but he loved Gabriele dearly. And he was proud of him, too. I once caught him watching a video of Gabriele dancing on stage, and when he looked up he had tears in his eyes. He said to me: *I didn't know he was this good.*'

I took a seat next to Sofia, pouring us each a mug of strong, black coffee.

'I bet Gabriele would love to hear that story.'

Sofia pulled her cardigan tightly around herself as though she was cold, although when I'd popped outside to clear our things from the night before, the summer sun had already been rising in the clear blue sky.

'I owe you an apology,' said Sofia.

'Sofia. You don't,' I said.

And I meant it – I'd come into her home expecting . . . what, exactly? That she was going to welcome me with open arms when her beloved husband had died weeks before?

'I do. I was . . . difficult yesterday. I was thinking only of myself. Perhaps we do that when we are grieving,' she said, with a wry smile.

'I think we probably do,' I said.

'When I saw you and Gabriele dancing out in the garden, I couldn't look away. I know it was strange of me to keep watching. You are probably thinking what a weird woman I am, watching two young people sharing a passionate moment meant only for them. But it reminded me so much of the night I met Enzo. Three decades ago now, back in Argentina.'

'Tell me about it,' I said. 'About him.'

Sofia rubbed her arms, as though the memory of him was making her shiver.

'He was in Buenos Aires for meetings. I was twenty-two

and had just left university, unsure what to do with my life. He was older – nearly thirty – and to me he had it all together. He knew how to talk to women, how to treat them, how to dress. How to be *charming*. He had come with his colleagues to watch an Argentine tango show at the bar at the end of my street. I was working there as a waitress, just to make some money while I decided what I actually wanted to do with my life.'

'Who does know, at twenty-two?' I said.

'Gabriele,' said Sofia, laughing softly. 'He always knew.'

'So that night, in Buenos Aires. How did the two of you get talking?'

Sofia's eyes misted over as she thought back to that night, to the moment she first set eyes on Enzo.

'He was so handsome, easily the best-looking man in the room. I could tell immediately that he was not a local – he was dressed too well, in his fancy shirt and expensive jeans and smart shoes. I was clearing his table when he struck up conversation with me in broken Spanish. His was so bad that eventually we swapped to English, which neither of us was perfect at, but my Italian was non-existent then, so we had little choice.'

I laughed, totally caught up in the story.

'What did he say to you?' I asked.

'He wanted to know if I could dance the Argentine tango. If all Argentinian girls knew how to dance it. I said that, yes, it was in our blood. He asked me to show him a step or two.'

I rested my chin in the palm of my hand, totally enraptured by the romance of it all. What a place to meet: hot, sultry Argentina, tango music everywhere.

'Could he dance?' I asked.

Sofia threw her head back, letting out an infectious roar. It was the first time I'd seen her properly laugh.

'He was terrible!' she declared. 'He wanted to learn the *boleo*, but he kept getting his legs all tangled up in mine. Eventually, I gave up teaching him the steps and simply tried to get him to connect to the rhythm of the music. Slowly, he began to understand the beat. Our hips were swaying together, we were looking into each other's eyes as though nobody else could see us, not even my boss who wanted me to clear more tables.'

'That's so romantic,' I said.

'We have barely been apart since,' said Sofia, her face falling again. 'I went back to his hotel room that night and by morning we had declared that we never wanted to be separated again.'

Tears began to slide down her cheeks and I instantly regretted asking her so many questions when it was clearly still too upsetting for her.

'I'm sorry,' I said. 'I shouldn't have—'

'Don't be sorry. I want to talk about him. It makes me feel that he is still here with me. I wish that you could have met him, and since you can't, I want to be able to tell you about him. Don't mind me if I cry. We Argentinian women are very emotional.'

'And the men?' I asked, thinking of Gabriele, who was a mixture of Argentinian and Italian.

'Not so much, as I'm sure you have noticed,' said Sofia.

Gabriele chose that moment to appear in the doorway. He looked nervous at first, probably wondering what I'd done to his poor mother to make tears course down her cheeks and her face flush.

'Everything okay?' he asked, looking from one of us to the other.

Sofia patted the chair next to her.

'Sit,' she said. 'I have just been telling Lira about your father. And about how I saw the two of you dance together and was blown away by what I saw.'

'Really?' said Gabriele, reluctantly taking a seat. 'Were you watching us, Mama?'

'A little,' she admitted breezily.

Then she turned to me, taking both of my hands in hers.

'I think you and I are going to be very good friends,' she said. 'I know you have your big dance career to pursue, and after seeing how perfectly you danced that rumba, I can understand that you have a talent that deserves to be nurtured and shown to other people for them to enjoy.'

I was so surprised I couldn't find a way to answer.

'You like Italy?' said Sofia.

'Yes,' I said. 'Very much.'

'And you like my son, yes?'

I glanced at Gabriele, who was looking utterly confused at the scene unfolding in front of him.

'Very much, also,' I said.

'Then I hope that you will come to visit us again. It will be nice for me to have some female company around the place.'

Gabriele looked at Sofia.

'Mama, are you feeling all right?'

He jokingly placed his hand on her forehead as though she might have a fever, and she playfully batted his hand away.

'The only thing that would make this even better would be for Enzo to be here to see how happy you have made my son, Lira.'

Gabriele groaned with embarrassment. 'Enough! Please, you two!'

All three of us cracked up. As I watched Sofia cry tears of laughter rather than pain, I thought how grief was a funny thing. How sparks of happiness could be found in even the darkest moments. And I had a thought. And I didn't know why it hadn't come to me sooner.

'Gabriele, would you feel up to dancing the final performance of *Slow Burn*? I'll do two nights in Florence with Tomas, but then you perform on our last night. It's *your* show. You should be there, up on stage, bringing it to its rightful end.'

'What a wonderful idea!' said Sofia.

'You'd come, wouldn't you, Sofia? You would come and watch Gabriele perform?'

She nodded. 'Of course I would. Sad as it would be without Enzo – because he was very proud of you, Gabi, you know. All he wanted was for you to be happy.'

'I do not know what to say,' said Gabriele.

'Say yes,' I said. 'And then let's call Carlos to tell him.'

CHAPTER TWENTY-SIX

Gabriele

The Teatro Verdi in Florence was completely sold out for the last ever performance of *Slow Burn*. There had been a time when I hoped it would not be the last. That perhaps there would be a Broadway run, or the UK tour Carlos was still trying to secure. That could still happen, but it would almost certainly have to go ahead without me, a situation I was still struggling to come to terms with.

When I peeked through the curtain to look at the audience, like I often did, I felt a sort of calm wash over me. For the first time in years, I saw faces I recognized. In the fifth row from the front sat my mother, all dressed up, wearing black because she was in mourning, but looking happy and excited. It was good to see her joyfulness come back, even if it was just for tonight. My throat tightened as I took in the

343

empty seat to one side of her, where my father should have been. And on the other side of her was Lira's sister, Sedi, who I had never met in person, but who I had spoken to on video call because I had had to give her directions from the airport to the farm; very kindly, she had hired a car and had offered to drive all the way out to collect my mother.

Lira and I had been rehearsing at the theatre since this morning, because it had been a few weeks since I had danced and I could feel the rustiness, that I was not quite so confident in every single step as I had been. Mama had not been up to coming with us and waiting around all day, so Sedi had stepped in to help, which Lira had been amazed about – she said she had not even had to prompt her.

It was surprising enough to her that Sedi had booked a flight to come to Italy in the first place, simply because she wanted to see her sister dance. It had been wonderful to see Lira so pleased that her family were putting her first for once, and Sedi was charming – she and my mother seemed have hit it off, too, and were laughing and joking around, pointing to something in the glossy programme Mama was holding.

Lira came up beside me, placing her hand on my arm. I shivered involuntarily as she stood on tiptoes to whisper in my ear.

'I see my sister managed to follow your very complicated directions,' she said.

I turned to face her, pressing my palm into the small of her back, bringing her a little closer to me.

'It feels wonderful to have family here to watch us, *si*?' I said.

Lira nodded sadly. 'I wish your dad could have been here, too.'

I swallowed hard. I could not let that thought consume me, not now, when I was about to go out on stage, possibly for the last time. I felt a small comfort in imagining that somewhere, somehow, he *would* be watching.

'Me too,' I said. 'But now we must focus on the task ahead. On enjoying dancing together again one more time.'

Lira looked at me with concern. 'And you're feeling okay? You're sure you're up to it? Because Tomas is in the audience and he said if we need him to step in, he'll be ready in a heartbeat.'

'I am fine, Lira. It has been helpful to have something positive to focus on. And I can't think of a better ending for *Slow Burn*. Carlos deserves that. *You* deserve that.'

I took Lira's hands in mine just as the stage manager gave the five-minute call and the lights backstage went down.

'I cannot wait to dance with you,' I said.

Lira squeezed my hands in reply.

When I looked up, I caught Daniella's eye – she was standing just behind us with the rest of the cast. She nodded, the trace of a smile on her lips – an indication, I thought, that there was no bad blood between us anymore. In silence, we stood together behind the curtain, each of us, no doubt, reflecting on the journey we had had together over the last six weeks. And then the audience hushed, the front-of-house lights went down, and the opening bars of our music signalled that we must take to the stage for the very last time.

Ecstatic to be in my home city, I danced every single movement to perfection, and Lira matched me step for step. And as the Argentine tango music began for the final number, Lira and I found our light and our starting position. It was silent in the auditorium, except for one loud whoop from the audience that I suspected was Sedi. This spurred me on even more – I wanted her to recognize what Lira could do, so that she could report back to her parents and tell them that Lira was the most beautiful Latin dancer she had ever seen.

As we glided around the dance floor, the evocative music getting faster and faster, our leg flicks becoming more and more intricate as we kept perfect time with the music, our lifts feeling light and effortless in a way they had not at the beginning of the run, I thought this might be one of the greatest moments of my life so far. The only thing missing was my father, but strangely I had almost felt him with me as we moved, and could imagine the look of surprise and joy on his face, as though he was sitting in the audience next to my mother, watching us. He would have been proud of me, I knew that now.

As the music came to an end, we performed our dramatic last step, culminating in Lira throwing herself backwards, safe in my arms, as I hoped she had always felt.

There was a moment or two of silence at first, then the

applause started, not slow and steady, but a sudden burst of noise and whistles and people shooting to their feet, and it got louder and louder and louder. I pulled Lira, who was folded into one of her spectacular back bends, up onto her feet and we beamed at each other before turning to face the auditorium. Mama was up out of her seat and so was Sedi – as was every single other audience member, from what I could tell.

Shouts of '*Bravo!*' rang out and it felt as though the entire theatre was about to erupt. With a sweep of my arm, I motioned for the rest of the cast to come out on stage and we all stood together, proud of ourselves, of each other, and of the show. I waved Carlos, who had flown out to Italy for the final show, onto the stage to join us and he bashfully ran on, generating yet another roar from the audience as they recognized who was standing in front of them, the world-famous choreographer who had just created another world-class show.

It was chaos backstage afterwards. Everyone wanted to hug me. Every other person asked me for a photograph, or to sign their programme. Sedi had Nolo on speakerphone because, apparently, she did not want to miss out and Sedi had sent her a video of our tango and she could not believe how beautifully Lira had danced. Lira herself had been scooped into the crowd, gleaning attention and congratulations of her own, and so all we could do was meet each other's eye every now and then, neither of us quite believing, I did not think, that *Slow Burn* had been even more of a success than we had hoped.

Finally I took her hand and led her away from the loudness of the bar and into a quiet corridor, where I could hear myself think for the first time that evening.

'Hello,' she said, smiling at me.

I smiled back, leaning against the wall, enjoying the peace. 'I have been longing to be alone with you all evening.'

She threaded her fingers through mine. 'We did it, didn't we?'

I nodded, drinking in her eyes, her mouth, everything that had become so familiar to me over the last few weeks. I did not want whatever this was to stop, and although I still did not know how any of it could work out, I had to at least tell her how I felt.

'I could not have done this without you, Lira, especially this last performance tonight.'

She nodded. 'It was only right that you should be up there with me.'

'Lira, whatever this is between us, I do not want it to end,' I said, buoyed by the high of the performance and the adrenaline coursing around my body.

She seemed surprised that I had come out and said it, that I had been so direct about my feelings and about what I wanted.

'But what does that actually mean?' she asked, looking serious now. It felt serious to me, too. 'Because when we're

348

together, I feel really connected to you. But then there's this other part of you, this part I keep hearing about from Daniella and the other girls, and even your mother, that you don't do relationships, you never have. So why would I let myself imagine that that's what you want with me? Because I don't just want to feel desired; I need somebody to want me in their life properly, not just for a quick one-nighter when the mood takes them. I know I deserve more.'

'Of course you deserve more,' I said, mortified that this was how I had made her feel.

'What do you want for us?' she asked, her voice little more than a whisper. 'Tell me. Spell it out. And be honest; think really hard about this. Because it's important that we tell each other the truth if we have any hope of doing things differently this time.'

It was on the tip of my tongue. I knew how I felt and I had to say it; this was not the time to hold back.

'I think I am falling in love with you,' I said, my voice strong and confident, choosing to ignore the self-doubt swirling in my belly. 'Is that truthful enough for you?'

Lira beamed. It was not the reaction I was expecting, although I presumed it was a good sign.

'Do you really mean that?' she asked, a little breathless, her eyes searching mine for a sign that I meant every word.

'Of course I mean it. And since we are being honest with each other, I think I fell in love with you that night in Paris and that I have been in denial ever since. And sure, people might say it was nothing more than an infatuation. They might say it was lust not love, but I know how I felt. How I thought of you almost every day for months, wondering where you were, who you were with, why you had left so abruptly, why I was not good enough for you.'

'You *were* good enough,' she insisted. 'In fact, you were *too* good. I'd resigned myself to the fact that I wasn't destined for a big, exciting life. I couldn't imagine somebody who looked like you, who danced like you, would be interested in seeing me again anyway, and I was scared of being rejected to my face. So I bottled it. Convinced myself that I was better off without you. That it was nothing more than a hook-up. A pleasant way for me to remember my last ever World Championships. Except, it wasn't pleasant to remember, in a way. Because there was this longing to see you again. And in my mind I kept going over and over what could have been.'

'Me too,' I said, shaking my head in disbelief. All this time we had been feeling the exact same way. 'I was travelling a lot then. Daniella and I were doing well in competitions. My father was young enough to run the farm single-handedly and I barely gave home a second thought. It should have been the happiest time of my life and yet it felt like something was missing. Or like I had had something special within my grasp and I had stupidly let it go.'

I kissed her then, not able to wait a minute longer.

'Are we really doing this?' I asked her, stroking her bare arms with the flats of my hands.

'But how? With you in Italy and me in Castlebury?'

'That is something we will have to work out, but we will find a way, I promise you,' I said, meaning every word.

'Then I'm all in if you are,' she whispered back.

'All in with what?!' asked Sedi, choosing that moment to burst noisily into the corridor with my mother following a few steps behind her.

'And here,' said Sedi, thrusting her phone at Lira. 'Mum wants to speak to you.'

CHAPTER TWENTY-SEVEN
Lira

I walked away from the group to take the call from my mum, not least because I couldn't hear a thing with an over-excited Sedi shrieking about how much she loved the show, and Sofia laughing in a way I'd never heard her given everything that had happened; I was glad that at least we'd cheered her up a little bit, and that seeing Gabriele up on stage had given her so much joy.

'Mum?' I said. 'It's me. Where are you?'

'Never mind that, Lira,' said Mum, sounding as though she was in a wind tunnel. Was she out on the deck of the ship? 'Sedi sent me the video of you and Gabriele dancing the Argentine tango. It was breathtaking, Lira. Really, I had no idea you were that good.'

A warm feeling spread through my body and I thought

that out of everyone who had congratulated me tonight, my mum being proud of me had meant the most.

'Thanks, Mum.'

'So listen, I've been thinking. And Daddy and I have been talking and we've decided that you should absolutely go and pursue the dancing career you should have had years ago. The studio has been running well with the stand-in teachers, hasn't it?'

'Yes, really well,' I said, confused. What exactly was she saying?

'So let's carry on like that for now. If you're okay to keep an eye on things remotely until we get back from the cruise, I don't think you need to rush back to Castlebury if you don't want to. And once we're back in the UK, Daddy and I will take over the management of the studio. It's our turn to step up and run the business we started and for you to get your chance to shine out on the stage.'

'Mum, are you serious?'

'Of course I'm serious! After the way you danced tonight? There's no way we can let you go back to managing the studio full-time, although I'm sure your clients would love to see you there now and again, whenever you can manage.'

'Of course! I'll be there whenever I can. There's no way I'm just going to abandon you all.'

'And you must get yourself an agent, Lerato. Can Carlos help with that?' said Mum.

'Probably. And Gabriele said he'd introduce me to some-one,' I replied tentatively.

'Perfect,' said Mum. 'That's settled then. I just wish you'd asked for help sooner, Lira. Please don't ever think you are disappointing me by going after your dreams. This is your time to go after what you want – don't think about us or anybody else. Especially not Gabriele Riccitelli.'

'Why on earth would I be thinking about Gabriele?' I asked, trying to laugh it off, as though he had been the very last thing on my mind.

'Mother's intuition. Promise me, Lira?'

I nodded. She was right – I hadn't come this far for nothing. Gabriele and I might have feelings for each other, but I couldn't let that impact the decisions I made next. Wanting to be with him didn't mean I couldn't put myself first for a while, now that I actually had the chance to.

'I promise.'

As I wandered back to the others and handed Sedi back her phone, still reeling from the conversation I'd just had with Mum, Carlos burst through the door leading through from the bar, joining our impromptu private party in the backstage corridor.

'I have something to ask you both,' he announced grandly.

I raised my eyebrows at Gabriele, who shrugged in response. Neither of us seemed to have a clue what he was talking about.

'I have begun working on a new production,' said Carlos, leaving a short pause for effect. 'And I am hoping to use the success of *Slow Burn* to accrue a big budget, big-name producers, a much longer run. *Broadway.*'

'Broadway?' I asked, my voice catching in my throat. I caught Gabriele's eye – I knew how badly he'd always wanted to perform on stage there.

'And, Lira, I have watched you over the last few weeks – your calmness, your intuition, your ability to bring everything of yourself to each and every dance. I want you in my next show. I want to take you to New York; for everyone to see this bright new talent I have discovered!'

'What?' I said, shaking my head in disbelief.

'You are the most beautiful dancer, Lira, surely you must know that by now,' said Carlos, looking at me with affection.

This was all too much, what with Mum's turnaround and everyone staring at me and Carlos saying all these lovely things. I felt as though my legs were about to crumble underneath me, and Gabriele must have noticed because he put his arm around me, pulling me close to him. Everyone clocked it, of course, and Sedi gave me a little wink and even Sofia nodded knowingly. It seemed like everyone knew what was happening between us before we'd even acknowledged it ourselves.

'And, of course, Gabriele, it goes without saying that I would like you to be my leading man,' said Carlos.

The atmosphere changed as Sofia's look darkened and Gabriele slackened his hold on me. I put my arm around his waist, letting him know that I was here for him now.

That I understood what a tough decision this was going to be to make.

Gabriele cleared his throat. 'Carlos, as I am sure you would know, there is nothing I would like more. But after what has happened with my father, it is not possible for me to be on tour right now, especially somewhere as far away as New York. I am not sure if it will ever be possible,' he admitted.

Sedi gasped, an audible reflection, perhaps, of what we were all feeling inside. He was too talented to give up everything he'd worked for; there had to be a way for him to be able to continue to dance. My mind was reeling with thoughts of the conversation I'd just had with my mum, about how things at the studio had been fine without me in the end, that it hadn't fallen apart because I wasn't there. And then a vague idea came to me – could what worked for me work for Gabriele, too? Could he help his family *and* continue with the career he loved?

I took Gabriele's hand and squeezed it. 'But what if . . . ?'

He looked at me. 'But what if *what*?'

'I have an idea,' I said, feeling my cheeks flush as it dawned on me that I probably shouldn't have this conversation in front of an audience.

Gabriele searched my face for clues. 'What idea?'

I glanced nervously at Carlos, and at Sofia and my sister.

'We should go,' said Carlos, taking the hint. 'Let you talk. Come on, everybody, let us return to the party.'

Once they'd gone, I turned to Gabriele. My heart was

hammering in my chest and I wondered what was making me so nervous – did I think he was going to reject my idea? That he'd think me silly for even suggesting it?

'I've been thinking about your family farm. About that building you showed me, the B&B your mum wanted to open. And I wondered if . . . this is a bit radical, so hear me out . . . I wondered if I could use my experience of managing the studio in Castlebury to help your mum set it up. Maybe you could host weddings – the wedding party could stay on site, and the reception could take place on the veranda, and maybe the ceremony in one of the vineyards. In the summer, when the weather is good. And—'

'Lira,' he said, running his thumb across my cheek. 'When did you think of all this?'

'Just now,' I admitted. 'After speaking to my mum. She's agreed to manage James Jive herself. She wants me to go and pursue my dancing.'

'At last she talks sense,' said Gabriele, smiling down at me.

'But what about you? I don't want you to have to give up dancing, either. Is there a way you could do both things, too? Help your mother on the farm – we both could – but then also be free to do Carlos's show, and other jobs that are too good to turn down. You said your father had staff and that your mother was worried about them losing their jobs – well what if they could take on even more responsibility? They know the wine-making business better than you, don't they? Surely they could manage if you weren't there on the farm with them every single day?'

Gabriele raked his hand through his hair, seemingly trying to take all of this in.

'And you would be there, too? With me, at the farm? In between shows?' he asked.

'Yes,' I said, being bold. 'If you want me there. Because obviously you might not be into any of this. You might think it's a terrible idea. And please don't think I'm forcing you into doing something that—'

'You are not forcing me,' he insisted, looking deep into my eyes and making my stomach swirl with hope. 'It is the most wonderful idea I have ever heard.'

He kissed me hard, then held me away from him as though he wanted to drink in every detail of me.

'It means that we have a second chance, Lira. And this time, we are absolutely not going to mess it up.'

EPILOGUE

Lira

One year later

I put Sedi and Nolo on speakerphone as I polished the glasses for the wedding reception taking place the following day. We were holding the reception outside in the vineyard – the bride and groom were wine-lovers, and they wanted their guests to be surrounded by grapes as they celebrated their union.

'What time's your flight tomorrow?' I asked Nolo.

'Don't remind me. I've not even started packing and Mum wants me to go straight to the studio. She's been banging on to her ballet students about me, and apparently they're all dying to meet me.'

'I'm sure they are,' I said.

'Well, if she thinks I'll be up for performing in front of twenty ten-year-olds after an eight-hour flight, she's sadly mistaken,' grumbled Nolo.

'Don't be like that,' said Sedi. 'They're kids. You were a ten-year-old once.'

'Imagine how inspiring it will be for them to see what they could achieve if they work as hard as you did at their age,' I added.

'I suppose,' said Nolo.

'That flight does take it out of you, though,' I said, fully empathizing now that it was a journey I did regularly myself. Gabriele and I had just come off of a two-month run of Carlos's new show, which had been a huge hit on Broadway and had an extended run until early next year. The two of us were taking a break to help Sofia on the farm, but we'd be back on stage in a few weeks' time, and although I absolutely loved it out here in Italy, I couldn't wait to perform Carlos's gorgeous steps again.

'How's everything in Tuscany?' asked Nolo.

I glanced around me, sometimes still not able to believe that this was my home for at least part of the year. When I wasn't here or in New York, I went back to Castlebury as often as I could, and when I did I would make a point of spending lots of time at the studio, taking some lessons, covering for the employees who now worked for us to give them a break. But it wasn't expected of me, and Mum was a permanent fixture there now and, as far as I knew, she and Dad weren't planning on heading off on any more world cruises.

'It's wonderful,' I said. 'Sorry, I know that sounds gushy, but it is. It's perfect.'

'Let's hope your happiness is catching,' said Sedi. 'I

think I need a bout of Tuscan sun and a romance with a hot Italian.'

'You'll have to find one when you come over,' I said. 'I'll ping over those dates for that big corporate awayday we're hosting – they want high-end dance performances and I'm going to put you at the top of the bill.'

'What about you and Gabriele? That's who they'll really want to see,' said Sedi.

'We'll be performing, too. One day I might get sick of dancing the Argentine tango with him, but I can't see it happening any time soon.'

'I'd never get sick of dancing with someone as beautiful as Gabriele,' said Sedi wistfully.

I tutted playfully.

'Sorry, is it inappropriate to have a crush on your sister's fiancé?' asked Sedi.

'Yes!' I replied, knowing she was joking.

I still hadn't got used to calling him that: my fiancé. He'd proposed right here at the farm on New Year's Day and we were planning our own wedding here next summer. But, in the meantime, we had myriad *other* weddings to help Sofia organize.

'Dad said Olive Grove Studios is the most googled wedding venue in Italy right now,' said Nolo. 'That's amazing, Li. You've all achieved so much in such a short space of time. Sofia must be thrilled.'

'Oh she is,' I said. 'She likes to keep busy, it helps her to not miss Enzo every minute of every day. She said she doesn't understand why she didn't turn the outbuilding into a hotel sooner. She's absolutely loved getting it ready for guests. Tomorrow we're hosting our biggest wedding yet – one hundred and fifty guests, no less.'

'With your crazily good organizational skills, it's going to be a huge success, and you know it,' said Nolo.

'On which note, I should go. I've got three crates of wine glasses to polish and chatting to you two is slowing me down.'

'Fine, but call us soon,' said Nolo, pouting. 'And think of me at home in Castlebury running ballet for toddlers.'

'It's about time you put some serious work in at James Jive,' grumbled Sedi, who had a newfound love for the mundanity of teaching after an adrenaline-fuelled tour of Australia with Barbed Wire. 'And teaching is more fun that you think, you'll see.'

'I'll take your word for it,' said Nolo, seemingly unconvinced.

I said my goodbyes and resumed the glass polishing, humming happily to myself while I mentally ran through everything I still had to do before the guests arrived the following morning. I was so caught up in the moment that I didn't hear Gabriele coming up behind me and wasn't even aware he was there until he wrapped his arms around my waist, kissing my neck softly.

'How is my exceptionally talented leading lady?' he whispered in my ear.

I laughed softly, melting into his embrace. 'Even better now you're here.'

'Mama is flying about all over the place,' said Gabriele, spinning me around to face him. 'She wants everything to be perfect tomorrow.'

'And it will be,' I said. 'It's lovely to see her so engaged and positive.'

Gabriele took me in his arms.

'I never could have imagined being this happy,' he said. 'Living with my two favourite women on earth. Making the farm business work for us all.'

He'd found a way to scale back the business while keeping Enzo's vision ticking over by hiring Gio to take over the management of the wine-making and distribution side of things. And with the studio fully booked for weddings and parties throughout the summer, supplying the guests with delicious bottles of local red and white was a lucrative side hustle.

Gabriele brushed his lips lightly across mine. 'Only you can manage to make an apron look sexy,' he said, untying the strings and hooking it over my head, casting it to one side.

'And you must be far too hot in that,' I said, slowly and tantalizingly unbuttoning his shirt.

I pushed it off his shoulders, revealing tanned skin underneath, his muscles even more defined after months of lifting and moving furniture around and digging in the fields. When he wasn't busy performing, he was really throwing himself into farm life.

'I love you, Lira James, in case I have not yet convinced you,' he said, lifting me onto a table.

'Do *not* smash any glasses, we're running short as it is,' I scolded him.

'I will be careful, I promise,' he said, sliding his hands under the hem of my skirt.

As I lay down on the table, looking up at the veranda, the sun filtering through the bougainvillea in misty strips of golden light, my beautiful husband-to-be looking into my eyes, I felt a rush of appreciation for how much my life had changed in just over a year.

How some things – Gabriele especially – had been worth waiting for.

Read on for an exclusive Q&A with Hannah Grace ...

Hannah: How much did your career as a professional dancer shape the characters you've created?

Oti: Oh, my dance career has shaped everything about these characters! Dance teaches you rhythm, emotion, discipline and storytelling, all of which are essential in creating characters that feel real and alive. Every dancer I've ever met has had their own story, their own struggles and triumphs, and I've drawn from those experiences to build characters that are full of heart, passion and determination. Whether it's the resilience of pushing through rehearsals, the joy of performing or the behind-the-scenes friendships and rivalries, it's all in there!

Hannah: What's your all-time favourite romance novel?

Oti: Ooooh, I love a good romance! It has to be *Me Before You* by Jojo Moyes. So emotional, so beautifully written, and it completely broke my heart, in the best way. I love a novel that makes you feel everything!

Hannah: Do you believe in happy ever afters?
Oti: Oh, absolutely! But I also believe that a happy ever after isn't just something that happens, it's something we create and could happen multiple times for one person. It's in the little moments, the laughter, the love we pour into our lives every day. Whether it's in dance, family or chasing our dreams, happiness is a journey, not just a destination. So yes, I believe in happy ever afters . . . because we have the power to write them ourselves.

Hannah: Favourite romance trope?
Oti: I love a good *enemies-to-lovers*. That slow burn, the tension, the moment they realise they actually love each other, it's like the perfect dance routine where everything just clinks in the end. But I also have a soft spot for *second-chance romance*, because who doesn't love a comeback story?

Hannah: Can you tell us anything about your next novel?
Oti: Oh, you know me . . . I love a good surprise! But what I can say is that my next book will be full of heart, passion and a few unexpected twists. It's a story that's been dancing around in my mind for a while, and I can't wait to bring it to life. Stay tuned . . . something exciting is coming!

ACKNOWLEDGEMENTS

This novel has been one of the most terrifying and thrilling things I've ever done, second only to dancing in front of millions in sequins and heels!

I have so many people to thank from the bottom of my heart:

To my husband, Marius, your love, laughter and belief in me never waver, even when I doubt myself. Thank you for reading the early pages, holding the baby while I worked and reminding me that I could do this.

To my daughter, you gave me the courage to show you that mums can chase their dreams too. I love you so much.

To my family, who taught me strength, resilience and how to tell stories with soul. You are in every word of this book.

To my incredible literary team, thank you for saying 'yes' when all I had was an idea and a whole lot of heart. Your guidance shaped this into something I'm so proud of.

To my readers, thank you for picking up this book, for

joining me on a new journey and for holding space for my voice in a new way. I danced for you, and now I write for you.

And finally, to the women who feel unseen, unheard or unsure: may this story remind you that you are powerful beyond measure and that it's never too late to begin again.

With gratitude and love,
Oti Mabuse

booksandthecity.co.uk

the home of female fiction

NEWS & EVENTS | BOOKS | FEATURES | COMPETITIONS

Follow us online to be the first to hear from your favourite authors

booksandthecity.co.uk

@TeamBATC

Join our mailing list for the latest news, events and exclusive competitions

Sign up at
booksandthecity.co.uk